AUGUST NACHT

AUGUST NACHT

by Joanna Pyplacz

Paperback ISBN: 978-1-7363485-4-3
ePub ISBN: 978-1-3932935-8-3
***

Written by Joanna Pyplacz
Published by Royal Hawaiian Press
Cover art by Tyrone Roshantha
Translated by Wieslawa Mentzen
Publishing Assistance: Dorota Reszke
***

For more works by this author, please visit:
www.royalhawaiianpress.com
***

Version Number 1.00

Table of Contents

Daß das Leben des Menschen nur ein Traum sei, ist manchem schon so vorgekommen, und auch mit mir zieht dieses Gefühl immer herum.

Johann Wolfgang von Goethe,

Die Leiden des jungen Werthers

Many people had an impression that human life is only a dream, and this feeling accompanies me constantly as well.

Johann Wolfgang von Goethe,

The Sorrows of Young Werther

Chapter 1

Il dottore della peste

October twenty-eighth, 1791, was unusually hot for a late season. On this day, Duke Martín Castro y Herrero celebrated his seventieth birthday. As always, on that occasion, he organized a masquerade ball, to which he invited the most notable inhabitants of Cantabria and Asturias to his residence in Valsombra. When it got dark, magnificent coaches and carriages started arriving at the palace. The door of the ballroom was swung wide open so that the sweet sounds of music mixed with the intense scent of white roses, still blooming outside.

Illuminated by the pale moonlight, the statues of Greek and Roman deities that adorned the garden gave the impression that the evil spell that had bound them was about to break, restoring their lost freedom of movement. The neatly trimmed hedge-maze, situated opposite the palace terrace, also seemed to be overwhelmed by the charm of the evening. The fountain inside it reflected a faint glow, as if there were some secret agreement between the water droplets and the moon.

The fairy-tale atmosphere of the garden contrasted with the splendor of the ballroom hall, shimmering with all the colors of the rainbow. Dressed in fancy costumes, the elegant guests looked like a flock of wonderful birds of paradise. The most unique creation was that of Carmen Jiménez y Castro, the niece of the duke, while the most interesting among the gentlemen was undoubtedly the son of the birthday boy, César, Marquis de Viciosa.

The austere, almost puritan elegance of his clothes contrasted strongly with the splendor that characterized the costumes of the guests, dressed as mythological characters, heroes of literary works, and even dangerous pirates or medieval monarchs. The only variation in César's appearance was a slightly different hair, more carefully styled than usual, and the presence of a mask. The black and white outfit was in perfect harmony with a beautiful face, with noble, slightly predatory features, and with magnificent, black curls, already sprinkled with gray in many places, tied with a black silk ribbon and flowing abundantly on his neck. Unlike his son, Duke de Valsombra looked like the epitome of wealth and splendor.

César rarely appeared in public. The exceptions were the celebrations on the anniversaries of his father's birthday. He spent most of his life in a residence away from Valsombra, situated in the heart of the old forest, devoting himself to the works of philosophers and various experiments in the field of physics and chemistry. His eccentric, alienated lifestyle had been the subject of all sorts of speculation and conjecture.

The interest in César was additionally fueled by the fact that among his very few friends was the famous Lord Harold Ravendale, who was sentenced in absentia to death in his native England, due to suspicion of ties with the French party of the Jacobins. He learned Spanish at an extraordinary pace, and in time he even managed to lose his strong English accent, which was now barely noticeable.

Despite his very pleasant disposition, Lord Ravendale's views prevented him from being liked widely. People whispered in the corners that he belonged to a Masonic Lodge. There was a similar opinion about César himself, but he was protected from the potential consequences of these accusations by the strong position of his father, as well as the duke's social ties with the influential Cardinal Mario Suárez.

Neither Martín nor his powerful friend had even guessed that César was in the process of working on a tome entitled *The History of the Inquisition in the Northern Lands*, a fact known only by Lord Ravendale, who could pride himself with the authorship of a dozen political and satirical pamphlets. He published these works in Paris in the late eighties of the eighteenth century, under a pseudonym and a false publishing address.

Even the name of the printing house was made up, though many suspected that there was a famous Parisian publisher hiding under the name *Associated French Printers in Switzerland*. Lord Ravendale intended to translate the *History of the Inquisition* into English and submit it to the "Swiss" publishing house of his printer friend. That evening he and César were busy discussing the terms of the possible publication.

The conversation took place in English - this language, unknown to any guest present in the room, served as a secret code. French was less safe, and "good Christians" - as Suárez called his secret scouts - were everywhere, listening eagerly, so that the cardinal could be informed of anything profane, and the ungodly perpetrator, caught red-handed, - captured and thrown into prison.

The orchestra was just playing a minuet from *Don Giovanni*, Mozart's newest opera, which quickly gained immense popularity also in this part of Europe. The duke first saw it in 1788, when he was visiting his cousin Antonia in Vienna [1]. Since then, the elegant minuet had become an inseparable element of all the masquerade balls he arranged in his residence.

"My dear cousin, what are you gentlemen talking about?" Doña Carmen asked, taking César by the arm.

"We cannot praise your beauty enough!" Lord Ravendale replied unexpectedly, bowing with exaggerated politeness.

"Liar!" She replied, coquettishly covering her mouth with a lace fan.

"How unfair you are, cousin," César interjected, clearly amused by his friend's move. "Lord Ravendale is the most truthful man in the world. It's also hard to find a person who would be easier to wrap around your finger."

"Your cousin is right, lady. And there is no more excellent dancer!" The Englishman said, making a theatrical bow.

The girl laughed.

"A minuet is the only thing I can really dance," he whispered to César.

"Since you boasted so much, it's time to prove your truthfulness and unparalleled dancing skills. I'd love to see how you do."

"Cousin, what about you? You're not dancing?" Doña Carmen was surprised.

"I'm not in the mood."

"Oh, your eternal melancholy! You'll be a complete eccentric soon!"

César responded to this innocent malice with a pleasant smile and an elegant nod of the head, which were immediately returned.

As Lord Ravendale and his lovely partner mingled with the dancing ranks, César headed for the garden. He was not interested in dancing or the merry company. His thoughts drifted inevitably towards the forest shrouded in eternal fog, where he left the unfinished chapter of his treatise on the Inquisition, and the unfinished reading of *The Monstrorum Historia* by Ulisse Aldrovandi.

He walked slowly down the stairs of the palace terrace to the garden, plunged in the twilight. As he walked among marble sculptures and neatly trimmed bushes, he wondered what would happen if he finally had the courage to challenge the world he came from, but whose hideous secrets he had learned well enough to separate himself from them in his forest stronghold, completely overgrown with ivy and wild vine.

Another object was on his mind as well, namely the mysterious figure that he had been seeing for some time in the clearing near the residence. It was a young woman with a pale complexion and dark auburn hair, casually pinned up. She always appeared just before dawn or just after dark, but César had never found the courage to approach her. He always watched her from a distance as she walked alone in the woods, engrossed in reading a book.

It was only because of his natural resistance to all kinds of witchcraft and superstition, which he knew perfectly well that the stranger walking among the old oaks was not a ghost or a phantom, but a human being of flesh and blood. Weary of the superficial coquetry of well-born ladies, and the hypocrisy and greed of the families of his few would-be brides, he decided to stay as far away from them as possible.

He was snapped out of his reverie by the rustle of leaves, coming from behind the plinth on which one of the statues stood. César turned back abruptly. Instinctively, he grabbed the hilt of the dagger he always carried with him. He paused motionless, waiting. A few long seconds of deep silence passed. Suddenly, a figure emerged from behind the conically trimmed crown of one of the shrubs.

It was a tall man, clad in a black cloak with a cape, and a triangular hat of the same color. His face was covered with a white mask in the shape of a bird's beak, known in Venice as *il dottore della peste* [2].

"What do you want?" César asked, taking a step forward.

The stranger slowly raised both hands and removed the mask, revealing a face with very regular, statuesque features, surprisingly similar to those of César. The light blue irises seemed translucent, and a strand of long, almost white hair stuck out from under the hat.

The man smiled, showing a set of gleaming teeth. It was not a friendly smile, but an ominous one, as perhaps the one the Germanic warriors bestowed upon the cornered Romans in the Teutoburg Forest, before they took to their swords.

"I have a business with the duke," he said. He spoke with a foreign accent.

"Tell me what matter it is, and I will gladly take you to him," César replied politely.

"I'm afraid it is not possible. I have a message of exceptional importance for him, but so confidential that I must pass it on *in persona* [3]," he said, looking at his interlocutor with contemptuous superiority.

At the same moment, his pale eyes fell on César's right hand, which was still gripping the hilt of the dagger. It was not this, however, that caught the attention of the foreigner, but rather the elaborate coat of arms signet on the ring finger.

"César Castro y de Abaroa!" He said softly.

"In person," César confirmed dispassionately.

"After all those years..."

"I do not understand. Who are you to my father?" César asked.

His voice took on a slightly aggressive tone.

"Sein liebster Freund!"[4] - replied the stranger with a mocking smile, again covering his face with the Venetian mask, then headed towards the palace. He was walking quite fast, as if the matter couldn't wait another minute.

César thought for a moment what to do. He was afraid for his father's life, because he knew perfectly well that the foreigner was by no means his friend. With the utmost amazement, he realized that the stranger had an excellent understanding of the territory of the duke's residence. His eyes widened with surprise as he saw the intruder direct his steps towards the rear part of the building, opened for the ball.

Without waiting any second, he followed the man. The latter had already disappeared into the narrow staircase for servants that led straight to the corridor, along which the ducal apartments stretched. César paused at the top of the steep stairs, staring in amazement as the stranger disappeared through the office door. A cold shiver ran down his spine. "How did he know my father has gone to the study? He must have been watching the windows from outside and noticed him inside," he thought. "I'll stay here just in case."

As if guided by a strange intuition, Martín left the ballroom for a moment and went to his office. The stranger, noticing a faint glow on the floor, entered without knocking. Unknowingly, he left the door slightly ajar, allowing snippets of a very strange conversation to be heard. It showed that the duke and his interlocutor knew each other well, or at least had mutual friends.

"Could this man really be my father's friend?" César wondered. "If so, why have we never met? Why was he not invited to the masquerade ball, but just showed up unannounced?"

The stranger says something in German and then in Spanish, but quite softly, so César did not understand much. He could only guess that it was about a third person that both men knew very well.

"When did this happen?" Asked the duke in a voice that was barely audible.

The tone of his speech indicated that he had just received news of someone's death or some unfortunate incident.

César did not understand the answer, as the stranger spoke mostly German (which the duke knew perfectly well), interjecting the words in Italian and Spanish. Moreover, the men were talking so quietly, that even through the slightly ajar door it was difficult to hear just a single sentence. César only caught the word *impostor* [5]. At one point, the intruder suddenly knelt down in front of the duke, crying and hugging his knees. The latter stepped back however, violently pushing the intruder away.

Not understanding much from the scene he witnessed, and fearing for his father's safety, César decided to stay hidden and wait for the stranger to leave the office. It happened within a minute. The man left with his mask on already, but he chose a different way back than the one that led him to the duke apartments. The orchestra played the famous minuet from *Don Giovanni* again.

César watched in amazement as the stranger turned right and ostentatiously descended down the marble steps into the ballroom. In his black outfit and frightening white mask, he looked like a ghost from the bottom of the hell, who had come to recover some unpaid duty from the living, which bound them to him for all eternity. César guessed that this man was some kind of demon from the past, and that he had decided to claim his rights with the duke.

At the sight of *il dottore della peste* majestically walking down the stairs, the guests parted to two sides of the room, creating an open line, with which they instinctively separated themselves from him. One lady slumped on the hands of her companion, two others, close to fainting, set their sumptuous fans in motion. "He looks almost like the ghost of The Commendatore," thought Lord Ravendale.

César saw a similarly dressed man for the last time in Italy, many years ago. He even remembered the day he saw him, because it was shortly before his mother's sudden and tragic death. Martín, his wife, Teresa, and his three-and-a-half-year-old son spent time then in Venice, in the palace of a scientist, half Spaniard and half Italian, with whom the duke had been bound by a long friendship, dating back to his early youth. It was in this house that César first encountered Aldrovandi's wonderfully illustrated works.

They were going in a gondola to Teatro San Giovanni Crisostomo for a performance of the Albinoni's opera *Il trionfo d'Amore*, when at one point César noticed on land a black-clad figure in a bizarre mask in the shape of a bird's beak. Before he could share this insight with his parents, the weirdo had already disappeared into one of the dark, narrow alleys.

The vivid memory of this extraordinary bird-faced creature, disappearing in the impenetrable depths of darkness and the evening mist, which had left its mark on his overly vivid, slightly neurotic imagination, returned at the sight of the masked stranger. César also remembered that since that visit, his father had never visited his beloved Venice.

1   The Vienna premiere of *Don Giovanni* took place in 1788, second after the Prague one in 1787 (all footnotes are from the author).

2   Italian: *a plague doctor.*

3   Latin: *personally.*

4   German: *His dearest friend.*

5   Spanish: *a*   *fraud.*

Chapter 2

Hyoscyamus niger

The deafening rumble of a lightning, which struck the withered tree in the clearing, bounced from the cave's ceiling with a terrible echo, rousing Iduna from a deep but restless sleep. Tears were still flowing profusely down her cheeks, covered with a dense mesh of deeper and shallower wrinkles. Opening her wet eyes, she sat down on a bed of animal skins and various fabrics, listening to the wonderful symphony played by the torrential rain on the surfaces of leaves, stones, and mosses.

The suddenly interrupted dream was an unspeakable torment for Iduna. It had been returning every night for over forty years, giving her no respite. Each time, the same scene was played out here and now. Same piercing scream, same barking of hunting dogs, same smell of fresh blood. And then, when it was over, the same texture of the damp earth, its wet, sweet smell.

A bird scream, piercing through her brain, snapped her out of her reverie.

"What do you want, Álvaro?" She asked.

The magnificent peregrine falcon, perched on a ledge, cocked its head to the left, making a series of quieter, prolonged sounds. His wise black eyes shone in the dark like two crystal balls. Slowly, he raised his massive wings until their tips touched, then stretched each one individually.

"Did you hear somebody?"

The bird responded with another series of longer and shorter squeaks.

It is not known where Álvaro actually came from. One winter day, Iduna went to get firewood. Suddenly she noticed a streak of fresh blood on the snow. Following the lead, she found a falcon that had apparently lost the fight against some other predator. His belly was almost completely open, and all the flight feathers from one wing were torn out. Iduna carried the bird into the cave, disinfected the wound with a tincture of pine cones and mandrakes, and sewed it together. To her immeasurable surprise, the animal survived. From that day on, he became her faithful and inseparable companion.

Having wrapped a thick woolen shawl around her shoulders, Iduna stepped outside the cave. Álvaro was right. A few steps from the entrance stood a man, wearing a black cape and a triangular hat, with very fair, slightly wavy hair hanging from under it. In his hand he held a white mask with a funny elongated nose resembling a bird's beak.

"August Nacht!" She cried out.

"Hello, Iduna," the man said hollowly.

"I know why you came here," said Iduna.

"Really? I don't bring you good news..."

"Dorothea... She died happy. Her last words were, 'August grew up to be a smart boy'."

"What are you talking about? Did you talk to my mother? But she died in Venice!"

"Never mind."

August looked at Iduna in disbelief.

"How?" He asked, his voice breaking. His eyes filled with tears that began to run abundantly down his cheeks.

"Suddenly I felt I had to go to the pond. Yurde always lets me know this way when someone close to me is dying."

Yurde lived less than seven years. Iduna gave birth to him on the edge of a pond in the middle of the forest. The childbirth was very long, but they both survived. The boy was not only gifted with beauty and exceptional dexterity, but also had a pleasant disposition.

One day, the duke organized a deer hunt. A herd of pointers rushed through the forest like crazy in pursuit of the timid animal, which, in a surge of supernatural strength, managed to jump onto a rock located near Iduna's cave. Unable to reach it, the enraged pack directed their anger at little Yurde, playing near the rock. At the sight of the dogs, he ran away and he would probably have avoided death, if it had not been for his fatal fall. The little boy slipped on the mossy boulder and fell flat. He tried to get up to run, but the pointers were faster - they tore him alive in front of his mother. Iduna stood frozen at the entrance of her stone house, helplessly watching the strong jaws clamp on the boy's shoulders, thighs and face.

When it was all over, she staggered to where what was left of her son, lay in a pool of blood. Picking up from the ground the barely recognizable remains, covered with the blood and mud, she filled the forest with a terrible howl. Wild wolves echoed her from afar, as if they were lamenting the death of this ever-smiling, golden-haired child together with her.

When the dusk fell, Iduna carried the boy's body to the same place where she gave birth to him. She buried him at the foot of an ancient yew that grew on the shore of a small pond in a clearing that had been known since medieval times as Claro del Agua.

Soon after Yurde's death, the elderly, nearly 100-year-old herbalist Iñigo reached the end of his years. In the morning Iduna heard her son's voice from the distance. She seemed to hear him singing a folk song about a little thrush, with which she greeted him just after his birth. As a newborn baby, he reminded his mother of a newly hatched chick. Yurde got naturally familiar with this peculiar lullaby, and at the age of two he knew all its verses by heart. The beginning was like this:

Little thrush, tiny thrush,
all speckled...

Hearing this graceful child song, whose verses were intertwined with a silvery laughter so familiar to her, Iduna felt at the same time an irresistible inner compulsion to go to Claro del Agua. When she got there, she saw a large black moth on her son's grave. The butterfly sprang up and, after dancing a lovely sarabande in the air, flew towards the lake, then vanished as if it had dissolved into the sultry summer air.

Iduna knelt over the mirrored surface of the pond. The child's laughter stopped and the forest immersed in a dead silence. At one point, the water shook slightly, blurring the perfect reflection of the treetops and multi-story clouds that were gliding majestically across the sky like royal ships. Iduna fixed her eyes on the surface. Her long-haired figure, leaning over the forest waters, resembled the painter images of the mythical Narcissus.

She knew the signs couldn't lie, and waited patiently for news from the depths of the pond. It didn't take long, only a few moments, but for Iduna they were an eternity. The surface of the water had already returned to its original tranquility, when it suddenly turned cloudy and darkened. The reflections of the spruce and fir tops gave way to a vague blur that after a few seconds took the shape of a human face.

"Iñigo! Is it really you?" Iduna called.

In response, she heard only a vague whisper.

"What can I do for you?" She asked.

She knew the old man was dying.

"Stay here," he grunted.

"I'll stay, my friend," she said, biting her lips. "But does it have to be like that? I have only you..."

"You will not lose me. I will look at you from the branches, from water, from raindrops... Isn't such a friend better than a sick, coughing, old man?"

Iduna smiled as she wiped her damp cheek with a strand of hair. Iñigo closed his eyes, then the vision vanished.

"See you later," she whispered.

A black butterfly appeared again over the water. It flapped its wings just above the place where the old man's face had appeared, then dissolved into thin air.

August was staring at Iduna with his blue eyes.

"There was always an extraordinary bond between you and my mother..." he said after a long silence. "What you say seems unbelievable, but I know very well that it is true. I remember the day you saved both of us from death as if it was today. I even remember the smell of the dagger blade with which my poor mother was going to kill me and herself..."

Just like in some ancient tragedy!

Iduna remembered the scene. One day, while she was sitting on the stone in front of her cave, busy patching her autumn cloak, she noticed an exceptionally beautiful woman, who was walking rapidly towards the darkest part of the forest, pulling a loudly crying little toddler by the hand. The blade of the dagger gleamed in her other hand. Her very pale hair and a strange, hard-sounding but melodic language in which she spoke to the boy revealed that she was a foreigner. Incomprehensible, broken words alternated with loud sobs.

Iduna realized immediately that the woman, blinded by a sudden surge of madness or despair, was going to murder the boy and possibly, subsequently, to commit suicide. She jumped up, ran to the stranger and knocked the sharp dagger out of her hand in one rapid movement. The woman gave her an empty gaze.

"Thank you," she said in Spanish.

At first she did not want to say where she came from, but finally revealed that her name was Dorothea Nacht, and that she was an opera singer. When she was at the top of her fame, she left her native Germany and settled in Venice. Unfortunately, due to a serious illness, she lost her voice, which had previously been her working tool. Although she recovered, she never regained it, leaving her destitute. To make matters worse, the father of her five-year-old son August, a man of high standing, had just refused to recognize him. Unable to come to terms with shame and rejection, and with the prospect of living in extreme poverty, she decided to spare herself and her child from suffering.

Though Dorothea had never revealed the name of her son's father, Iduna could easily guess that it was Martín. In little August's blue eyes, she saw the same spark of cold cruelty she had seen in the Duke de Valsombra. Despite the very fair, almost white hair, and an alabaster complexion, the boy looked very much like him. When she looked at the now grown man, she found that his resemblance to his father was striking.

"You're coming from him..." she guessed.

"He rejected me just the same as when I first came here with my mother. So I came to this forest in the hope of meeting you, my long-time beloved friend."

"You can always count on me. I will do for you what I failed to do for my son."

"I trust you completely."

"And I trust you. We must work together."

August kissed her wrinkled hands that smelled of thyme, wild mint, and bird feathers. He remembered vividly from his childhood the dry touch of these hands, and their characteristic herbal scent, that soothed his burning mind like a magic Band-Aid.

"How great was my stupidity! I tried to win my father's favors. I thought that by bringing him the news of my mother's death, I would become closer to him. Meanwhile, I met the classic fate of a bad news messenger."

"Martín is cold and ruthless. The only human instinct he shows is fear for his own skin. He never loved your mother or his wife. He is in love with himself only."

"You knew him well..."

"I know people," Iduna said shortly, not wanting to go back to the painful memories that still burned like an open wound. "I have my reasons for not wishing him well."

"Mother was right. I have nothing to look for here. I, the older son, live like a miserable tramp, while my younger brother is overflowing with riches, titles and honors."

"César means to him as much as you do."

"Are you saying he doesn't care about him at all?"

"Not at all. He might as well not exist. Martín is completely absorbed in himself. He is interested in operas, hunting and women. Don't think about César. He poses no threat to you. Even if he suddenly vanished from the face of the earth, the duke would still not recognize you. The only thing left to you is to take revenge on the man who is your father only in name. What father treats his own children in this way? He hurt you and your mother and he cuts you off again. So forget about blood ties and help me get revenge on Yurde's murderer."

"What if my brother would really disappear from the face of the earth?" August asked, puffing up his nostrils violently and pressing his lips tightly together.

His pale blue eyes turned icy in color.

"It won't do you any good. Sooner or later, César will end up miserably. He got involved in some political scandal together with that troublemaker, Lord Ravendale. Believe me, this doesn't lead to anything good. This Ravendale is a good-hearted fool, who, like your brother, considers himself the savior of mankind."

August's eyes widened. The woman's extensive knowledge of the latest activities of César and his friend amazed him. "How can Iduna, who spends her whole life in her forest cave, have an idea of the nuances of politics, the secret meetings, and secrets of the aristocracy?" He wondered.

"I can see from your face that you wonder how I got all this news," she said with a smile, as if reading his mind.

"I was going ask you about it this very second!" August exclaimed.

"Wait," Iduna ordered.

She got up from her seat, then went to the room at the back of her large cave, where she used to store the most important medicines, poisons and antidotes. She came back with a small box that contained some dried stuff.

"What is this?" August asked, studying the grayish substance with interest. "Looks and smells a little familiar..."

"It is *hyoscyamus niger*," Iduna replied solemnly.

"A doctor I know in Venice showed me this plant once. As far as I can remember, he used it as a painkiller."

"That's it. It not only soothes the pain of the body... but also brings out the pains that plague the soul."

"I don't know what you're getting at..."

"In one of those horrible dog hunts your father is so fond of, and because of which I lost my only son, Martín's trusted servant named Ausencio fell off his horse. He didn't break anything, but suffered a very unpleasant sprain due to the fall. It happened not far from here. I was sitting quietly in the cave, watching Álvaro relish eating a piece of deer meat stolen from the hunters, when suddenly we heard the piercing scream of this young man. Knowing that someone from Martín's entourage had been injured, I decided that this was an excellent opportunity for me to help the wounded man and thus win his friendship, so that I would have access to the latest news from the palace. My choice fell on this dried powder, which I tried on myself. By testing its properties, I found that it works not only on the body, but also on the mind. So it was an ideal drug. I took a small amount with me and set out to fulfill my mission. When I got there, Ausencio was lying on the ground, writing in pain. The dislocated arm began to swell rapidly. I sprinkled the swelling with this powder, then spat and rubbed the resulting mixture into his body. After a moment the swelling began to subside. The boy asked me to give him a bit of this "magic" panacea for the next days, so that he could get rid of his ailment himself if it would recur. I refused, because it is a poisonous plant and, if used inappropriately, it can lead to disaster. But I promised him that he would get help whenever he would come to my cave. He showed up the next day, still in pain, but his arm looked a little better already. A month later, Ausencio recovered, but continued to visit me. I entertained him with a nice conversation on topics of interest to him, such as game, minerals, and the like, into which I skillfully weaved various questions."

"You old witch, how skillfully you wrap young men around those skinny fingers!" August joked, kissing her hand.

They both laughed.

"The old Iñigo, from whom I learned about the existence of this plant, revealed to me that inhaling the smoke from its burnt leaves works more effectively than applying ointment. I gave this medicine to this young man. Not only have the aromatic vapors completely restored him to health, I have also learned during our meetings many of your father's secrets, that even César surely does not know about."

"Iduna, you are a real genius!" August cried out, staring adoringly at his friend.

"It's not me, it's nature. It created these wonderful plants, fungi and minerals. Without them, even the greatest genius would be completely helpless."

"Does this boy visit you often?"

"Of course. We spend a lot of time together. With time I gained his trust. He tells me literally everything. Because of our conversations, I am up to date with everything. Ausencio is very close to Martín. He knows about most of his activities."

"Such an acquaintance is a real treasure."

"And precious one too! Thanks to him, we will be able to complete our joint plan. Of course, he can't find out about anything. He is too kind for this, and the good ones often end up badly and drag others with them."

"We'll avenge my mother and your son," August said with tears in his eyes.

Iduna kissed his forehead.

"And ourselves," she whispered.

"And ourselves," August repeated.

Chapter 3

Viciosa

The Duke de Valsombra remained until the very end of the ball in his office, wherein he locked himself. César said goodbye to the guests on his behalf, explaining his father's absence by a sudden indisposition, allegedly caused by the weather change. It was guessed, however, that the reason for the duke's ailment was not the impending storm at all, but rather the unexpected visit of a mysterious man in an *il dottore della peste* costume.

As the guests departed home, César ordered his coachman, Francisco, to prepare a carriage and horses. It was late, but he had no intention of being in his father's palace a minute longer. He had hated this place from the moment his mother died. Every corner of the magnificent mansion reminded him of the irretrievably lost moments he had spent with her as a little boy.

His father's lavish parties made him think of a ball that was held on the last day of his mother's life. Teresa de Abaroa y de Vicente arrived at it accompanied by her husband, dressed in a white lace dress, pale as if she would be about to dissolve in the cold January air. She smiled, then just stared away with her absent eyes with unnaturally dilated pupils. This is how César remembered her.

He knew something terrible was going to happen that night. He sensed it would have to do with his mother. He had no chance to say goodbye to her. In the morning he heard from the tearful servant that the Duchess de Valsombra was dead. The doctor stated that she had died a natural death, although César secretly suspected that she had been deceptively poisoned. This was also suggested by the sudden disappearance of Serafín, one of the ducal couple's servants, which was discovered the next day.

Some said that Teresa consciously took her own life, unable to bear the constant affairs of her husband. Despite loving his father, César blamed him for his mother's death. He was deeply convinced that had it not been for his numerous flirts and romances, the duchess would still be alive, or at least would not have died prematurely at the age of only twenty-six. Occasionally, he also considered the murder hypothesis.

After Francisco had groomed the horses and prepared the carriage, César ordered him to take him to Viciosa as soon as possible.

"Lord, it's late! The road leads through forests..." the coachman tried to protest.

"Let's go!" César repeated the order. "I'm going to leave this terrible place as soon as possible."

Two black horses with shiny coats raced through the fields lit by the pale moonlight. The roar of the sea gradually grew quieter. César looked thoughtfully into the distance at the advancing black wall of trees on the horizon. The road to his mansion led through a dark, impenetrable forest, the subject of legends that could make even the hottest blood freeze in the veins.

One of them talked about an old woman, sometimes seen in that old forest, bending over a stream, washing a bloody scarf. Those who met her, said that their eyes never saw a face more monstrous. It was the face of a corpse, devoid of eyes and nose, with a great wide open mouth. From that endless abyss flowed a mournful lament, resembling a wolf's howl. Everyone who saw this woman, died shortly thereafter in gruesome circumstances and indescribable suffering.

No one knows where such a legend came from. It is said that it comes from a time when Cantabria and Asturias were only inhabited by their native people, the Celts. The source of this story was lost in the memory of even the oldest generations, however, the fear that this figure had aroused survived the Roman conquest, the darkness of the Middle Ages, and the progress of civilization. *La lavandera* [6] still instills terror in everyone coming to explore the wild corners of the local forests on their own.

César was not a superstitious man, so he approached all of these stories with an ironic distance. Nevertheless, he instinctively avoided with his thoughts the ghastly laundress who filled him with a subconscious, irrational fear. A barely noticeable twitch crossed his face as the carriage plunged into the black abyss of the forest. After a while he smiled to himself, realizing how tainted with superstition his seemingly enlightened mind, familiar with the most difficult issues of science, had turned out to be.

"The stories people come up with", he sighed.

The carriage now rode along a narrow line of old trees with knotty trunks and fantastically twisted limbs. Some of them were partially decayed, while others were in the final stages of their long and silent agony. The remains of life still smoldered in a few morbidly transparent leaves on the ends of their branches, which fluttered sadly in the wind like souls in purgatory.

Every now and then you could hear the howling of a lone wolf, or the calls of owls and other night birds. Francisco was terrified of these creatures, so he rushed like crazy, slashing the horses' backs mercilessly with his whip. Concerned by the too frequent whistling of the thong and the warning neighing of the animals, César leaned out of the carriage.

"Francisco, are you out of your mind?" He exclaimed.

His jet-black eyebrows joined over his eyes in an expression of impatience.

"Lord, you ordered to go as fast as possible!" The coachman explained.

"I told you to go, not rush blindly! Take it easy, because once the horses rebel, nothing will protect us from local thugs."

"Lord, these birds are going to drive me crazy. Every now and then it seems to me that Güestia is coming for my soul... "-lamented Francisco.

Güestia is a procession of the dead. Souls, dressed in flowing white tunics reaching all the way to the ground, carrying torches made of human bones that miraculously ignite themselves, walk slowly through the darkness in a long, gloomy retinue. It is not known where they start and what direction they are going. Only one thing is certain: whoever sees the procession, will surely die. If they stop before the human household, death will come there soon.

César smiled.

"It will surely come for both of us if you don't slow down immediately!" He made fun of the superstitious servant.

"Lord! For God's sake!" The coachman exclaimed, his teeth chattering with fear. "We must not laugh at it, because we will be punished by God!"

"You are babbling nonsense, my good Francisco. It's a shame to listen to it! You're a grown man. You know perfectly well that there are no ghosts. I am also not convinced about the prospect of a divine punishment."

"Lord," whispered the despairing servant. "We're lost!"

"Calm down immediately!" César rebuked him sharply. "You should not be afraid of phantoms that someone once saw, but of the thieves, the most real in the world. They do indeed prowl these areas and have murdered many people. We also have to watch out for pirates, because they come here at night to hide their treasures in the caves. If our carriage gets derailed, we will be an easy prey for them. And if the horses bolt, we will surely die in a very unpleasant way. Then no force, human or supernatural, nor prayers or magic spells will save us from the miserable fate that you will arrange for us by rushing like madman and tormenting horses!"

"Alright, my lord, I swear I'll drive wisely!" The embarrassed servant promised.

"You don't have to swear, just apply a little common sense, about which you always talk so much!"

The carriage arrived at the destination unscathed. César looked out of the window with satisfaction at the eastern side of his residence, covered in a shroud of a night mist. The moon just peeked out from behind the cloud, casting cool rays on the stone terrace, covered with vines. The deep colors of the ivy and vine seemed even darker in this light. While the vivid red of the wild vine was of deep bloody hue, the gray-green ivy gave the impression of being completely black.

The late Gothic castle, where César resided, looked abandoned. Its construction started at the end of the fourteenth century, for strategic and defense purposes, and then, for reasons not fully known, the work was stopped. It resumed briefly in the fifteenth century, but after the surrender of Granada, which ended the era of feverish fortifications in the north, it did not get completed.

It was the first Marquis de Viciosa, the childless deceased cousin Domingo, who adapted this majestic building for residential purposes. He ended his life at the age of only forty-five as a result of a fatal fall from a horse during a hunt, shortly after the residence was arranged to be lived in. The castle and its title were inherited by César.

From the outside, the small but dignified building was tightly wrapped in exuberant vines, the hue of which changed depending on the season, giving color to the entire castle. The eastern, residential part of the building was arranged very simply by Domingo, so that the refined, contemporary style would not be in a grotesque contradiction with the gloomy austerity of the late Middle Ages.

Like his cousin, César did not like luxury, so he felt at home in the castle. He equipped the rooms he occupied with his characteristic thrifty elegance, while he left the rest of the building in its original state. His aesthetic preferences were not shared by the servants, which were terrified by the dark, narrow passages, pointed gothic window arches, labyrinths of corridors and cavernous cellars.

There were many stories about the uninhabited western part: some ridiculously naive, others chilling to the bone. César entrusted its care to Aitor, a fearless, red-haired strongman from the Basque country. Despite the fact that he had been completely illiterate until recently, he despised the local superstitious way of thinking, considering it a symptom of incurable stupidity.

Aitor coped well with the tasks that most of the castle's inhabitants found impossible. His enormous height, fiery red hair and deep voice, as well as his unrestrained, insane courage, not only caused universal respect, but also helped to keep the most wayward youths in check. César trusted him greatly, knowing that he was an honest man and completely immune to both superstition and intrigue. He taught him to read, write and perform basic mathematical operations. Thus, Aitor became his master's right-hand man and in time, began to act as the manager of his residence. Whenever he found a spare moment, he hid in one of the chambers in the western part of the castle, where he spent his time reading books on medicine and botany. He chose this refuge quite consciously, knowing that it was the only place where his peace would not be disturbed by any of the household members, who fearfully avoided the gloomy stone gate, leading to the unused wing of the building.

Francisco took care of the carriage and horses, and César went to the library, where he suspected he would meet his steward. Indeed, Aitor sat on the floor beside the bookshelf, carefully studying the titles, calligraphies in Gothic capital, on the parchment backs of the works on poisons and antidotes on the lower shelf. The giant was so absorbed in his activity, that he did not even notice that someone had entered the room.

"Aitor! Hello my friend," César greeted him. "I see that I haven't taught you things for nothing."

Aitor immediately rose from the floor.

"Forgive me, my lord," he said, bowing low. "I have not noticed your Excellency!"

"I don't see any Excellency here," César replied, bursting out with laughter. "All this title mania makes me sick. Mother always said that the interpersonal communication was most hindered by the grotesque conventions."

"Except I'm still somehow uncomfortable addressing... you without using any title. I know it's funny, but I also realize that in your circles a title is sacred."

"In my private house it is ridiculous and unnecessary," replied César. "I know what others think about it, including members of my own family, but the last thing I want is to turn into an old, arrogant peacock in a gaudy tux and a powdered wig."

Aitor, who secretly fully shared this opinion, replied with only a discreet nod of the head. "The fact that César, the Marquis de Viciosa, spoke so nonchalantly about people equal to him in birth and wealth does not mean that I, Aitor, the son of an illiterate blacksmith, have the right to argue about their tastes and customs," he thought.

"What are you studying so hard at this hour?" César asked.

"It's very interesting, my lord. This knowledge may be useful to us someday!" Said the servant, handing César the Spanish translation of Pedanios Dioscorides, published in Salamanca in 1570.

"I know this book! I remember that when in my early youth I did not want to learn Greek, my teacher gave me the original work, knowing that this would encourage me to learn."

"The Greek original? I would love to read it, but unfortunately I only know my own language and the local language here..."

"You don't need the Greek yet. However, if you learn Latin properly, you will be able to read most of the volumes you see here! If you like Dioscorides, I also recommend Pliny the Elder to you."

Aitor sighed deeply as he looked around the magnificent library. Shelves filled to the brim with manuscripts and prints reached all the way to the high ceilings. Unfortunately, so far he could only read books that were either written in Spanish, or were Spanish translations of the works of authors writing in other languages.

"I will also teach you the basics of mathematics and chemistry - then your knowledge of poisons and other substances will be more complete."

Aitor's face lit up.

"There is only one condition," César said seriously.

"What is it, my lord? I will obey any of your orders," Aitor promised.

"This one is very simple: never call me 'Your Excellency' again!" César replied, laughing.

Aitor straightened, taking care not to hit his head against the huge chandelier, whose arms, casting around elongated shadows, resembled the legs of a giant, poisonous spider.

"You're right, your knowledge of poisons may turn out to be useful," César said, watching these mysterious shapes thoughtfully.

6   Spanish *washerwoman.*

Chapter 4

Atropa Belladonna

César left Aitor, completely immersed in reading the work of Dioscorides, in the library. He himself went to his chambers. As often happened to him at such an hour, he went out to the balcony with a view of the forest wilderness. It was a new moon that night. Every now and then, the heavy wings of owls and other night birds silently crossed the almost cloudless sky, extremely rare at this time of the year and in this part of the country.

As César returned to the chamber, his sleepiness left him. So he decided that he would go for a short walk to his favorite clearing near Castillo de Viciosa, to let his eyesight, hearing, and smell enjoy the unique beauty of this autumn night for a while. Having armed himself with a dagger, just in case, he went down the servants' stairs and quietly opened the gate leading outside. The forest air, infused with the fresh scent of resin, thyme and rosemary, was like a magic elixir for him.

The planned several-minute stroll turned into an almost all-night walk in the forest. Looking at the metallic, smooth, mossy and corrugated leaves of the various trees and shrubs, César remembered Aitor's words. He tried to find in his memory which of the plants he encountered were potential cruel murderers, and which the natural miracle workers were. He also realized that his botanical knowledge was now far more modest than that of Aitor. "If this passion for learning does not fade away as fast as it was born, I will take seriously to his education. He is still young, he would make a great medic!" - he thought. At the same time, César's attention was attracted by a rather inconspicuous shrub with dark purple, shiny fruits that seemed completely black in the dim light. He was convinced he had seen the plant somewhere before, but he could not remember either the place or the circumstances.

The fruits gleamed like precious stones, carefully polished by a seasoned jeweler. There was something attractive and at the same time terrifying about them. César plucked a twig with leaves and two berries. "I think I've seen something similar somewhere... It's probably a deadly poison. My home-grown botanist will be delighted!" He thought, intending to show Aitor the find. "I wonder if he will decipher this puzzle and find an antidote, if this beauty is indeed poisonous!" He carefully placed the plant behind his coat, and then followed the overgrown path known only to him, leading to a picturesque clearing.

César liked this place especially because of the presence of night birds. Observing them gave him great pleasure. He was far more interested in the great performances in the form of hunting, noiseless flights, fierce battles for territory and elaborate mating rituals, than in participating in lavish parties organized by his family members, boring balls or pointless discussions about politics and religion, in which he had never been able to participate fully due to the inability to reveal his true views.

The second reason that made this charming place even more special to him, was the frequent presence of the mysterious, pale-faced stranger in the clearing or in its vicinity. Several times he wondered what was the reason for those walks, during which she exposed herself so recklessly to the attack of pirates or thieves. Sometimes he imagined that by watching her from a distance, he was keeping her safe. Such fantasies gave him great pleasure. He felt like the hero of some extraordinary medieval legend.

Sometimes he invented yet another scenario, according to which the stranger, as a figure from the afterlife, attracted mortals with her beauty, and then gave them an unenviable fate, dragging them into a whirlpool or turning them into insects.

As César was busy watching the enormous owl, flying in wide circles above the clearing in order to catch some fearful rodent in its massive claws, he heard a soft rustling of leaves behind him. Instinctively, he placed his hand on the hilt of his dagger, then slowly turned his head. The young woman he'd been thinking so much about lately, stood only a few steps away.

It was the first time he saw her up close. She was much more beautiful than he thought. She had pinned her hair up very carelessly. A few long, disobedient strands fell on the white, almost transparent forehead. Two large, black eyes stared curiously at César, who stood mesmerized, not knowing what to do so as not to scare or offend the stranger.

He also noticed that this time, she showed up without any reading. "Perhaps I should ask if she lost the book or why did she leave it at home?" he wondered, as he formulated the question he was going to ask her in his head. But he was unable to speak up to her. The woman stood motionless for a moment, watching him curiously, as if she wanted to remember every little detail of his person.

Then, quite unexpectedly, she came a few steps closer. César bowed gracefully, but stayed where he was, fearing to make any mistake that could prove fatal. The stranger approached again. When she was only half a meter away from him, he was surprised to note that her eyes looked as if they were composed of the pupils only. "I guess she's really out of this world!" He thought as he watched the woman with a feeling that was a mixture of almost religious adoration and an irrational fear. "I guess there is no salvation for me anymore, I am destined to fall into her trap, whoever she is!" He still couldn't believe that his secret dream to see this extraordinary face up close, came true.

The rational side of his mind waited with a truly scientific curiosity for any action on her part, friendly or hostile. The woman approached even closer, then stood on her toes, ran her hand through his hair and kissed him unexpectedly. He had never experienced anything like this in his life before, so he wasn't sure if it was a bizarre dream or a reality. He closed his eyes and kissed her back.

When he opened them, the stranger was already some distance away. She walked quite slowly but decisively, as if, embarrassed by her erratic behavior, she decided to leave the place where it had happened.

"Lady, don't run away like that!" César called after her.

The woman paused, nervously brushing a strand of hair from her forehead.

"Will you do me the honor and tell me your name, madam? It would be unbearable not to know the name of the person who gave me something so wonderful," he asked, finally finding the courage.

She didn't answer. As she turned her face away, César saw that she was smiling. "Why did I deserve such an honor?" He asked himself, still not believing what had just happened. "I need to know who she is at all costs," he decided, watching her bright figure disappear into the darkness of the forest thicket. "I wonder why her eyes are devoid of irises..."

When he returned to the castle, it was already three in the morning. He tried to fall asleep, but every time he closed his eyes, he could see the face of the beautiful stranger in front of him, and his memory stubbornly recreated the entire unusual scene, in which he participated. In his mind, everything was replaying over and over again, for the first, second, hundredth time. He suddenly remembered the plant he had brought from his walk and intended to show to Aitor. "Probably nothing is left of it now," he thought.

The twig, however, was still fresh. The dark fruit, reminiscent with its color and size of very ripe cherries, shone in the dark as beautifully as a few hours earlier. The leaves of a regular, elliptical shape were also in good condition. César placed the plant in a cup, into which he poured water from a decorative decanter on the cupboard, a memento of Duchess de Valsombra.

As he looked at the cup and then at the fruit, which he suspected had poisonous properties, his gaze drifted down to the decanter. A shiver ran down his spine. "Could it be a sign?" - he thought. Sometimes he suspected that a poison was behind his mother's sudden death, but these were mere speculations, unsupported by any evidence.

True, the doctors did not find anything suspicious, and the duke himself and other family members were of a similar opinion. However, César, for reasons he did not himself understand, somehow could not agree with their rational explanations. He sat down at the desk and stared at the gleaming fruit, hanging from the twig. The sleep came unexpectedly, closing his eyes.

Heavy footsteps on the stairs woke him up. A moment later, someone knocked on the door. It was Aitor.

"Is everything all right, sir? Are you well?" He asked.

"The healthiest in the world. I will go down to the dining room in a moment," César replied.

At that moment, old Enrique entered the bedroom with a basket of clean linen. While César was talking to him, Aitor noticed the decanter with the mysterious twig on the desk. He picked up the dish, then looked carefully at the leaves and fruit. "I am sorry, I couldn't help myself!" - he excused his curiosity.

"You have nothing to apologize for. I plucked this twig specifically with you and your natural interests in mind. I suspect this plant is poisonous. I've seen it somewhere before. If you have the time and feel like it, you can identify it. I remember that in one of the atlases..."

"No need for an atlas. This is *belladonna atropa*, one of the most poisonous plants. Rare species, but how deadly! It only takes a few fruits to poison a child and about ten to finish off an adult."

"So my hunch was right!"

"Absolutely."

"Do you know if there is an antidote to this beauty?"

"I'm just trying to find out. This is an extremely interesting plant. As soon as I learn something, I'll tell you everything right away."

"Thank you, Aitor."

"Where exactly does the name *atropa belladonna* come from?"

"*Belladonna* means 'beautiful woman' in Italian. It is indeed a captivatingly beautiful shrub, but its beauty is also extremely deceptive. Whoever succumbs to its spell, dies. *Atropa* is a word of a Greek origin. Atropos was one of the three sisters known as Moirah who spun the thread of human life. It was her who cut the thread..."

"A terrible story!" Enrique interrupted, looking scared.

"As terrible as the local legends about an old laundress by a stream, or about forest processions... If one of the boys hears it, they will not sleep at night!" Aitor laughed.

"Better have mercy and don't tell it, especially at night," advised César.

"If one of them gets under my skin, I will know how to give him a scare! Just before going to bed, I will tell him this: 'If you continue being so obnoxious, a certain Greek woman will come with scissors and cut off your nose and ears!'" Enrique said sternly, wagging his finger as if one of the wayward young men were in the room.

At the sight of his comical expression, bulging eyes and theatrical gestures, Aitor and César couldn't help but laugh.

"My dear Enrique, how many times have I told you that you should have become an actor?" César said finally, still laughing.

"He's wasted his talent, but at least he helps me keep this bunch of rogues in check!" Aitor added.

When Aitor and Enrique left the room, César became serious again. He kept thinking back to the forest clearing, and to the strange meeting with a pale stranger with unusual eyes. Had it not been for the unexpected kiss she had given him, he might have believed that the whole event was only a dream, or the product of his unusually vivid imagination, which had already made a cruel mockery of him several times in his childhood and early youth. As a small child, he had strange daydreams. Sometimes they got mixed up with the reality. There were also times when he saw terrifying, sunken faces of the dead on the trees bark, and the gaping throats of drowned people on the surface of the water. Several times he dreamed that his mother came to him. He barely recognized her features, distorted and blurred by death.

But he knew it was her, he recognized the lace dress, the same one she was wearing the last time they saw each other. She reached out with her cold hand, with shreds of skin hanging from it, to touch his face, as she used to do when alive. César, however, pushed this disgusting apparition away from himself. As he desperately resisted her touch, tears of blood poured profusely from her cloudy eyes. He would wake up with a piercing scream that put the entire household on its feet.

It was because of these nightmares, among other things, and because of his innate aversion to human communities, that César was a dark and introverted boy, and later - a little more sociable, but still overly serious young man. Despite this, he had the grace inherited from his father, and a sense of humor, the mask under which he skillfully hid the eternal anxiety of his soul.

As an adult, he still had these terrible dreams, but they haunted him less and less, giving way to other visions, more detached from reality, but equally disturbing. The last time he saw his mother was a month ago. But she was no longer as terrifying as she had been on her earlier visits, when he was a little boy. This time he dreamed that he saw her unclear, blurry figure. She came for a moment, uttered some incomprehensible words, and after a while she dissolved into the haze of the night fog.

César sensed it was a sign. On the one hand, he missed his mother very much, and on the other, he was terrified of those night visits. As an eight-year-old, he liked to go to her grave, where he stayed for days. It was then that his mother started visiting him in a dream. But the delusions of a child's brain were so confusingly similar to reality, that after the first "visit", little César swore he would never go to the family chapel again.

This radical decision of the frightened boy caused even more suffering. He inadvertently confided to his guardian of his visions, which soon ceased to be a secret. When the duke told his friend, Father Mario Suárez, about his son's condition, the latter decided that the boy had been possessed by the devil, and that exorcism could be the only cure for his condition.

For this purpose, Father Suárez brought his cousin from Burgos, Father Felipe Velázquez, a famous Castilian exorcist. At the mere memory of him and his practices, César's pulse rapidly accelerated till this day, as if his heart wanted to break free from his chest and throw itself into an abyss, while his forehead and temples covered densely with drops of icy sweat. Father Felipe was even more terrifying to him than the ghost of his dead mother, haunting him.

Terribly thin and bald, with a hoarse voice and a face that looked more like a medieval gargoyle than a living man, he looked nothing like his rather handsome cousin. He tied little César to the bed with all his strength, so that his silhouette resembled a person stretched on a cross. He was spraining all his joints doing this, and the coarse rope rubbed the boy's ankles and wrists until they bled. César struggled madly, trying to break free from his bonds.

The monk, endowed with the strength that was almost superhuman and utterly disproportionate to his meager stature, was just waiting for it. He then rolled up the sleeves of his habit and tightened the boy's fetters with all his strength, reciting Latin formulas. At the end, he took out a glass bottle with some cloudy liquid, which he forcibly poured down the boy's throat. Within seconds, the substance was beginning to foam abundantly.

The last stage was the least oppressive. Father Felipe handed César a metal crucifix to kiss. As the boy raised his head to complete the ritual and shorten his suffering, a foamy, white substance oozed from the corners of his mouth. Since the presence of the foam proved that the demon was about to leave the body of his victim, in order to finally cast out the devil, the monk raised his hands to heaven, reciting the following formula in a theatrical voice:

Crux sacra sit mihi lux
Non draco sit mihi dux
Vade retro Satana
Numquam suade mihi vana
Sunt mala quae libas
Ipse venena bibas

After the rite was completed, Father Felipe untied his arms and legs, put the strings, stained with blood, into the yellowed cloth bag, and left the room without a word. César remained motionless, staring blankly at the ceiling, accompanied by the babysitter, who was saying prayers until dark. At night he dreamed of the face of the sinister monk, and the formulas he was reciting mingled in his tormented head with the echoes of his own screams. It was like that every time.

He always wondered what Father Felipe used to season the holy water. One day, completely by accident, he managed to solve this mystery. While browsing one of the botanical books in his library (for a completely different purpose), he came across a description of a plant called *saponaria officinalis*, the root of which acquires strong foaming properties in contact with water.

"*¡Hijo de la gran puta!*" [7] - César cursed at the memory of the cruel exorcist, and returned his thoughts to his night stroll through the forest, and the extraordinary meeting it resulted with. "Who are you?" He thought, then rested the back of his head against the back of the chair and closed his eyes, recalling the memory of the kiss he had unexpectedly received. He recreated the entire scene in his imagination.

7   Spanish: *Son*   *of*   *a*   *bitch!*

Chapter 5

The Count de Aciago

Ramón Suárez y Montero, Count de Aciago, was reaching the age of forty-seven. Like his seven years older brother, Cardinal Mario Suárez, he was characterized by a strong physique and impressive height. His dark, angular face with an extremely repulsive expression was additionally marred by a broken nose, a reminder of the duel he fought in his youth, in which he barely saved his life.

Count de Aciago enjoyed a well-deserved fame as a crude and cruel man. He lived with his newly wedded wife in the enormous Palacio Aciago, near César's residence. He got married late in his life. His choice fell on the daughter of a teacher from Reinosa. Don Carlos Morales, whose only fortune were two sixteenth-century Bibles and the title of a doctor of philosophy, obtained in Salamanca in his youth, reportedly descended from an old lineage of the completely impoverished *hidalgos*.

In mid-June 1790, the count went to Reinosa at the invitation of his older sister Francisca. On the second day of his visit to this city, tired by the afternoon heat, he decided to stop by a tavern located on one of the main streets, to drink cool wine. He took a comfortable seat by the window, where he could see all the other guests. His attention was caught by the person of an elderly man with carelessly untied gray hair. He sat across from the count, but a few tables away, his head resting on his left hand. He looked drunk. Moments later, a beautiful young woman with dark hair and an exceptionally fair complexion entered the tavern, dressed in a simple brown dress, whose coarse, unfashionable cut was a mismatch to her extraordinary beauty. She walked over to the old man and kissed him on the forehead.

"Father, it's time to go home. You're not going to sit here until the night, are you?" She asked, trying to grab the old man's arm.

He pushed her away with his elbow, then rested his head on his left arm again.

"You'll be sick again, you know very well you mustn't drink so much. You are not helping either yourself or me with this," she tried to negotiate.

The old man pushed her away again, cursing violently. Count de Aciago immediately took advantage of the situation to introduce himself to the woman, whose beauty amazed him. He did not care about the drunkard's fate, and was even glad that he had managed to slide down to the bottom of society, for he knew that his daughter's desperation could work to his advantage. He got up from behind the table, leaving his wine half-drunk, carefully slid the chair behind the counter, and walked over to the bench where the man was sitting.

"Could I help you with anything?" He asked politely, addressing the young woman directly, then made a deep bow.

"That's very kind of you, but I think we can take care of it without any help," she said, looking him straight in the eye.

"I see your father is not well. I could give you a ride home," suggested the count, not giving up.

"There is nothing wrong with him, except that..." She broke off, blushing with shame.

"Y-yeah, o-of course, you'll now say I'm drunk! And that is no-not true at-at all! I am ab- absolutely sober! This obnoxious girl wo-wo-won't let me live, she fo-follows me everywhere!" The drunk exclaimed indignantly, emptying the glass in front of him all the way to the bottom.

"Father, calm down right now! You know full well that I have not come here to upset you, but to escort you home. I'm worried about your health. You have not been well lately. You will also catch a cold this time, if you come back late, and besides, the road to our house, although very picturesque during the day, can be dangerous at night," she persuaded, trying to force her father to get up from the chair. The old man jerked away violently, mumbled few unclear words, staggered from the table, then fell flat to the floor. The count immediately sent for a doctor. A young medic arrived almost immediately and found the initial stage of *delirium tremens*. The count took the drunk home, where he also came the next day, under the pretext of concern for his health.

Carlos slowly began to sober up and was feeling a little better.

"This gentleman saved your life," said Blanca, for that was the girl's name.

"I don't know how to thank you. I am terribly ashamed of my behavior yesterday. Apparently I got drunk again and passed out!" The old man groaned, shedding tears.

"You had early delirium. Fortunately, this gentleman called a doctor in time."

"I would like to give this up, it's a terrible disease. Unfortunately, it turned out to be stronger than me."

"I feel sorry for you," replied the count, pretending to be concerned with his interlocutor's fate. "Certainly, some misfortune must have befallen you that pushed you into the grips of the addiction. You don't seem like a typical profligate to me."

"My father has been drinking since my mother died," Blanca explained.

"Poor Ana!" The old man howled pitifully.

"She was taken from us by an unfortunate accident..."

"Hopelessly stupid woman! She drowned in the well!" Carlos suddenly shouted, switching unexpectedly from mourning to uncontrolled anger. "I would have shown her how to get water properly, but I was not there. She always had to ruin everything, just like her daughter. A faithful copy of the mother!" He exclaimed, wagging a swollen finger in the air.

"I believe you are acting very unfairly," the count protested. "A misfortune can happen to anybody. Accidents also affect smart people, not just complete idiots."

"I apologize for these antics. My father is not feeling well yet" Blanca excused him.

"And who asked you for your opinion?!" Carlos exclaimed. "That girl is my punishment! She follows me like a nightmare, babbling nonsense, while she should keep her mouth shut. I will not obey a chick's orders!"

"You are terribly ungrateful, Mr. Morales," concluded the Count. "I would give anything to have a being as beautiful and wise as your daughter care for me as she does for you. I have everything, but this one thing I look for in vain..." he added, looking at Blanca.

"Have courage, your nobility will be rewarded. You deserve this and much more," she returned the compliment politely.

"I'm afraid that the moment I met you, my possibilities have been drastically limited..."

"How is that?!"

"You are the only one that could make me happy. You wouldn't lack anything..."

"I respect you very much, but..."

"Shut your gob!" Carlos shouted.

"I am very sorry that my words have sowed a grain of discord among you," said the Count de Aciago. "It wasn't my intention. I will be on my way back tomorrow at noon. I will come to say goodbye. Meanwhile, take care. Be well, sir! And you, lady..." Having said these words, he bowed almost to the ground.

After he left, Carlos didn't say a word to his daughter. Deep in thought, he lay with his head supported on his shoulders, staring at the ceiling. Blanca guessed what was causing this behavior. She knew her father and knew that if he persisted in doing something, he would persevere in his decision, however ridiculous it might be, until his death. She had been terrified of rejection since she was a child, and now she was almost sure that this terrible moment had just come.

She was also aware of the bad financial situation both of them were in. The last pennies left of Ana's dowry, Carlos lost for drinking and in card games. Had she accepted the count's proposal, she would have saved her father, freeing him from the misery and, perhaps, from drunkenness. Her own fate would also be significantly improved. She would have a widely respected husband, a roof over her head, and the necessary livelihoods.

She liked neither the count himself, nor his exaggerated kindness and overly smarmy behavior. He did not inspire her sympathy or trust, on the contrary - the thought of him filled her heart with both fear and disgust. She sensed something very insincere in his behavior, she also saw a flash of cruelty in his eyes. However, she would be willing to accept a proposal solely for her father's sake.

She hadn't closed her eyes all night long, wondering how she might regain Carlos's lost respect and at the same time avoid the dreadful prospect of entrusting her entire life to a man she had met only twice, which was however quite enough to make her genuinely hate him. She imagined him as Pluto, who rose to the face of the earth on his dark chariot to lure her into the land of eternal lamentations.

The next day, the count appeared on time. His overly elegant clothes contrasted grotesquely with his angular face and broken nose. When Blanca saw out the window an ornate carriage drawn by four huge black-roan horses, she felt that her life was draining from her. She turned away from the window, digging her fingernails into both hands until they bled, then walked slowly down the stairs to open the door.

The count bowed low when he saw her. He did so with expressive exaggeration, just as everything else.

"Welcome back, Count," she greeted the guest politely.

"I hope that the disagreement that my bold proposal provoked between you is gone forever, and that I did not offend you in any way."

"Of course not. It's an honor for us," Blanca replied, smiling at him with the last of her strength.

The count noticed her cool eyes. He also noticed her deathly pallor, a sign of lack of sleep.

"I am very happy to hear these words," he said with a smarmy smile.

"I'll take you to my father."

Like his elder brother - the cardinal, Ramón had the ability to sense human emotions. He knew perfectly well that Blanca had no sympathy for him. Moreover, he was fully aware that she disliked him. While another man in his place would have been devastated by such a discovery, the Count de Aciago did not feel the slightest offense. On the contrary - this arrangement suited him very well. He had always been most attracted to those women who sincerely hated him. The more they avoided him, the more he strove for them. He felt his greatest pleasure when they were afraid of him. He fondly remembered the moment when he had managed to lure a certain planter's sister into his bedroom. She wasn't particularly beautiful, but she seemed scared to death. After a few days, however, the spell was broken.

Fear and hatred gave way to fatigue and resignation.

So he let her go.

Blanca was different - she was perfect. Not only was she in a regrettable situation, but she also possessed an exceptional, unique beauty and - as he immediately noticed - great intelligence. She met also another important criterion: she considered him a monster, as he could read from her icy gaze. He knew she would try to stand up to him till the end. This was exactly what he wanted: a difficult but unequal struggle with a perfect opponent, who despised him.

Carlos was sober. He waited impatiently, in a clean shirt and with a clean shaven face, for the count's visit.

"My daughter has something to tell you," he said.

It was the first time he had addressed Blanca since the count's previous visit. She expected a similar behavior, so she was prepared. She knew that refusing the proposal could in the long run poison her life even more than accepting it. If her father would die of grief over her selfish pursuit of her own happiness, she would not be able to live with the thought that it was her decision that directly contributed to his death. And old Carlos - as she knew well - would not fail to make it clear to her. So she decided to submit to fate.

"Say it for me, Father," she replied.

"Well then: my daughter accepts your proposal. She actually accepted it yesterday already, but your proposal, Count, fell on her like a bolt from the blue, so unexpectedly, that she did not know how to behave properly, for which I apologize to you."

"An apology is absolutely unnecessary here," the count protested coaxingly. "Thanks to you and your daughter, I will soon become the happiest man in Spain, and perhaps in the whole world. Moreover, I already am one!"

With that, he kissed Blanca's stiff and icy hand.

The wedding took place less than two weeks later in the Suárez family chapel, near the palace. The bodies of all the ancestors of Count de Aciago were buried in it. The ceremony was held personally by the cardinal. He noticed the intense sadness on the bride's face. Looking at her blank gaze and slow movements, he inadvertently remembered the memorable party given by his friend Martín, where he had last seen his wife Teresa. She died unexpectedly that same night.

Blanca wore a dark red gown that matched her very pale complexion and dark chestnut hair with a dozen large Atlantic pearls breaded into it. Her face assumed a completely indifferent expression, and her large gray eyes seemed to be staring at some distant point on the horizon. There was something sublime and tragically beautiful in this absent gaze and fierce indifference.

Count de Aciago appeared dressed in a courtly fashion. His cream-colored tailcoat, embroidered with gold thread, and a slightly darker shade of vest and pants were refined in every detail. The outfit was complete with a carefully combed gray wig and an elaborate muslin jabot. Unlike his fiancée, he triumphantly scanned the pointed arches of the chapel's vault, the medieval stained glass windows, and the faces of the guests.

The wedding reception lasted for several days. Carlos Morales, who promised himself not to bring shame to his high-born son-in-law, kept his word and did not touch a drop of wine. Abandoning his drunken rudeness, he behaved in an extremely dignified manner, getting into a scientific debate with a Catalan astronomer who could not praise enough the old man's quick-witted mind and the broad spectrum of his scientific interests.

Blanca didn't talk to anyone except her husband.

Her pale face resembled that of a porcelain doll.

She stared blankly into the distance, answering the count casually. From a distance, her eyes seemed much darker than they really were. People whispered in the corners that the bride had never smiled, and various speculations were made about it.

Some saw the source of this melancholy in some mysterious, unrequited love, others - in Carlos' drunkenness and generally ill health, yet others - and those were right - in dislike of the newly married husband. The most perceptive of the guests immediately noticed that the Count de Aciago, fully aware of the state of affairs, not only did not worry about it at all, but, on the contrary, took unhealthy pleasure from it.

As soon as the wedding celebration ended, Carlos became seriously ill. Two trusted medics were summoned, but they were helpless, unable to find the cause of the disease or identify its symptoms. Mr. Morales was buried very quickly, the next day around noon, as the body began to decompose almost the second the soul left it. Blanca did not appear at the funeral. She was last seen   at   her   own   wedding.

Chapter 6

Ausencio

Despite his twenty-one years, Ausencio Cabrera had the face of a child. Over time, Iduna began to like him very much, although at first he was just a source of valuable information for her. His wavy golden hair, smooth complexion, and round brown eyes reminded her of Yurde. She often wondered what her son would look like if death had not taken him from among the living in such a sudden and brutal way.

She enjoyed these meetings, from which she benefited doubly. On the one hand, the naive young man introduced her to ever new, dark secrets of Duke de Valsombra, which she longed to learn, and on the other hand, the sight of his childish, freckled face pleased her, because she imagined that this was what Yurde might look like if he lived to adult age.

Ausencio was an orphan. He was from Castro Urdiales. After his parents died in a house fire, Roberto, one of Martín's most trusted household members, took him in. The nice, fair-haired boy immediately gained the sympathy of the servants, and his conscientiousness and extraordinary diligence won the duke over to him. Ausencio quickly became his favorite. Over time, Martín began to entrust him with tasks that required complete confidence and discretion.

The old duke trusted no one. He also did not like his own son César, considering him a madman and a freak, who, with his radical views, eccentric behavior, and suspicious friendships, dishonors his family and disgraces his title. It happened, therefore, that for lack of persons to whom he could turn for advice or comfort in various distresses of a personal nature, he shared these matters with the young servant.

Ausencio was given his rare name in the memory of his great-uncle, a hermit. It meant "absence," which further captivated the duke. Despite the fact that Martín had many influential acquaintances whom he entertained with spectacular balls and parties, and despite his numerous affairs with beautiful women, he was in fact a very lonely man, and as time went on, he suffered more and more with the feeling of emptiness.

Ausencio became an inseparable companion of his loneliness. Whenever Martín became ill, got excessively drunk, or taken over by melancholy, he summoned the young servant, who in time became his chief confidant. This role was a burden to him, but he had no choice. His entire future depended on the duke's sympathy, so he made every effort to meet the growing expectations and not to disappoint his increasingly capricious employer.

Burdened by such a great responsibility, Ausencio subconsciously wished that the favorable fate would endow also him with a close soul to whom he could entrust his innermost troubles and worries. This spot was filled by Iduna, who in a short time won his unlimited trust, replacing his long lost parents to him. Whenever he found a free moment, he would go to the wilderness where the new friend was waiting for him.

That day Ausencio had the afternoon off. As usual, he went to the forest, where Iduna was waiting for him at the appointed time. He showed up on time.

"Hello, my young friend!" She exclaimed cheerfully. "Look what I have prepared for you!"

She proudly pointed to the hearth, above which there was a metal bowl, full of finely ground, dried *hyoscyamus niger* leaves. Next to it was a basket of nuts and dried fruit.

"You are not looking well, my dear Ausencio," she said at the sight of the dark circles under the young man's eyes. "Is something bothering you?"

Ausencio looked listless.

"I'm well, however, I didn't sleep well that night. In fact, I never closed an eye."

"You couldn't fall asleep?"

"As for me, I have never had the slightest problem falling asleep. It was his Majesty who was tormented by terrible nightmares, so he went down to the palace dining room, where he also summoned me. He offered me a large glass of sweet wine, with which he had managed to get himself quite drunk even before I came. He was very depressed."

"How barbaric it is not to let a man sleep because of someone's own nightmares. Indeed, your master behaves like a spoiled child," said Iduna.

"If I had such nightmares, I would probably also get drunk or even do something even stupid. Fear changes people a lot... and especially the fear of such monstrosities..." Ausencio tried to excuse his master.

Iduna looked at him curiously. She knew dreams were always related to the past, and sometimes shed more light on certain events than a fully rational interpretation of them. She wasn't mistaken about her intuition.

"Every now and then his majesty has dreams, which could even be fatal to a less resilient man," Ausencio began. "I don't know what would happen to me if something similar happened to me. In fact" - here he deeply inhaled the smoke from the burnt leaves - "I am beginning to fear for my own health... If I dream the same, I might die or go mad like the Marquis de Viciosa.

Apparently, he suffered from something similar in his childhood, I know it from his Majesty."

"Perhaps César inherited a vivid imagination from his father..."

"It's not the imagination, Iduna. She came to him first. It was so terrible that the mere sight of her drove him completely insane. At first, everyone thought the boy was possessed by the devil. There was even a series of exorcisms that had little effect... but she hadn't come to His Majesty until yesterday."

"She who"?

"Duchess de Valsombra."

"Hmmm... your lord dreamed about his dead wife..." Iduna picked up with a slight sneer.

"My master has been saying for some time that he feels very lonely. He remembered her in conversations. Until he cried the proverbial wolf. She came at night."

"What do you mean she came? In a dream?"

"The duke was not asleep yet. As usual, at this time, he was writing his diaries at his desk when he suddenly saw a shape in the window. So he went to see if his strained eyesight was simply failing him, or if maybe Inés had not cleaned the glass again. It was then that he realized that the shape he was seeing in front of him was not a smudge on the glass, but a reflection of someone in the room. At the same time he felt a gust of icy air on his back, 'the breath of the grave,' as he put it. When he turned his head, he almost died of terror. The figure of a woman in a white lace dress stood before him. It was his late wife. She visited him looking just as he had seen her at that unfortunate ball."

"You just said she was terrible. What is terrible about seeing such a beautiful woman as Duchess Teresa?" Iduna asked, frowning.

"I'll explain everything to you. As his ducal majesty stared at the figure in front of him in disbelief, at first she looked just as he remembered her. However, her face gradually turned gray, her eyes and nose sank in... After a while, instead of the beautiful duchess, her decaying corpse stood before him, and soon - the skeleton itself, which rattled miserably in the shreds of the ball gown. The musty smell of the cemetery filled the room. My master stepped back in horror and barely had time to sit down in his chair, when the apparition suddenly vanished. His heart stopped beating for a moment. Then, with the last of his strength, he called Roberto and told him to call me."

Ausencio rubbed his eyes with his fingers several times, as if he wanted to erase from them the horrible vision that influenced his young imagination very strongly, although it did not happen to him personally.

"It seems that her ducal highness comes to her relatives at the moment they miss her. When his Excellency Marquis de Viciosa was a child and he missed his mother very much, he had similar visions," he said.

Iduna got thoughtful. She remembered perfectly well this sweet, dark brown tincture, which Serafín was to mix with aged wine and serve to the Duke de Valsombra at the moment of toasting "the beloved friends, present and absent." But something did not go as planned. The duke survived, while his wife became the innocent victim of the plot. Serafín, on the other hand, disappeared without a trace the next day. Thus Iduna could only guess how the tragic mistake had come about.

"Did your master mention the circumstances of his wife's death?" She asked, staring at Ausencio with her piercing black eyes.

"He only said one sentence about that: 'One second of madness has condemned me to life in hell'," Ausencio replied, inhaling the aromatic vapor from the hearth. "I have no idea what he meant."

"Didn't he say anything else?" Iduna continued.

"Absolutely nothing. He hid his face in his hands, then suddenly he struck the table with all his strength, with such force that the massive goblet with unfinished wine, standing on it, immediately fell over. Fortunately, it did not break - it would additionally upset my master. This cup belonged to his father, the famous Duke Leonard. My master does not part with it."

"It seems there has been some tragic mistake," said Iduna, pretending that the subject of the duchess's death was completely foreign to her. "But what could it be? I think we'll find out sooner or later."

"I don't think so," replied Ausencio. "When his grace the duke mentioned this unfortunate accident, he was already drunk. This morning he ordered me to forget about that night and not to mention it to anyone, threatening 'dire consequences'. But I trust you, Iduna."

"You can trust me. Someday your master will get drunk again and then perhaps he will tell you what is bothering him. Martín is a very lonely old man who obviously can't quite deal with the ghosts of his own past," said Iduna. "You are his only confidant," she added in a whisper.

"I'd rather not be one..." Ausencio sighed.

"It looks like this cruel man has murdered his own wife! This is the only way I can understand this one second of madness," Iduna thought. "But how did he know that the cup contained a deadly poison?!" She looked out of the corner of the eye at Ausencio, who had just raised his head, thoughtfully watching the flock of birds flying across the sky. "Serafín could not say anything because he owed me a debt of gratitude. And yet...? He's a traitor after all. If he had decided to murder his master, why shouldn't he betray me as well?" She thought bitterly.

Ausencio was still staring at the long line of birds that just crossed the clear sky. The position of the sun showed that the time of his visit was slowly drawing to an end and it was almost time to return.

"I feel so good here..." he sighed, "it's a pity I have to go back home. This palace always filled me with dread."

"There is something about it that upsets even me, so I try to avoid it," joined Iduna.

"I will come to see you as soon as I can. If I don't find you in, I'll wait."

"I will be looking forward to your visit," she answered, adding in her thoughts, "Perhaps you will manage to find out more   about   the   duchess's   death."

Chapter 7

Dorothea Nacht

After the medics had almost miraculously ripped her from the clutches of a terrible and mysterious disease that had completely devastated her body, Dorothea Nacht never returned to the opera stage. A colorful bird with a magic voice, which melted the hearts of the doges, dukes and patricians with its singing, fell silent forever. The big world forgot about her very quickly. After leaving the luxury apartment overlooking the Grand Canal, the once beloved opera goddess and her young son August moved to a dingy porch in the fishing district.

Realizing her position and the very uncertain fate awaiting them both, Dorothea invested the last of her savings in a trip to Spain, where her former lover and August's father, Martín Castro, lived. She hoped that the wealthy duke would recognize the five-year-old as his son and save at least him from a miserable fate. She wasn't counting on anything for herself.

It was then exactly eight months since Teresa's death, but Dorothea had no idea of the misfortune that had recently befallen the duke. When the mother and son finally arrived at their destination, after three weeks of tiring journey through the sun-scorched south of Europe, they stayed on the outskirts of Valsombra, in a small inn with a rather bizarre name El Rincón Oscuro - "Dark Alley".

The inn was located in a 17th-century homestead, whose characteristic frame wall reminded Dorothea of the so-called Prussian wall, well-known to her from her homeland. She smiled at the sight of the wooden beams, blackened from frequent rainfall, and the contrasting lime white.

"That's a good sign, son!" She said to August.

But the boy didn't answer. He fixed his eyes on the aged street spice vendor.

"Mom, look!" He called, dragging Dorothea over to the stall.

"Come on, August, what we need the least right now are spices. After all, we will not cook anything, we will eat dinner at the inn," she argued, pulling the child away from the man.

The boy obeyed his mother's command, but he could not take his eyes off the table, which was entirely covered with wooden boxes full of various herbs, dried bunches of plants, and mysterious-looking bottles with colorful liqueurs.

The salesman pressed a sprig of rosemary into his hand and said goodbye to both of them with a toothless smile.

"*Vielen Dank, Signor!*" Dorothea said in a mixture of Italian and German, waving a muslin handkerchief at the old man on leaving, as she used to do in Venice during her heyday, when she greeted this way the devotees who followed her home after the concert through canals and narrow sidewalks.

"Mom, what's he like?" August asked, excited about the near prospect of meeting his father.

"Intelligent, musical..." Dorothea began to enumerate. "He's also very wealthy, so if all goes well, he can ensure your education. Perhaps you will stay here for a while, who knows..."

"What is education?" The five-year-old wanted to know.

"Education is the most important thing in the world. Apart from you, sonny."

She bent down and kissed the boy on the forehead.

"Does that mean I'll go to school?"

"Yes, honey, to the best school. And then to university. Who knows, maybe you will become, for example, a scientist or a famous doctor? Such a son is a treasure, you will take care of your ailing mother."

"Then I'll become a doctor."

"Fine. Your father's help can make things a lot easier for you. He is a well-educated, but also well-to-do man."

She remembered Martín dimly. His image became more and more blurred in her memory, so that with time only his dark green eyes with penetrating gaze remained, the expression of which August had inherited from his father, and a noble profile with a prominent but perfectly proportioned nose, somewhat reminiscent of a bird of prey. It also seemed to her that her son had the duke's smile, although it was rarely seen on the child's face.

Like César, little August was a dark, withdrawn child. He was also distinguished by remarkable intelligence. He began to talk very early, at the age of only a few months, in full, grammatically correct sentences already, although he said them quite rarely. He also quickly learned to add and subtract. From an early age he was fascinated by trees, herbs, mushrooms, minerals and various chemicals.

He spoke only German with his mother, which did not prevent him from learning Italian. Over time, he was able to distinguish between the Venetian and Tuscan dialects that sounded in the streets and canals of his hometown. When a certain medical student, Giovanni Anastasi, moved into the building where they lived, August often looked into his room through a crack under the door, from where he watched the young man measure the tibia, cut frogs and mix various concoctions.

Giovanni was August's first teacher. Having caught the little boy red-handed, watching him clean the surgical instruments, he invited him over. From that moment on, he became August's mentor and friend. It was thanks to him that the boy learned the basics of correct Italian, and became interested in mathematics and natural sciences. August assisted Giovanni in his studies almost every evening, learning something new from him each time.

This pleased his mother, whose only goal in life was to give education to the boy, so that he could fulfill his childhood dreams in his adult life. She knew he was stubborn enough that if he liked something, no force could distract him from it. "At the sight of this little smarty panty, Martín will completely melt away. How can you not love such a child?" She thought hopefully.

After they left their luggage at the inn and slept off the hardships of the journey, Dorothea decided it was time to go to the palace. It stood on a small hill, and the road to it led through the main street of Valsombra, the same one El Rincón Oscuro was located at. Dorothea dressed in her best gown, the only one left from her stage triumphs. She kept it for "special occasions". The outfit for August was sewn by her own hands, although it looked as if it came from under the needle of a seasoned tailor.

As they walked towards the palace, Dorothea's long golden hair and the original beauty of her son attracted the eyes of passersby. Over the years spent in Italy, she had already gotten used to the southern spontaneity. The whistles and other taunts the young men gave her did not make any impression on her anymore. She responded with complete indifference or a cold, slightly dismissive smile.

As they reached the palace gates, Dorothea's heart sped up and drops of cold sweat appeared on her forehead.

"Mommy, what's wrong with you?" August asked, squeezing her wet, icy hand.

"Mom is nervous because she wants to do well at the meeting with your father. You also have to try your best. You are not allowed to say anything or go anywhere without my specific instructions. OK?"

"OK!" The boy replied. "I promise I will not let us down!" He added, embracing his mother's leg.

"We're so close. We will be able to breathe a sigh of relief this evening. You will finally meet your father, isn't that great? It's time for you to be introduced to each other..." said Dorothea, reassuring herself with these words.

"I wonder what he is like..." the boy said to himself.

When the two doorkeepers let them into the palace, Dorothea stood motionless for a moment, gazing in awe at the sumptuous interior. She had not seen such riches even in Venice or at the most eminent European courts where she performed. She was awakened from this amazement by the sight of a little boy, about four years old, with a swarthy complexion and shiny black curls, who suddenly ran through a side door into the palace hall, laid with pinkish marble. He was followed by a young girl, apparently a babysitter.

Seeing August, the little boy suddenly got gloomy. He stopped, watching carefully the fair-haired boy, a little older than himself.

"César, welcome the guests. Show me how nice you can bow."

The boy greeted them with a graceful bow. Dorothea looked meaningfully at her son, who immediately obeyed her instructions and returned the bow.

"*Como te llamas?*"[8] asked the nanny, walking up to August and stroking his blond hair.

"*August. Un piacere*"[9] - the boy introduced himself, brilliantly recognizing Italian sounds in the Spanish words and guessing their probable meaning.

César was studying Dorothea and her son seriously.

The fair-haired boy with cold eyes aroused incomprehensible fear in him. The sight of César, in turn, filled little August with unspeakable sadness, as if he understood that the place at his father's side had already been taken. He looked away from him and the girl accompanying him, then stared at one of the two stately gargoyles, crowning the marble railings of the stairs.

When Roberto entered the hall, Dorothea handed him a letter addressed to the duke. The servant looked closely at her and the child, then nodded and went to his master's quarters to deliver the letter to him. The duke made them wait for a long time. Two hours passed before he finally made his way downstairs in slow, majestic steps. Dorothea noticed that he looked much older.

He was dressed in a black tailcoat and a gray vest, tied with a black silk sash. He looked coldly at Dorothea, ignoring August entirely.

"I wasn't expecting this visit," he said coldly.

"I will explain everything," said Dorothea, "but first, I'd like to introduce someone to you."

Her heart was racing madly, like that of the game animals when they were on the verge of dying at the hands of a hunter.

The conversation was in German.

"This is your son, August."

"What an absurdity!" Said the duke in a theatrical tone. "I have only one son, named César. By the way, I am amused by this coincidence... both boys have Roman names," he added with a smile.

"Indeed, a strange coincidence. August is a popular German name. I gave it to him out of nostalgia."

"Good thing you haven't named him Martín. It would be extremely embarrassing," the duke said sarcastically.

"I didn't know you had a son," said Dorothea. "He's a little younger than mine..."

"Unfortunately, he is my only son," he replied, emphasizing the adjective "only."

Dorothea felt her heart leap in her throat.

"My wife passed away eight months ago."

"I am very sorry... How unfortunate the timing we came here... Forgive me for this tactless visit, I had no idea that such a terrible misfortune has befallen your family... "

"I don't blame you."

"Also know that I would never have come here, if the situation in which I found myself didn't force me to do so."

"The famous Dorothea Nacht in a difficult situation? This is some news..." said the duke, expressing his mock surprise in his typical theatrical way.

August swallowed. His eyes narrowed.

"Soon after the birth of August, I fell seriously ill. One of the symptoms was swelling in the airways that nearly resulted in suffocation. Somehow I managed to survive, even though the medics had already written me off. Unfortunately, I never regained the voice that was my working tool. You can't hear it when I speak, but I'm not able to sing anything anymore. We have lived for some time off the savings we had accumulated over the years, but these are starting to run out. I don't know how long I'll be able to support August. It is about him, not about myself, and I am asking you only to help me raise him and educate him. He is your son too after all..."

"I have absolutely no certainty that August is my son. After all, you are not a nun, but an opera singer..."

"We didn't come here to be insulted by you. May God reward you handsomely for how you dealt with us!" she replied, and she and her son hurriedly left the sumptuous residence.

Once they were some distance from the gate, Dorothea knelt on the ground and burst into tears.

"Don't worry about me, Mom. I don't want a father like that at all. He is nasty!" He said, embracing her. "May he die!" - he added in his thoughts.

"It's over now. Never in my life has anyone humiliated me more than this pompous, selfish, conceited man! This is the end!"

In an instant, she got up from the ground, grabbed the boy's hand and, dragging him behind her, and quickly headed towards the forest.

"Mom, where are we going?" August asked.

He sensed that despair had taken away his mother's reason, and that she was going to do something terrible.

"*In die Dunkelheit!*"[10] exclaimed Dorothea.

At that moment, August noticed that his mother was holding a shiny object in her hand. It was the same dagger she usually carried with her in Venice, in case she was attacked by bad guys, numerous in their neighborhood. The boy, however, immediately understood that she had not taken it from her purse in order to defend herself against bandits, but for a completely different, terrible purpose. So he started screaming loudly and crying, hoping that this would attract people's attention and save them both from his mother's madness. That's when Iduna saw them.

They spent the night in her cave, from where, after restoring themselves with a meal of mushrooms and a wild goose she had hunted, they set off on their way back in the morning. When their money ran out, they stopped at a different tavern every night, where Dorothea managed each time to collect a few pennies in exchange for washing dishes and tables and cleaning the guest rooms. When they got to Venice, she was completely exhausted and fell ill again.

After she recovered, thanks to the quick intervention of Dr. Carlini, brought by Giovanni, she immediately began to look for something to do, so that she could provide for herself and her son. After a few weeks of feverish searching, she finally got a job as a seamstress, which helped her pay off her rent arrears and provided her with a temporary, very modest but relatively steady income.

Despite his age, August was well aware that even this job was beyond the strength of his increasingly ill mother. He knew that the only way he could save her from dying, would be for him to start some kind of work as soon as possible. Giovanni had a pharmacist friend, who was in dire need of a diligent messenger. When he brought little August to the pharmacy one day, Matteo Mattei burst out laughing.

"Isn't' he your neighbor's son? This kid doesn't speak a word of Italian!

"You're wrong, sir" August interrupted suddenly. "I don't speak as well as you, because I'm not Italian, but I can do it. My mom is sick, you must accept me."

"I assure you with my own head that this toddler will be of more use for you than a hundred other messengers. He is stubborn as a donkey, incredibly hard-working, and when he likes something, he puts his whole soul into it! He is like a little adult" - Giovanni praised his little friend, then added in his thoughts: "His crazy determination scares me a little..."

"All right then," Matteo Mattei agreed. "You'll get a fair salary, so you can help your mom. But remember, you must not be late once! You start tomorrow morning."

Giovanni shook his friend's hand, then stroked the boy's fair hair. He was glad that he could be of help, at least in this way, for Dorothea, whom he had secretly loved for a long time. He also knew that Matteo Mattei was reliable, and one could be hundred percent sure he would deliver on his promise. He was sure of the same about August.

The boy showed up at the appointed place half an hour early. Standing in front of the still closed pharmacy, he stared with delight at the small display window, decorated with dried herbs and jars, bottles and boxes containing salutary drugs, as well as deadly poisons. He immediately remembered that old trader in Valsombra and his stall, full of various treasures.

"*Tinctura menthae... tinctura salviae... cnicus benedictus... cyanidum... acidum carbolicum...*" he read aloud the calligraphic labels.

Matteo Mattei came in at a quarter to seven.

"I did not expect this!" he exclaimed appreciatively as he saw the little boy waiting patiently outside the pharmacy and passionately repeating Latin names.

"It is wonderful!" August marveled. His blue eyes glowed.

"I see medic material in you," Matteo Mattei said. "If you become a doctor, your mom will never be in financial trouble again! You just need to work hard and study diligently, no pain - no gain."

"I like to work," replied the boy, staring seriously at his employer.

August started working on the same day. He did great. He quickly won the sympathy of the pharmacist and his wife, Anna Maria. They had no children of their own, so the ambitious and hardworking boy quickly became their favorite. Already at the age of eight, he helped in the pharmacy while attending school. Matteo Mattei gradually introduced him to the innermost secrets of the pharmacy, and August turned out to be an exceptionally talented student. As a sixteen-year-old he was accepted to medical school, where he could finally learn the secrets of the medical profession. Like previously Giovanni, then already a respected surgeon known as *Il Dottore Anastasi*, he brought home bones and collected a variety of specimens, the sight of which made Dorothea sick. However, she never said a word about it, because she knew that her son's peculiar workshop was indispensable to his studies. At the sight of the handsome and eminently gifted young man, his mother's heart was bursting with pride.

August quickly established himself as a diligent and competent physician. Whenever someone in Venice became seriously ill, especially when he had an extremely rare condition, the first specialist to be sent for was *Il Dottore Nacht*. He also treated his mother, whom he diagnosed with a very atypical case of severe, chronic rhinitis. Thanks to him, she lived to the age of fifty-eight, although under normal circumstances the disease would have wiped her off the face of the earth at least ten years earlier.

However, the brilliant doctor had a second face. His extensive pharmaceutical knowledge, acquired during ten years of working in a pharmacy, also allowed him to prepare sophisticated poisons and find effective antidotes. After he saved the life of a Doge's son, whose dinner had been sprinkled with arsenic, his grateful father presented him with a purse full of gold coins.

Some time later the doge sent for him on a very confidential matter. It was about eliminating a certain inconvenient senator. August fulfilled the order perfectly, for which he received another purse, and a precious ruby signet ring with a monogram A.N. and a motif of three connected stars referring to the name Nacht [11], made on special order by the most famous Venetian jeweler. From then on, August always sealed letters with it.

After some time, the talented physician received another order, and soon another one. He quickly discovered that he was rewarded much more generously for taking a life than for saving it. The gratitude for the removal of a rival, or for the avenged insult, was a thousand times greater than the gratitude for the saved wives in labor and newborns, disinfected wounds, operated fractures or timely antidotes. August's secret knowledge and skills were the object of desire for vengeful politicians, deceptive careerists and betrayed wives.

He was doing very well, and his mother, proud of August, did not suspect anything. Soon they moved to a very cozy apartment on one of the nicer streets, where they were not bothered too much by the dampness coming from the canals, the unpleasant smell of rat droppings, and the constant raids of mosquitoes. However, Dorothea's health began to decline again. Despite August's and Giovanni's best efforts, she was fading before their eyes. She died with a smile on her face.

After arriving in Valsombra, August, once again rejected by his father, decided to stay in Spain, intending to avenge his harm sooner or later. The fire of revenge, burning in his chest, was fueled by the meeting with Iduna. Just like she had saved Dorothea from taking hers and his life years ago, also this time she poured consolation into his heart again. It was only thanks to her that he managed to emerge from the abyss of despair that was sucking him in, and began to rationally plan his revenge.

He checked into the El Rincón Oscuro inn - the same one where he and his mother had stayed once. After a few days, he met a judge from Oviedo named Pelayo Lorenzo. This man, obsessed with fear for his own safety, decided that the heavens themselves had sent him a savior in the form of an eminent expert on poisons and antidotes. He invited him to his beautiful estate, which August gladly accepted.

The circle of patients, until now limited to Pelayo Lorenzo, quickly expanded to include his father, suffering from gout, his wife suffering from all diseases of the world, his cousin struggling with anemia, and numerous friends. They took advantage profusely of not only August's excellent medical skills, but also his pharmaceutical knowledge and less official services, which, as in his native Italy, made him a trusted friend to many influential sufferers.

8   Spanish: *What's your name?*
9   Italian: *Nice to meet you.*
10 German: *Into the dark!*
11 German: *Night.*

Chapter 8

Blanca Morales

Count de Aciago opened the door to his bedroom. He looked around, but Blanca was not in the room.

"¡La perra maldita!"[12] - he drawled through his teeth.

Blood was pulsating rapidly in the swollen veins at his temples. He immediately left the chamber, slamming the door behind him with all his might, then ran down the marble stairs into the hall. He looked like enraged Polyphemus who, as soon as he discovered the trick of the cunning Odysseus, rushed out of his cave onto the seashore to curse his tormentor.

The moon just peeked out from behind a screen of dark blue clouds, casting a bluish light on his broken nose. Not able to find his wife anywhere, he called his servant Adrián.

"Saddle Blue!" he ordered. "Immediately!"

"Lord, it's only three in the morning!" The surprised servant replied.

"No discussion!" The count snapped, puffing his nostrils in rage.

"Has her Majesty disappeared again?"

"She must have gotten out of here a while ago. This mad woman will drive me crazy. I'm going to look for her!"

"I will go with you," Adrián offered.

"You're not going anywhere. This is my business, my disgrace!" The count shouted.

As soon as Adrián managed to saddle his horse, he mounted the mighty animal in one skillful move, and thrusting his spurs into its sides until they got bloody, he sped blindly into the dark of the forest. Whoever saw him from a distance would surely think he was seeing a dark apparition, or enraged Pluto, who got out from hell to earth. He could also be mistaken for Death itself, in the form of a mighty rider on a black horse.

The count's mind was completely taken over by the thought of punishing his wife for showing him such blatant disregard and making him the laughingstock of the service. He frantically looked for her pale figure between the trunks of the trees and in the sinister-looking thickets along the Arroyo Oculto creek [13], where half a year before his death, one of his recently deceased friends saw a corpse-pale old woman, dressed in long torn rags, washing bloody cloths in icy water.

A shiver of terror ran down his wide back. The murmur of the stream echoed the long groans of the night birds and the mournful howls of wolves. In the count's burning head, these sounds merged into a big sinister symphony. Having confused two similar-looking paths, he had just entered the wildest part of the forest, completely overgrown by thorny bushes, through which a stream ran. By the time he realized his mistake, it was too late.

The horse screeched terribly and reared up, scaring the nightjars, owls and other birds carelessly dozing on the branches of ancient trees. Blood spurted from the horse's spiked flanks and his thorn-torn legs, and foam rolled copiously from his mouth. Mad with pain and fear, the animal kicked madly, trying to throw off its rider at all costs. The desperate attempts to control the horse and stay in the saddle did not work, and Count de Aciago fell heavily to the hard, rocky ground. Ignoring the wounded, Blue ran deeper into the forest. In the morning the count was found by the servants. He miraculously survived.

At the same time, Blanca went to her favorite clearing. She quietly hoped to meet again the stranger she saw there so often, whether she was watching the stars or looking for night creatures. She kept thinking back to the moment when in a sudden rush of madness that she did not understand, breaking all the rules of etiquette and good manners, she gave him a kiss.

She knew that Count de Aciago might appear in the woods at any moment. She was also aware of the unpleasant consequences of the disobedience to her husband. With time, however, she stopped thinking about them. Moreover, while until recently she had feared enraging the count, now, on the contrary, knowing that she had nothing to lose anymore, she even relished his frustration and spasmodic attacks of anger.

When she reached the clearing, there was no one there except for a few stray deers, which scattered in all directions of the forest at the sound of her footsteps. She looked up at the sky, but even the faint glow of the moon hurt her. With time, she tolerated light less and less, and preferred to spend her time in a darkened room in the north wing of the palace. That was why she longed for the night to come, so that she could enjoy a walk or reading in the fresh air.

Initially, she did not think much of this strange ailment, ascribing its appearance to the distress caused by her father's death and her husband's unbalanced behavior. Eventually, however, she began to wonder why, in just a few months, her life had begun to be confined to the night and the hours of very early morning or late evening, after the complete darkness.

"What is happening to me?" she thought, hiding her face in her hands. When she looked up at the sky again, she felt a strong dizziness. She didn't want to go back to the palace, she preferred a hundred times more to spend even the whole night in the forest than in the bedroom. She had already managed to control the fear of her husband, which at first paralyzed her, and a strong disgust with his perfidious character, but she preferred to use every opportunity to avoid returning to the hated marriage bed at night.

Every evening she waited impatiently for darkness to fall. As soon as the world fell into the darkness she desired, she hurriedly left the palace. The Count de Aciago ordered the old servant named Jaime to close the gates for servants just before dark. The latter, however, while diligently following the order every night, obtained a copy of the key, which he secretly gave to Blanca.

At one point, she came across a path leading into the parts of the forest that had been unknown to her till now. She decided to check it out. "I have a lot of time, and later come what may," she thought, then plunged into the dark abyss. After a dozen or so months, her eyesight adapted to living in the dark to such an extent, that she began to see in the dark almost as well, and with time even better, than in the light of the sun or candles.

The barely visible path, frequented only by deer and wolves, was guarded on both sides by huge trees with stocky trunks and massive boughs, twisted in all directions. Some of them resembled hooded monks, others - dried mummies, still others - grotesque dwarfs. Blanca flinched at the sight of these shapes, but decided not to retreat into the clearing, but rather to check where this rarely traveled trail led to.

Her inborn curiosity and the need to face challenges had always led her to the mysterious and the dangerous. From her earliest childhood, she eagerly visited abandoned houses, neglected gardens and old, mossy cemeteries. So when her eyes suddenly stopped tolerating daylight, she quickly got used to living in darkness and among shadows, and in time she even liked them.

The overgrown path turned out to be much shorter and less winding than Blanca had first thought. It led directly to a small courtyard of a medieval castle. The gothic building was tightly covered with ivy and vines. The eastern part looked inhabited. It appeared to Blanca that there was a faint light in one of the rooms adjoining a large terrace. The west wing, on the other hand, was ruined and entirely overgrown with wild vine.

An elegant black carriage, standing in front of the building, indicated that its owner was in the castle. So Blanca decided it would be best to look at the building from the west part, which looked poorly guarded, if there was any living soul there at all. She was captivated by the sight of aggressive vines, gradually breaking apart the solid, stone structure. "I wonder why nobody lives here," she wondered. "Certainly there must be a story associated with this place... but who could tell me about it?"

At that moment, her heart sped up rapidly, then stopped for a split second. Behind her, she heard the rustle of leaves. When she turned her head, she saw in front of her a man of enormous height with long, reddish hair.

"Don't worry, I won't do you any harm, Madam. My name is Aitor. You probably got lost in the woods. How could I help you?"

"I got lost a bit. I don't want to trouble you, I know the way back. Whose property is this?"

"It's Castillo de Viciosa. The castle and its lands are the property of César Castro y de Abaroa. I am his servant."

"So I got to Viciosa..." she said, admiring the structure thoughtfully. "Your master must be very happy here. This is a beautiful area!"

"My master loves this place. The more the castle blends with the rest of the forest, the happier he is. Just look, these insolent vine shoots are breaking even into his bedroom!" Aitor said, pointing to the terrace in the east wing.

There was still a faint light in the room.

Blanca thought with disgust of the Count de Aciago's palace, almost as old as the castle, but partly rebuilt and full of ostentatious splendor. She did not consider it her home, but rather a tomb in which she was imprisoned while still alive.

"Why don't you come in for some wine and dinner? Would you like to meet the Marquis de Viciosa? As you can see, he is still awake. Your flattering opinion on his preferences will certainly please him very much."

"You're a good man. However, the last thing I would like to do right now is to cause you trouble and to irritate your master. The Marquis de Viciosa certainly has better things to do than talking to random people."

"He writes something all night long or walks in the woods."

"Your master must be an extraordinary man."

"The most extraordinary I've ever met. He is also one of the noblest people I have ever dealt with."

"Even someone as noble as your lord might get upset if he were suddenly distracted from some interesting activity at such a late hour. I don't think he would see your spontaneous idea appropriate."

Blanca felt the ground move away from under her feet. "What a horrible situation!" she thought. "Certainly the stranger towards whom I acted so inappropriately was the Marquis de Viciosa himself. The same one that is the subject of legends. Apparently he is not crazy at all, as Ramón and his siblings claim. Unfortunately, now he probably thinks I'm crazy. It is amazing how much damage I caused myself in this one moment..." She also knew that even if she hadn't jeopardized her pride that night by acting in a rather extravagant manner, she wouldn't be able to accept the invitation. "We'd all have to be talking in the dark," she thought resignedly.

Aitor snapped her out of this gloomy reverie.

"If you need anything, I'm at your service," he said, examining her face carefully.

His attention was drawn to large, black eyes that looked as if they were missing irises. "I've never seen eyes like this in my life," he thought.

"Thank you for your concern, my friend. I don't need anything," replied Blanca.

"I can take you back in a carriage, or if you wish, you can go on horseback."

"I would only cause unnecessary trouble for you and your master. I need to go back. It's time for me."

"Do you live far?"

"This, unfortunately, I cannot reveal," she replied mysteriously, knowing that the kind hearted giant could discreetly escort her out of fear for her safety.

If Count de Aciago saw him by accident, Aitor could even pay for it with his life.

The way back to the palace was much more difficult than Blanca had thought. Not having a good understanding of the newly discovered area, she confused the narrow path that had led her to the castle with another, quite similar one, making exactly the same mistake as Count de Aciago had made before. She realized it late, already halfway there. She was afraid of predatory animals for which she could become an easy prey. So she quickened her pace and kept walking, not looking back. "Sooner or later I'll get out of here somehow," she reassured herself.

Her heart beat faster and faster. Suddenly her knees gave way. In front of her, a dozen or so steps away, was a black horse. Its mouth was open and foamy, and huge thorns stuck out from its bloody sides. The suffering animal scratched its hoof irritably, snorting every now and then.

"Blue?!" Blanca called, recognizing the count's horse. "Where's Ramón?"

The horse replied with a terrifying neigh, shaking his long mane, ruffled by thorny thickets.

Blanca slowly approached the animal, grabbing it by the bridle and gently stroking its face. When she was sure the horse would not kick and hurt her, she pulled the first thorn from its side, a millimeter thick and a few centimeters long. A moment later she pulled out another, and another, and another... Blood spurted profusely from the animal's wounds each time.

"He must have had an accident," she thought. "I think he treated Blue the same way he treated me on the wedding night." At the mention of that terrible night, a violent shudder of disgust ran through her body. "It's terrible to wish your husband die... but I hope he's dead!" She pressed her cheek against the thorn-gutted side of the animal and stood still for a moment, inhaling the sweet scent of blood into her nostrils.

After a while, no longer thinking of anything other but relieving the tormented horse in suffering, she wiped its wounds with her shawl, then removed most of the thorns from the other side of the animal. Unexpectedly, she heard the sound of human voices. She immediately recognized Jaime and Andrés, a newly recruited servant, favored by Count de Aciago.

Though she had already grown accustomed to the count's crudeness, Blanca felt a strong fear of this servant. Always insolent and self-confident, he treated all the household members with contempt, and his eyes had a ruthless expression. The way he looked at her disgusted her even more than all the atrocities she had experienced on the part of her husband. Andrés was from Galicia. Hearing him speak with old Jaime with his singing accent, she instinctively dug her nails with all her strength into the skin of both hands until her own blood mixed with the horse's.

At the sound of Andrés's melodious voice, Blue snorted and slammed his hoof violently against the rocky path.

"Shh Shh!" Blanca hissed, not wanting the servant to notice her.

The horse seemed to understand immediately. It was completely still, so even Blanca could not hear it breathing.

"Somebody is here!" Andrés exclaimed, characteristically prolonging the last sound.

"Damn thug!" Blanca thought. "Good thing he came with Jaime. If it weren't for this old good man, probably all that would be left for me would be to pray for death!"

"My beautiful lady! How worried we were!" Andrés said, bowing with exaggeration.

There was a hint of mockery in his voice.

"Where is my husband?" Blanca asked.

"Countess…" Jaime began.

"Has there been an accident?" Blanca interrupted. "During my walk, I came across Blue. He's hurt. Where is my husband? Has he survived?"

"The Count fell off his horse. He is in bad condition, but medics say he will live."

"For such am offense, the beast should end up in the slaughterhouse," Andrés said.

Blanca didn't answer, aware that the impudent servant was clearly provoking her. All the time she felt his gaze on her.

"As far as I know, the Count makes such decisions, not you, youngster!" Jaime said. "If necessary, I can afford to buy him out from the butcher. My brother's mare has just died, so if the Count decides to get rid of him, Blue will be a blessing for him."

"Be it as you want, old man," Andrés replied with an ironic smirk to Jaime, who was half a head shorter than him.

It was dawn when they returned to the palace. The rays of the morning sun blinded Blanca, so she quickly headed towards the palace, covering her eyes with her hand, and then disappeared into a narrow, side staircase. During the day she used it very rarely, because the way from that part of the palace to the rooms of Count de Aciago led through the rooms occupied by the servants. This time, however, seeing that Andrés had gone with Jaime towards the stables, she decided she could go that way without fear.

When she reached the chamber and opened the door, her eyes narrowed instinctively, as the light of the candlesticks immediately hurt her. She found her husband in the company of two medics, who were arguing fiercely over how best to treat an open collarbone fracture, apparently having no idea what to do.

Count de Aciago was pale like death, and a cold sweat ran profusely down his forehead.

"My beloved!" He groaned, trying to make her feel guilty. "It's because of you that I got these horrible injuries. I went out looking for you."

"I'm sorry about your accident," Blanca replied.

The timbre of her voice sounded so indifferent that the medics, who had just been close to jump at each other's throat a moment before, exchanged knowing glances in unison.

12 Spanish *Damn bitch!*
13 Spanish   *Hidden*   *stream.*

Chapter 9

Palacio Aciago

While the count's other injuries healed reasonably well, the shattered collarbone had turned a suspiciously blue color. The two medics alternately argued over this and nodded their heads in concern. They gazed at the ever uglier wound with resignation, exchanging knowing glances whenever they were asked about the health of the Count de Aciago. Realizing that the state of his health was deteriorating significantly day by day, the count trusted these specialists less and less.

Two days after the accident, Mario Suárez visited his injured brother. He arrived in a gilded carriage, pulled by four slender gray horses with neatly combed, silky manes. As usual, the cardinal appeared dressed in his ostentatiously exquisite manner. He shared the love of glamour that characterized his younger brother Ramón. The clergyman's clothing was refined in every detail, from shiny shoes to elegant headgear.

Andrés greeted him, theatrically kneeling down and kissing his grand ring. This flattered the cardinal, who regarded his brother's new servant with appreciation. "Ramón has always had a good eye for people, especially when it comes to choosing a service. With women, he is a bit worse, although on the other hand, I would be a complete hypocrite if I pretended that I did not see the beauty of my sister-in-law," he thought.

More than the count, Mario wanted to see his wife. Therefore, before he greeted his brother, he supposedly inadvertently opened the door to the darkened office, adjacent to the bedroom. Blanca was immersed in reading works of Propertius.

"Are you, my beautiful sister-in-law, studying the classics again?" He asked. "A woman as well read as you is a real rarity."

"Nice of you, my dear Mario, that you value good literature," Blanca replied, smiling coldly at her brother-in-law. "I owe being well read to my late father, who taught me Latin."

" 'My dear Mario' - how beautiful it sounded..." the cardinal noted with satisfaction, then placed a long kiss on her hand. "I am also very pleased when such an angel addresses me in this way."

He was still holding her hand. Blanca jerked away quickly, struggling to hold back the spontaneous urge to rub her hand on her dress. Her inborn tact did not allow her to make such an ostentation.

"I see that my beautiful sister-in-law is not in the good mood today. You are probably troubled by your husband's illness," said the cardinal diplomatically.

"I am very sorry he is in pain," she replied flatly.

The cardinal laughed knowingly to himself, then left the room.

Left alone, Blanca was no longer able to concentrate on her reading. Her mind was overwhelmed by uncertainty mixed with fear. She tried in vain to chase away the terrifying visions of what would await her if she were suddenly left at the mercy of the impudent Andrés, who unofficially, though with the express approval of the Count de Aciago, had become the self-proclaimed administrator of the palace. Fragments of Ramón's conversation with his brother, which she had accidentally overheard through the wall, also broke her concentration.

Now, in turn, she had a new fear - of aging Mario. As he left the office, her heart was pounding as if it was about to break out of her chest. With a trembling hand, she opened a desk drawer, hoping to find in it the key to lock the door from the inside. In vain. "I have to find Pilar. Even if Ramón has hidden the key somewhere, or perhaps the key has been lost because of someone's neglect, Pilar must have at least one more copy," she thought with satisfaction.

In the next room, she heard Jaime's voice. So she took a strategic position by the door to get his attention as he would be leaving the chamber. Indeed, after several minutes, the old servant stepped out into the corridor. Through a crack in the ajar door, Blanca saw that he was alone. She extended her hand and made an inviting gesture. Fearing that the conversation might be overheard, she pointed to the lock and drew the letter "P" in the air, which was the initial of the keymaster's name.

Good-hearted Jaime understood immediately. He also figured out why Blanca was so anxious to get the key. He had noticed how Andrés was acting toward his mistress, and he did not fail to notice the meaningful glances that the cardinal himself gave her. "I hope one of these two does not come up with the same idea! I hope Pilar is not so utterly stupid as to give someone the key to my mistress's room! May there be only one copy!" He thought, and then, without wasting any time, he headed for the small room near the palace kitchen, which was by occupied Pilar.

At the same time, the cardinal and his brother were wondering with whom to replace the two elderly medics, who turned out to be completely useless. Count de Aciago was very weak, and a rather serious infection developed in his broken collarbone.

"I know someone who can heal you. He is a young German educated in Italy. He's arrived here recently. I met him personally during my last stay in Oviedo, at the house of Pelayo Lorenzo, who praised his extraordinary abilities to me," the cardinal said, examining the infected wound. "Apparently he is a genius who can cure almost any disease. He also knows herbs well."

"Pelayo Lorenzo? You mean Judge Lorenzo?" The count asked.

"Indeed."

"If Pelayo Lorenzo praised him, it means that the gentleman deserves the highest esteem. Do you know where this man has stayed?"

"He is reportedly in Cantabria. Pelayo told me that he met him at the El Rincón Oscuro inn in Valsombra, where he checked in at the time."

"Send for him. I'm afraid that at the moment only a true medical genius will be able to help me. What's the name of this German?"

"The last name I remember: Dr. Nacht. I believe his name is Anton or August. However, all you have to do is send someone from the service to Valsombra with orders to inquire about a German medic named Nacht. They will surely find him."

Without a moment of delay, Count de Aciago sent Adrián to Valsombra, where he was tasked with finding the talented doctor. The servant immediately headed for the old inn. When he asked the innkeeper if there was a young German there, she knew immediately who he meant.

"Dr. Nacht has just left to see a patient. Apparently it's a tough case. Shall I give him a message when he gets back?" The woman asked.

"He is urgently needed at the Palacio Aciago. This case is also difficult. My lord, Count Ramón Suárez, has had a serious accident. Only a doctor as good as doctor Nacht is considered to be, can save him."

Adrián shoved two golden escudos into the woman's hand to make sure she would deliver the message. Squeezing them tightly, the innkeeper smiled with satisfaction.

"I will definitely pass it on," she whispered happily.

While the count and cardinal were busy talking, Jaime managed to get the key to the office where Blanca was staying.

Fortunately, he found Pilar in her cell, where she was crocheting while singing an old lullaby.

"Always coming in here and rummaging through drawers. Take what you want and don't disturb me!" she ordered.

Jaime, meanwhile, retrieved the key to the office from a drawer marked "2" and immediately went upstairs to hand it over to Blanca. When she saw the key, she kissed the old man's rough cheek.

"I don't even know, my good Jaime, how to thank you. Bring me also a bed to sleep on and a change of gowns. I do not intend to return to my room" - she whispered, at the same time gesturing to him that he should leave quickly so as not to arouse suspicions. "They seem to be talking, but their vigilance never sleeps!" she thought.

As soon as dusk fell, having prudently equipped herself with a dagger, she headed as silently as she could for the servants' section, from where she could easily get out through the side exit to which she had the key. She held her breath as she passed the room Andrés occupied. Every crack of the old parquet or stairs made her dread.

She had already mastered the art of tiptoeing down the spiral, almost vertical stairs to perfection. Over time, she was no longer afraid of the giant spiders that lived in the gloomy, narrow staircase, though it took several months for her to become accustomed to seeing them. She was also used to the shadows, cast by the openwork balustrade on the long unbleached walls.

After getting outside, she took in the cool night air in her lungs, then, enlivened by its freshness, headed for her favorite clearing. She was almost certain that the stranger she saw in those areas, whom she had suddenly kissed for reasons unclear to her, was César Castro, and that sooner or later they would be introduced to each other. So she decided to forget about the "unfortunate event" and not to avoid the only place where she could forget at least for a moment about the ubiquitous atmosphere of fear in Palacio Aciago, becoming more and more unbearable every day.

The enormous mansion that her husband had inherited from his parents, owed its bizarre yet grim name to the misfortunes that had befallen the family of Ramón's ancestor, the famous Balduino, more than a hundred years ago. Pilar knew his story best among the household members, and told it to Blanca once, in secret from the count. It is said that this Balduino murdered his cousin in a fit of rage.

Isabel, because that was the name of the woman, was his adolescent love. Although Balduino married Count Ortega's daughter, María, he did not give up his secret trysts with his still unmarried cousin. After the death of María, who was said to have died of grief, Balduino proposed to marry Isabel. However, perhaps due to remorse, she refused.

Balduino then became furious and slashed her throat with a razor. It happened late in the evening. By the time he recovered from his insanity attack and realized his terrible deed, it was too late. Having laid Isabel's body on the bed next to him, he spent the night mourning the crime he had committed and pleading with his cousin's soul to punish him accordingly. The request was answered within the same twenty four hours.

In the morning, the eyes of the two doormen saw a terrible sight. The massive palace gate suddenly swung open.

Isabel walked slowly out through it. A thick trickle of partially clotted blood ran from her slit throat onto a white muslin dress. Her eyes were wide open, but they were already a little cloudy. Shrouded in deadly white, they stared motionlessly into the distance.

She led Balduino, who followed her obediently, squeezing her icy hand. Paralyzed with fear, the watchmen watched in astonishment as the lovers disappeared into the mist of the morning fog, holding hands. When they recovered, they alerted the rest of the servants and the whole family. Almost every corner of the Pueblo Aciago was searched, including the so-called Hanged Men's Cemetery, where, according to local legends, witches gathered herbs. Indeed, mandrake, among others, grew there.

There was no trace of Balduino and Isabel, but the memory of them remained alive. Despite the fact that successive descendants of Balduino made every effort to ensure that this macabre event was forever erased from the history of the family, the servants, as well as the numerous enemies of the clan that was closely associated with the Inquisition, were eager to tell about it. The liveliness of the legend was also successfully fueled by villagers, who claimed to see this terrifying couple every now and then, walking in the early morning hours in a forest clearing near Palacio Aciago.

Taking her place on her favorite stump at the edge of the clearing, Blanca suddenly remembered that terrible legend. "Like humans, houses have memories," she thought. "The memory of that terrible Balduino remains in his palace. Maybe there is a curse on it and that's why I'm slowly sinking into darkness..." A gentle rustle of leaves from the mouth of the path that had taken her the last time to Castillo de Viciosa, snapped her from her somber reverie.

When she looked that way, her eyes saw the characteristic figure of César. She easily recognized his statuesque features and long black hair that fell down his back. The words of Aitor, who described the Marquis de Viciosa as "one of the noblest men," emboldened her. "If he really has such a noble character, he will not judge me by my last indiscretion," she decided in her mind.

She rose from her comfy seat, sliding a silk bookmark into the precious 1727 Amsterdam edition of the Elegy of Propertius. "It's all because of you, Sextus! After so many years, your works continue to stimulate the imagination..." - she thought, smiling to herself. César greeted her from afar with a beautiful bow, which she courteously returned.

"*Sunt aliquid Manes: letum non omnia finit...* [14]" he said, looking meaningfully at the *Elegiarum libri quatuor* that Blanca still held in her hand.

"It's my favorite elegy," Blanca remarked, raising her eyebrows.

"Mine too. Especially its first sentence... When I was a child I used to repeat it over and over again because it gave me hope."

"I understand that you lost someone very close..."

"My mother. She died suddenly, I didn't even have time to say goodbye to her."

"It was similar with my parents. My mother drowned herself in the well, and father died of a strange disease that no one could even identify. I know how you feel. This is one of the most painful sufferings..."

"I missed my mother so much that in my mind I often begged her to come. I wanted one last look at her, which was not given to me the day she died. One night I realized how unreasonable these childish pleas were..."

"Why?"

"Because they were heard. I saw my mother... It was such a terrible sight that I almost died myself. Worse yet... I'm sorry, I don't know why I'm telling you such horrors. We do not even know each other!"

"I am honored that a stranger has placed so much trust in me," Blanca said.

"I haven't even introduced myself! César Castro y de Abaroa, at your service!"

"Blanca Morales," she said.

He kissed her hand.

"I owe you an explanation... I believe you can guess what I'm talking about..."

"Indeed. I am your debtor and will remain so until my death. This wonderful kiss brought back my will to live again. This is the most beautiful gift I have ever received."

"I have received a beautiful gift from you too - your trust. It is also a priceless gem, much more precious than that one kiss. Beautiful, but also obliging. You trust me, that's why I should warn you about myself..."

"I don't understand... What do you mean?"

"At first I did not intend to tell you my story so as not to endanger you..."

"For you, Madam, I am ready to expose myself to any danger."

"I don't know if you are aware... You certainly know the Count de Aciago..."

"Of course."

"I thought so..."

"Are you related to him?"

"He's my husband."

César's eyes darkened.

"Now I understand why you seem to be afraid of something... Ramón Suárez does not enjoy a good opinion. If whenever..."

"Out of the question. I have no right to burden you with my own troubles. Nor can I bear it if you pity me."

"The Stoics believed that pity was a weakness of the soul. There is a lot of truth in that. I never have pity, especially on women as brave as you are."

Blanca looked him straight in the eye.

"Only very strong people want to protect others when they are themselves in danger," said César admiringly.

At the same time, heavy storm clouds covered the sky, releasing more and more drops of an autumn rain.

César covered Blanca with his black cape.

"Let's get out of here!" he suggested. "Otherwise you will get a nasty cold!"

"Where are you taking me?"

"We need to run from the storm."

"Do you know any place where we could hide?"

"There is a deep cave behind those trees. I often use it when I am caught by heavy rain during an evening walk."

The cave was behind four oaks grown into one. The narrow entrance they had to squeeze through led to the spacious interior. Once César and Blanca got inside, they were still covered with the same cape. Water poured down from the sky in streams, as if furious clouds decided to sink the whole earth in the blue depths of the flood.

"Thank you..." Blanca began, but at the same time César closed her mouth with a kiss.

14 Latin *The spirits of the dead exist, and death does not end everything.*   Propertius,   Elegy   IV.   7.

Chapter 10

Mandragora Autumnalis

It was already after dark when August returned to his inn. After reading Adrián's letter, he hurriedly fed and watered the horse, then headed upstairs to prepare all the necessary surgical instruments, and a couple of glass bottles containing precious solutions and powders. He packed everything in a large but handy leather bag that could be easily attached to the saddle.

A storm was brewing, but August knew that his patient's life would not wait for the weather to improve. He prudently took with him a thick cloak that effectively protected against the rain. However, it rained only late at night, when August was already in Asturias. The last leg of the journey, leading through the dark forest, awakened his old memories.

Even though he was now heading west, not east, as when he had returned to Italy with his mother after being rejected by the Duke de Valsombra, the ancient forest was very much like the one in which Iduna saved him and Dorothea from her act of despair. "This extraordinary woman has already saved me from death twice," he thought. "The first time by my mother's actions, and the second time by my own. May she live to see the day when I will take revenge on the man who does not deserve to be called a father!"

The monotonous sound of rain and leaves trembling in the wind made him sleepy. His eyelids grew heavier and heavier until he was about to fall asleep in the saddle. When he managed to open his eyes with the last of his strength, his eyesight was blurred and out of focus. It seemed to him that his path was crossed by a strange retinue of skinny figures dressed in white, ground length tunics.

"Mein Gott!" [15] he called, tugging on the reins sharply. The horse stopped violently, then stood as if petrified. August felt the animal tremble all over its body. He rubbed his eyes, believing what he was seeing was a mere hallucination, caused by accidentally inhaling the vapors when he was applying a painkiller ointment to his previous patient. However, the more he stared at the retinue, the more he realized that despite his great exhaustion, he had kept his sober mind and his eyes were not deceiving him.

The storm wind suddenly stopped, and the whole forest wilderness was deep in silence, broken only by the mournful choir of the pilgrims. The procession proceeded very slowly, singing some incomprehensible song, the melody of which resembled a grim wailing rather than any music. White figures with gray faces and sunken eye sockets held tibia bones in their hands, which burned like torches. Beads of cold sweat appeared on August's forehead.

The horse stiffened all over and its sides got damp. August stroked his back, which was also completely wet. Instinctively wiping his hand with a handkerchief, he realized with horror that the animal was sweating with bloody sweat. "If I am crazy, he is crazy together with me. What is all this supposed to mean?" August wondered, following the last pilgrim with his eyes.

For a moment longer he heard the mournful wailing of the procession and saw the faint glow emanating from the macabre torches. The horse, terrified to the core, stood motionless, and August fought the overwhelming weakness. "What a strange country this is!" he thought as he gently nudged the animal with his spurs to make it move. But the horse huffed and poked the ground nervously with its hoof. Only when August offered it an apple, having eaten the fruit, did the horse take its first timid steps.

In the morning he reached Pueblo Aciago, a small town that derived its sinister name from Palacio Aciago. The stately, late-gothic mansion, rebuilt in a contemporary style, exuded a dark aura around it. Exhausted from the all-night journey, August got off his horse with difficulty. Leading by a bridle the breathless and frothy animal, covered with bloody dew, he headed towards the gates of the palace.

He was immediately allowed into the hall and his horse was entrusted to Adrián. Andrés, who now served his master faithfully day and night, led August to the chamber where his patient was lying. He was awake, eagerly awaiting the arrival of the famous medic.

"Doctor Nacht in person!" Count de Aciago greeted the newcomer.

"At your service, enlightened count," August replied, bowing low.

"Were it not for the fact that I was expecting your visit, when I saw you, I would have thought that Death itself had visited my house. You're even paler than me!"

"It's the effect of dozens of sleepless hours. All day yesterday I was watching over a young man who, like you, fell off his horse and suffered serious injuries. Fortunately, I was able to reposition two dislocated joints. Then I spent the night in the saddle. Now let me see the wound."

As he approached the count's bed, he realized that the man was in a very serious condition. The collarbone was blue and very swollen.

"There is an inflammation, I'm afraid," August said carefully.

"Is it serious?"

"Unfortunately yes. However, please be optimistic. I have already dealt with a similar case in Venice. I know a medicine that can help you."

"Those two idiots I had held in high esteem until recently, gave me some horrible smelly potions that only made matters worse."

"You can trust me," August put a hand to the patient's forehead. "This substance will also lower your fever."

Saying this, he opened the bag, from which he took out surgical instruments and medicine bottles.

"I hope your potions smell better than that stinky stuff, which was ineffective on top of that!" Count de Aciago commented, eyeing the vials with greenish substances suspiciously.

For the first time in a long time, August smiled.

"Don't worry, count. My nose is as sensitive as yours," he replied. "I didn't come here to torture you."

While reviewing all the medicines he had taken with him, he noted that the grated mandrake root that Iduna had given him was missing. "How is this possible? I was convinced that I brought it with me!" He thought in surprise.

"Count..." he turned to the patient.

"I guess something is missing?!"

"Yes. In a hurry, I forgot to bring my sleep medicine. I will need it because your collarbone needs to be operated on as soon as possible. Fortunately, this medicine is growing literally everywhere here."

"Weeds again! What is this wonderful weed?" The count asked impatiently.

"Mandragora. It's not a weed, it's a root. Raw one has similar properties as grated. It not only puts you to sleep, but also disinfects and relieves pain."

"I know what you mean, doctor. Adrián boasted about seeing this plant at the Hanged Men's Cemetery!" Andrés put in helpfully.

"Excellent, Andrés! I can always rely on you. And now off you go to the Hanged Men's Cemetery!" The count ordered.

The boy turned pale.

"But, your Excellency..."

"No discussion," the count cried. "Out of here now!"

The frightened servant swallowed, then bowed as low as he could and left the bedroom. Shivering all over his body, as if he had been consumed by a deadly fever, he descended to the hall down the stone stairs with a slow, resigned step, clinging to the railing. His legs seemed to buckle under him as if they were all skin.

"Why was it to me, the most faithful of the household, that the count assigned such a task? What cruel ruthlessness made him sacrifice just me? Why didn't he send Jaime or Adrián?" As he contemplated his situation, the overwhelming fear that constrained his every move, even his breathing, merged into a terrible whole with a fierce and bitter anger at his ungrateful employer.

It was still dark when he went outside. He knew the way to the Hanged Men's Cemetery well, as it was located near Palacio Aciago. The road to this legendary place led down a path that was not used by anyone, overgrown with weeds and thick cobwebs. There were various stories about the Hanged Men's Cemetery - it was, among other things, a meeting place for all kinds of bandits.

Thieves and murderers were not afraid of ghost stories. The superstitious fear, with which the inhabitants of Pueblo Aciago gave this place wide berth, not only did not put them off, on the contrary - it made them feel safe there, sharing the goods plundered on wanderers, drinking rum and planning new attacks. Many times the superstitious locals mistook these bandits for ghosts, which closed a vicious circle.

For all his insolent arrogance, Andrés was mortally afraid of all supernatural beings. His almost obsessive fear of demons came from his native, tiny village among forests in the very center of Galicia. The mandragora was even more terrifying. He remembered his grandmother telling him about the dangers of handling this plant.

But he was most afraid of the scream, which was said to be produced by its humanoid root as it was brutally torn from the ground. According to his grandmother, the sound was so terrible that it killed anyone who heard it. She told him that this was how she lost her first husband. The man suffered from rheumatism. When the deformed joints hurt a lot, a local healer rubbed the sore spots with mandrake root liniment and the ailments subsided.

One evening the pain worsened. The wife went to the wise woman, begging for a little miraculous panacea. It turned out, however, that she had not yet prepared the specific. So she promised the grandmother that if she waited patiently, she would quickly make the medicine and go to her husband immediately. She kept her word, and half an hour later she was holding an olive tree wood bowl filled to the brim with liniment.

In the meantime, however, the sick man felt even worse. The pain was already unbearable, and his wife was nowhere to be found. So the desperate man decided to deal with it himself. He got up from the bed, put on his shoes, then limped toward the tree where he knew his medicine was growing. From a distance he saw the characteristic, branched tuft of dark green leaves, surrounding the huge purple goblets.

When he got there, gritting the last few teeth remaining at his old age, he placed his horribly misshapen fingers on the damp ground and proceeded to uproot the plant. At the very moment that the little man-shaped tuber was forcibly torn from its nest, it gave such a terrible cry that the poor man died immediately.

When Andrés remembered his grandmother's tale, he almost fainted. His brain was bursting with visions of a screaming root and imminent death. However, not wanting to waste time on unproductive deliberations, which only fueled the fear, he decided not to think about anything, run to the Hanged Men's Cemetery, pick up the herb indicated by August, and run back to the palace.

He went through the shadowy corner with his eyes half closed. He rushed ahead like mad, hurting himself painfully against thorns and nettles, and panting like a fish taken out of water. When he realized that thick cobwebs that he had torn while running stuck to his face, he let out a short cry of disgust and vomited. He wiped his mouth on his shirt sleeve. His eyes saw the sinister sight of broken, ivy-overgrown tombstones.

He could already see the purple mandrake goblets from a distance of several steps. With a slow, staggering stride, he walked over to the grave where their concentration was greatest. Clenching his teeth and eyelids, he dug his fingers into the ground where the most magnificent plant grew, then carefully lifted a humanoid bulb from the soil. At the same moment a piercing scream stabbed his ears.

Contrary to appearances, the sound did not come from the root, but from the owl that was just flying through the cemetery. Andrés felt that a weakness he had fought for some time, became unmanageable. He fell to the ground, still clutching the mandrake root tightly in his hand. After he came to, he looked at the fleshy leaves surrounding him and the purple flowers that moved gracefully in the wind.

"I-I didn't die!" he stuttered.

His heart beat very slowly and an icy sweat covered his body. But he didn't have a moment to waste, he had to get to the palace as soon as possible. It seemed to him that the earth span above his head and the sky below his feet. The stronger he gripped the root in his hand, the more paralyzed his hand was, all the way to his shoulder. "There must be some poison in that damn weed!" he thought, then with the last of his strength he tore off a piece of his sleeve and wrapped his catch in it.

At the same time, August strolled impatiently around the room, coming to the window again and again.

"Please operate me without a mandragora," ordered Count de Aciago. "I'm not going to die because of that idiot!"

"I have no doubts about your courage, and I know well that you would bravely endure even such a painful procedure."

"So what the hell is going on?"

"Count, this root is not only anesthetic, but also a disinfectant and anti-inflammatory. I'll be completely honest. Unfortunately, your wound is already heavily infected and if we don't control the infection, it may be fatal."

At that moment, the bedroom door opened and Andrés burst into the room. He handed August a bundle of sizable root, then staggered and fell to the floor. August set down the package and leapt to him.

"Bradycardia," he said, measuring his pulse.

"What's that supposed to mean?!" The count cried. "What is this stupid youngster doing? Probably got drunk at the inn!"

"He's not drunk. It's my fault," admitted August.

"How is that?!"

"I forgot to warn your servant that the mandrake can also act through the skin, causing the heart to slow down, and even a fainting. He'll be fine, he's just been in contact with this highly intoxicating plant for too long."

Saying this, he sliced one of the root branches with a lancet into thin slices, and handed some of them to the count.

"Just don't tell me I have to eat this!" The patient protested, turning his head in disgust away from August's hand.

"Yes, and immediately," said the medic.

"You use some strange methods, I don't like all this!" the count said, then followed the order reluctantly.

"Indeed, mandrake has been used since antiquity and many doctors now consider it a relic of the past. However, there are at least two famous surgeons in Venice who have treated very serious wounds and other diseases with it. I tried this drug on myself."

"Well then, I put myself into your hands," replied the Count.

He sighed deeply, then closed his eyes and fell into a deep sleep. When his breathing became deep and steady and his pulse slowed considerably, August chose from among his tools the ones he deemed most suitable for the operation, and, having rubbed the previously diseased spot with the cut surface of the mandragora root, proceeded to work.

15 German *My* *God!*

Chapter 11

Anagnorisis

A gray glow shone at the mouth of the cave.

"It's almost dawn," Blanca said, brushing a strand of hair from César's forehead.

He didn't answer, playing thoughtfully with a slender stem of a rickety one-leaf plant that, for some unknown reason, managed to germinate in this dark and hostile place. Blanca also looked at the plant. The huge leaf contrasted with a thin transparent stem.

"I wonder how long it will live..."

"As long as it has the will to fight," César replied.

"I don't know whose position is worse, it's or mine," thought Blanca. "On the one hand, this plant is doomed to live in a cave, unless someone replants it to a more convenient place. I, on the other hand, can get out of my prison for a short time, but this prison is a thousand times more terrible than this cave. Secondly, I can not be sure Ramón will not imprison me in Palacio Aciago permanently in the future..."

"What are you thinking about? Are you concerned about the fate of our green friend?" César joked.

He could guess, however, what was the subject of these considerations.

"I'd rather not share such thoughts with you. I don't want worries to poison the memory of the wonderful few hours we were able to spend together," she replied.

"You're not worried about this cruel man's health, are you?" César asked.

"On the contrary!" Blanca replied, suddenly bursting out with laughter.

"All our hope is in his good-for-nothing doctors. I have heard only unfavorable opinions about these two gentlemen."

"But I don't think they will stay long at the Palacio Aciago. Ramón plans to get rid of them. Yesterday, as I stayed locked up in my office adjacent to my bedroom, I accidentally overheard his conversation with his brother. Mario recommended a brilliant German to him. My husband immediately ordered to send for this medic, as soon as he heard about him."

"You say he's German?" César asked with interest.

Suddenly he saw the figure of the stranger in the mask of *il dottore della peste*.

"Yes. Apparently he grew up in Venice, but his parents, or at least one of them, were of German descent."

César turned pale.

"What's wrong?" Blanca asked.

"A German born in Venice…" repeated César.

"You know him?"

"I'm not sure. Recently, at a masquerade ball for my father's birthday, I met a very strange man. He spoke with a German accent and was hiding his face under a Venetian mask of *il dottore della peste*. He was acting very unfriendly and arrogant. During a short conversation, he made me understand that he knew me. I don't know where from, I can't remember him at all…"

"Maybe he heard from someone about you?"

"Maybe…"

Blanca suddenly burst out laughing again.

"I've heard things about you too... My husband didn't have a single good word about you!" she said.

"If the Count de Aciago has unflattering things to say about me, it must be a good sign," replied César, clearly amused. "But back to that German... He must have some connection with my family, or at least with my father."

"Perhaps it's an old friend of his who showed up at the ball by accident," Blanca suggested. "After all, masquerades attract various freaks..."

"I think he's a good friend. And he told me that he was his friend. Besides, my father talked to him for a long time. What a pity that I didn't understand the entire conversation, just snippets of it."

"What was the main topic?"

"I realized this man had come to my father to notify him of the death of a third person they both knew."

"It must have been someone important to both of them if he decided to notify the duke in person."

"Probably all of this has to do with my father's frequent trips to Venice during my early childhood. He looked much moved by the whole matter. However, I have no idea who it might be."

"Maybe a woman..."

César got thoughtful. Blanca's suggestion that this mysterious deceased might be an old love object of his father, brought back a vague recollection of an event that had taken place when he was still a very young boy. It was late summer, maybe late August or early September. He was playing in the library under the watchful eye of his guardian, Juana, when he suddenly heard that unexpected guests had come to the palace.

Having heard the doorman's voice coming from the hall, and then a woman speaking in a hushed tone in a foreign language, he ran out curiously of the library. He saw a very beautiful lady with very pale golden hair and pale blue eyes. She was holding the hand of a little boy of similar features. However, unlike his mother, who looked more like an angel from paintings than a human being, there was something very repulsive about the beautiful child.

César remembered the moment when Juana, who had run after him, told him to say hello to the boy. The babysitter's words, said in an instructive tone: "Caesar, welcome the guests. Show how nice you can bow" echoed in his ears again, with almost the same intensity as when he stood in front of this strange boy, not much older than himself, staring at him with icy eyes.

Later in life, César saw such a look only in the mysterious man in the *il dottore della peste* mask. The moment the stranger said his full name sneeringly, he was looking at him in exactly the same way the boy had looked at him many years ago. César began to combine everything into one whole: the same fair hair, the same eyes, foreigners, meeting with the duke, Venetian mask, medicine... there were too many similarities.

César also remembered that the boy had introduced himself to Juana in Italian. He did not know the language himself, but during his trips to Venice he had become familiar with some basic expressions. So he knew that *un piacere* was the Italian equivalent of *un placer.*

"I think I remember something..." he said thoughtfully. "Soon after my mother's death, a woman and her son visited us. She spoke a foreign language, I think German... Her son introduced himself in Italian... Only now have I realized that the man who came to the masquerade ball was probably the same person! The little boy I remember had very distinctive eyes. I haven't seen anyone else with the eyes like this, except this stranger at the ball!"

"It had to be that man. He probably came to inform the duke about the death of his mother..."

"Unbelievable! The medic who treats your husband could be my brother!" César said, opening his eyes wide.

Blanca looked at the mouth of the cave. It was dawn. She leaned over César, giving him a long goodbye kiss.

"I'll be waiting at the same time tomorrow," he said.

"If I don't come, don't look for me. It's dangerous," Blanca warned him.

She got up from the makeshift bedding of César's black cape, and ran her fingers through her hair. They hurriedly bid their farewells, then Blanca walked briskly towards the Palacio Aciago.

"This is the only command from you I will never follow!" César thought, then, after waiting until she was some distance away, he followed her, careful not to step on any crackling twig or a noisy stone, that would reveal his presence. When he saw that Blanca was already in the courtyard, he followed her with his eyes to the side gate of the palace where she had disappeared, then turned back to his castle, overgrown with vines.

Using the key to the service gate that Jaime had obtained, Blanca quietly opened the door, then headed up the spiral staircase. She barely climbed the three steps when she heard footsteps at the top. For a moment her heart stopped beating. Instinctively, she reached into the small, secret pocket on the right side of her dress, in which she hid the dagger, then leaned against the wall and took a few deep breaths. After a while, when she was already completely confident and determined to face the possible threat, she began to climb up.

While August was cleaning the wound he had cut, still removing dozens of tiny fragments of bone, Andrés was slowly recovering. Seeing that the operation was in progress, he silently rose from the floor. August was so preoccupied with the complicated procedure that he didn't even notice the servant's awakening. It was already dawn, but the candles were still burning in the room, for without them the medic would not be able to complete the operation. Looking at the cut humanoid root on the table, Andrés flinched fearfully.

His mind was still under the intoxicating influence of the mandrake. His heart was beating with a normal rhythm already, but the imagination had not yet broken free from the yoke of delusions and hallucinations. When he looked at the mutilated one-legged man and the lancet lying next to him, he was overwhelmed with horror, as if he was subconsciously afraid of the revenge of the Mandrake Demon, about whom his grandmother had told him many times.

After leaving the bedroom as quietly as he could, he headed for the servants' quarters, dirty, sweaty, and very hungry. His shirt was only good to be thrown away. Due to the early hour, however, he still had enough time to thoroughly wash and dress before breakfast, which he always ate in the kitchen with the rest of the servants.

As he reached the top of the spiral staircase, he thought he heard footsteps at the bottom. He paused for a moment and listened. Hearing the footsteps getting closer, he decided to go down a few steps to see who it was. "I hope no thief has invaded here as I am completely defenseless!" he sighed.

At the same moment, the figure of Blanca appeared before his eyes. Her heart stopped for a moment when she saw the servant. But she thought about the dagger hidden in the folds of her dress and her courage hardened. The fear left her completely when she noticed the state Andrés was in.

"Good morning, your Majesty," he greeted her, bowing to her deeply. There was none of the old arrogance heard in his weak voice.

What's more, he tried to get out of her sight as quickly as possible. He felt humiliated that she saw him like this.

When Blanca reached the office, which had also been her bedroom since the incident of the Count de Aciago, she saw the door handle of the adjacent room move. Right outside the door, a male voice spoke with a strong foreign accent. After a moment, the door opened and a tall, fair-haired man with a cold gaze emerged from her husband's bedroom. "Probably this new medic," she thought.

The stranger greeted her with a beautiful bow.

"Who do I have the pleasure of addressing, sir?" she asked.

"My name is August Nacht. I am the new physician of the count," he introduced himself. "Your husband is not in any danger any longer, lady. He will have to rest a lot as the wound was already very infected. However, I was able to piece the bones together and control the infection."

"Thank you on behalf of my husband for your care," Blanca replied with a cold politeness, cursing the young medic and his talent in her mind.

August couldn't take his eyes off her. For the first time in his life, the sight of a woman aroused in him feelings that were different than a filial affection. The stream of heat that suddenly seeped into his icy heart was also very different from medical curiosity. Until now, every woman, just like every man, child or animal, aroused in him a desire to learn about their entire anatomy and general health.

He felt this desire both towards women who were hunchbacked, lame or afflicted with any other ailment, as well as towards those beautiful and desired, for the love to whom his Italian friends lost their heads, got into various fights or even died in duels. Old Dr. Carlini was the only person who understood this urge for knowledge, which dominated all other instincts.

"This doctor Nacht is a very strange man!" thought Blanca. "On the one hand, his cold eyes terrify me, and on the other - he has something of César in him..." She easily recognized the expressive profile that characterized the Marquis de Viciosa, as well as the characteristic, reserved and distanced manner of being. However, August differed from his brother not only in skin and hair color, but also in his eyes.

César's gaze betrayed his innate intelligence and a very restless mind, while the ruthless, insane determination, beaming from August' eyes, evoked metaphysical anxiety, even fear, in anyone who came into contact with him for the first time, as if everywhere where he just appeared, he were bringing a blast of the frosty north wind.

"Please excuse me," Blanca said, opening the door to her office.

August could not get a word out. He nodded goodbye. Blanca gave him a friendly smile, then quickly disappeared into the darkened room. After she closed the door behind her, August religiously kissed the silver-plated handle she had just touched, as if the object had become a precious relic or had acquired magical powers.

Chapter 12

Arseni trioxidum

It was not long since Ausencio's last visit in his friend's forest kingdom, when he came there again, this time early in the morning. Iduna spotted him already from a distance. She hadn't expected him to pay her a visit so soon. Sensing that the boy was carrying some important news, she impatiently walked out to meet him.

"Hello, my dear Ausencio!" She greeted him happily.

The young man kissed her on both cheeks.

"Hello, Iduna! I hope I haven't distracted you from any important activity."

"Not at all. The more often you come, the better. Your visits make my sad old age more pleasant," she replied.

"And for me, they bring a respite. In the palace I have nowhere to hide and to whom to entrust my worries, and there is enough of them... I must be ready for every call of my master, who has not been well lately..."

"Did he get sick?" Iduna asked, pretending to be concerned about Martín's health.

"He looks very sick, but his suffering is not of a physical nature."

"Of what nature then?"

"Two days ago my lord almost fell victim to a perfidious plot against his life. Someone in the house tried to poison him."

"Poison?!" Iduna repeated. "Who might want to poison him?"

"I'll tell you everything..."

"Let's sit down in a quiet place," interrupted Iduna. "I'll prepare some fruit."

When they reached the cave, she disappeared into its depths for a moment. Meanwhile, Ausencio made himself comfortable on the flat boulder at the mouth of the cavern. After a while, Iduna returned with a basket full of tasty fruit. There were ripe figs, grapes, and a whole lot of dried berries and nuts.

"How did you get it all?" Ausencio asked, admiring these wonders.

"It's a gift from a woman whose child I saved."

"What was wrong with it?"

"It was bitten by a snake. The mother heard somewhere that I know medicines and I can help. She brought to me the child who was already in agony. I used the only antidote I had at hand and fortunately it brought the desired effect. The child quickly recovered."

"So you know not only about medicines but also about poisons?" Ausencio asked, staring at Iduna as if enchanted.

"Of course. I also know a bit about antidotes, although it is a very difficult science."

"It's good to have a genius like you among friends!" Ausencio said appreciatively.

"My dear Ausencio, you are one of the few people who appreciate this art. People usually turn to me for help out of extreme desperation. They point their fingers at me, calling me a witch. It's a miracle the Inquisition hasn't gotten interested in me yet!"

"I was supposed to tell you about this strange incident with poison... it will definitely interest you, especially since you know about these things."

Iduna looked at him closely.

"The story is like this: two days ago, his Majesty the duke was sitting in his office, as he used to do in the afternoon, reading a book. At one point, Inés brought him a carafe of his favorite sweet wine. She half filled the goblet that was on his desk and left the room. It wasn't even a few minutes before my master called her back. Inés returned from him completely shaken. She told us that he had asked her a whole series of meticulous questions, including where she got the bottle from, who opened it, who recently had access to the basement, and so on. Inés replied truthfully and according to her own knowledge, but she was afraid - fortunately unnecessarily - that the master did not believe her words. His Majesty then ordered Roberto to summon me immediately. When I came, he told me that the wine Inés had brought was poisoned. He also revealed to me how he discovered the trick that allowed him to survive. Well, the chalice he inherited from his father, Leonardo Castro, has some extraordinary properties."

"You mean it detects poison?" Iduna asked, intrigued by Ausencio's story.

"Indeed," he confirmed. "Well, Duke Maximiliano, father of Duke Leonardo, received this unusual vessel as a gift from a certain Turk. The goblet is made of special glass with tiny particles of silver and gold embedded in it. It changes color depending on the angle at which the light falls and what liquid we pour inside. In this way, the owner of the dish can be sure that he will never be poisoned."

"The conclusion is obvious: the person who wanted to poison the duke is certainly not aware of the unusual properties of this cup."

"Only my lord, perhaps the Marquis de Viciosa, and now also me know about them. Apart from me, no one from the servants has any idea that the cup is capable of indicating poison. Each substance colors the chalice differently. The duke is convinced that the wine was spiked with arsenic."

"Now I already know what Martín meant when he said, 'One second of madness has condemned me to life in Hell,' " thought Iduna. She began to wonder aloud.

"I wonder if your master also drank wine from that cup on the day of Duchess Teresa's death?"

She trusted Ausencio, but chose not to mention Serafín's involvement just in case.

"Certainly. He never leaves this... Jesus Christ!" The young man exclaimed, crossing himself.

"I thought so... Remember that you told me what your master said about 'one second of madness'? You then said that you had no idea what he meant. We know everything now!"

"It's terrible! My master is moody and often malicious, but I never suspected that he could murder his wife."

"I do not care what the Duke de Valsombra was guided by. The only reasonable conclusion that can be drawn is this: someone was trying to poison him. However, when he noticed the change in color of the goblet, he realized that the wine contained poison, and offered the drink to Duchess Teresa."

"Holy Mother!" Ausencio exclaimed in horror.

"That's probably why he has been dreaming about his wife's ghost lately. He has a guilty conscience," said Iduna.

"But who tried to poison him this time?"

"I have no idea," she replied.

"Only August, or possibly Serafín, if he was still alive, could have done that," she mused. "Serafín had reason to hate him... But it's more likely that August is behind it, as he has recently returned to this area, while Serafín has fallen off the face of the Earth. He is probably dead, as he was already very ill then..."

It was Serafín's disease that indirectly caused him to hate Duke de Valsombra with all his heart. He suffered from a very unusual condition, as a result of which his entire body, including his face, was densely covered with disgusting blisters and warts, ranging in size from microscopic grains to huge tubers. Even though the disease was not contagious, many people avoided Serafín for fear of being infected.

There were also those - including the duke - for whom the man's disability was the subject of crude jokes and mockery. The duke nicknamed him "a toad", and constantly ridiculed him in front of the rest of the household as well as the guests whom he often invited to visit Valsombra. Once, at the annual birthday ball, he had the unfortunate man dance a gigue with beautiful Alicia, whom all the servants loved. The contrast between Serafín and his beautiful partner, and at the same time a great dancer, was aimed not so much to ridicule the cripple, as to punish the girl for repeated and decisive rejection of the duke's advances. Alicia couldn't stand this horrible show. Suddenly she stopped, then, after kissing Serafín's forehead, covered with disgusting growths, ran out of the room. After this event, nobody saw her again.

"I don't know who would want to poison the duke," said Iduna after a long silence. "It's a mystery we won't solve now."

"I can't wait for August's visit," she thought. "He came to Valsombra specifically to take revenge on his father. Secondly, he worked for many years in this old Italian's pharmacy, where he learned the secrets of poisons. Besides, Serafín's horrible appearance would have attracted the attention of the household at once, so the poisoner had to enter the palace completely unnoticed. He also had to know the inside of the mansion well."

When she became convinced that the attempt on the duke's life was most likely the work of August, her heart began to burst with mad pride. She knew that her Venetian friend's cool and utterly determined mind had tirelessly pursued the only goal - at least till now - to take revenge on his selfish father, who had humiliated his mother and rejected him with such contempt.

She did not know yet that August, who so far, apart from the revenge on his father which he had passionately pursued, had been only interested in medicines, poisons, antidotes and rare cases of various diseases, suddenly fell in love with the same woman as his younger, hated brother. This feeling, from the moment it was born in August's indifferent heart, grew with each passing second into a dark, devastating obsession.

When Ausencio left the forest kingdom of Iduna after several hours' visit, she was left alone with her thoughts. She could only share them with Álvar. The bird was just sitting on a branch of a sprawling oak, carefully cleaning its feathers.

"If you only knew, bird, how much it hurt me that Martín survived..." She sighed heavily.

At the sound of Iduna's voice, Álvaro paused the grooming for a moment and listened intently to his mistress's words.

"I wish you could understand this..." she said. The falcon stared at Iduna for a long moment, then suddenly cried sharply.

"If I could entrust you with the mission of avenging my child, you would certainly have done it flawlessly, especially since you do not like this vile man yourself!"

One day the Duke de Valsombra was riding a horse near the cave. He didn't notice Iduna inside, but she could see him perfectly. She was standing at the mouth of the cavern with Álvaro sitting on her shoulder. At the sight of the duke, her heart, flooded with grief and anger, began to beat as hard as if it was about to burst. The falcon sensed this unease. He tilted his head first to one side and then to the other, as if he were recording Martín's face and entire figure in his memory. Then he sank his beak into his mistress's hair, as if in his own way to comfort her.

"Do you remember Duke de Valsombra?"

Álvaro kept looking at her with his wise, shining eyes. A series of long, high-pitched screams that he used to make during a hunt, escaped from his spotted chest.

"Is it possible you understood what I said?" Iduna asked, holding out her arm.

The falcon tilted his head, then flew off the branch and landed on the offered arm so accurately, that he did not even scratch it with the tips of his powerful, curved talons. And just as he did when they watched together the Duke de Valsombra ride through the forest, he sank his beak into Iduna's gray hair.

Chapter 13

El sol de los muertos

A heavy, late autumn downpour was just rolling over Valsombra. The duke stood at the west window of his library. He watched thoughtfully as streams of rain ran down the face of the stone angel placed on top of the ancestral chapel, where the remains of his ancestors and his tragically deceased wife were buried. The Angel of Death looked straight ahead majestically, leaning firmly on his long sword, towering over the palace garden.

The beautiful, somber figure, carved in white limestone, filled the duke with anxiety from the earliest years of his life. When he was a child, his grandfather once scared him that if he did wrong in life, the Angel of Death would fly from the roof of the chapel, come for him and throw him into Hell. This tale, intended only as a scarecrow for a naughty boy, took root deeply in Martín Castro's seemingly enlightened mind, invariably arousing in him an inexpressible terror.

"I wonder when he'll come for my damned soul..." he wondered. Then a sudden ray of sunshine broke through the streams of rain, filling the entire garden with warm afternoon light. The figure of the angel flashed like a great torch, almost blinding the duke, who admired this amazing sight with his eyebrows raised and eyes wide open.

"It must be a sign," he whispered.

The sudden blood pressure spikes he had suffered from an early age, had become more and more troublesome in recent years. Turning his head away from the window, he leaned both hands on the stone sill, then took a few deep breaths. After a while, the bothersome shortness of breath stopped. When the duke looked at the majestic statue again, it was slowly plunging into darkness.

The last ray of the sun fell on the gilded sword of the angel. The bright light reflecting off the shining surface almost blinded the old man again. "It's not time yet… Teresa, I am begging you for forgiveness! Don't take revenge on me in such a cruel way!" The duke thought, and without waiting any longer, walked away from the window. Donning his coat, he made his way down the marble steps to the hall.

He happened to find Roberto there, discussing something with one of the doormen. They both looked deeply moved.

"What are you discussing so lively?" The duke wanted to know.

"It's nothing important, Your Majesty," Roberto assured.

"In that case, enough of this chit-chat and go to work! In this palace, trivial matters are not discussed," the duke scolded them, then went outside.

The rain had almost stopped. The last, heavy drops either died in the collision with the stone heads of the statues of ancient deities, or they spectacularly splashed in the large puddles created by the downpour, to transform in the last fraction of a second of their short life into fancy crowns and brilliant tiaras. "How many years does it take to appreciate the beauty of such a simple thing as an ordinary raindrop…" thought the duke, watching the water that had accumulated in the cavity in the wall.

Having soothed his jangled nerves with this sight, he headed for the ancestral chapel. It stood at the edge of the vast palace garden, right next to the steel fence. The gothic building resembled a miniature cathedral. Despite the passage of several centuries, and the humid climate of this part of the country, the soaring pinnacles and intricate stone ornaments adorning this small architectural masterpiece were in perfect condition.

When the duke was only a few steps from the chapel, it seemed to him that a faint light was emanating from within. It was already dusk, so the pale glow immediately caught his eye. The duke's heart began to beat furiously, and a bead of cold sweat appeared on his brow. He reached into the pocket of his coat for a muslin handkerchief to wipe his face with it, when he suddenly froze motionless.

For it seemed to him that a hooded, stooped figure flashed before his eyes. It was already quite dark, so he couldn't see it clearly, but he noticed one detail: a horribly distorted hand protruding from beneath the black robe, densely covered with huge, repulsive blisters. The duke swallowed. He watched with his eyes wide in terror as the intruder got out through the gate in the fence.

"Serafín..." he choked out.

The face of the former servant, cruelly crippled by disease, stood before his eyes as if alive. The duke closed his eyes and remembered a scene from the past: Serafín, smiling, offers him a tray, on which, among crystal goblets filled with various types of wine, stood his own, surpassing the others in beauty and value. Taking the precious vessel in his hand, the duke noticed that the pinkish glass suddenly began to darken, and after a while it changed its color from purple to intense blue. Only he himself noticed the change - no one else, not even the Duchess, was privy to the secret of the Castro male line. Instinctively he looked at his wife standing next to him, who, staring at the tray held by Serafín, was not entirely sure which type of wine to choose. Without a moment's thought, the duke handed her his cup.

"It has long been my dream to drink from it at least once," confessed the duchess as she tasted the drink.

"As always, I took care of everything, killing two birds with one stone. Letting you drink wine from this precious goblet, I solved your dilemma at the same time," replied the duke.

"Delicious!" The duchess admitted, smiling at her husband for the first time that evening.

It was also her last smile - not only on that day, but in her whole life. Already in the middle of the ball, her pupils began to gradually dilate, and unhealthy, deep purple blushes appeared on her pale cheeks. She went to retire long before the end of the ceremony. She died in the early hours of the morning after a brief bout of convulsions.

At the mere memory of that scene a shiver of terror ran down the duke's spine. "The cursed traitor!" - he thought. "He's trying to kill me again! I will not be fooled by this cripple. Because of my own stupidity, I cannot demand justice for him, because I was the one who offered Teresa the goblet of poison... my hands are tied while he came back to torment me with his tricks!"

The veins in the duke's temples pulsed in agitation. "You won't oppress me like this! I won't let you, you shameless coward!" - he decided. But he knew the situation he was in was hopeless. Revealing the duchess's poisoning would inevitably lead the investigation to him, and then he would face not only death, but a disgrace, a hundred times worse than death.

The duke walked briskly to the small but imposing portal of the chapel. Thousands of long, thin candles were already burning with full flame. The brilliant light emanating from them dazzled his eyes, as the ray reflecting from the sword of the Angel of Death did before. The duke pressed the door knob, then pushed the grating, but the door did not budge.

"It's him!" He exclaimed indignantly.

He remembered that the set of keys Serafín used in his daily work had disappeared together with him. "After all these years, he still holds on to these keys..." he wondered. "He's a madman!"

At that moment, a violent gust of wind burst into the interior of the above-ground part of the chapel, extinguishing all the candles in one go. Gray smoke filled the room.

The duke, who suffered from breathlessness, coughed violently, chasing away clouds of acrid smoke with a muslin handkerchief. His irritated eyes began to water profusely. This natural reaction to the stench of burning, coupled with fear and anxiety, caused the old man to kneel on the floor, propping his head against the iron grate, and burst with a violent sob.

The sky was clearing - the evening downpour gave way to a clear, moonlit night. The duke got up from his knees, still clinging to the steel bars. For a short while he stared at the barely visible painting that was part of the small altar. Suddenly it seemed to him that the remains of the smoke blown by the wind, still billowing in the chapel, formed the shape of a woman in a white dress.

"Oh no, not that! Leave me alone!" he exclaimed, then returned to the palace as quickly as he could.

As he reached the hall, the doormen looked in horror at his deathly pale face and wide open reddened eyes.

"Doesn't our lord look as if he has aged a dozen or so years during this one evening?" one of them whispered when the duke was already at a safe distance.

"Who walks in the garden at this time?" His companion wondered, nodding his head.

"It seems to me that he misses The Duchess Teresa more and more as time goes on. They were not given reaching the old age together."

"I think there is a terrible secret behind her death. It is obvious that our master is troubled by something more than just longing for his dead wife. "

The doormen's conversation was interrupted by the arrival of Ausencio, who, as he did every evening, went upstairs with a tray on which he carried the duke's supper. From the earliest times, the duke did not trust cooks, and entrusted servants with the checking of meals. While the glass goblet reliably detected the poison in beverages, the food was more difficult to test.

Therefore, the duties of Roberto, and later Ausencio, included not only serving the table or taking meals to the duke's rooms, but also tasting the portions of each dish indicated by the lord. As a decoy, they also had to taste wine. Failure to test the contents of the chalice while controlling everything else very scrupulously, could lead to the discovery of the spontaneous participation of the duke in his wife's death.

When Ausencio brought dinner, the duke instructed him to stay with him in his study after tasting the roasted fish and vegetables.

"Your Majesty does not look well... Could I help your Majesty with something?" Ausencio asked obligingly.

"I just need the company of another human being. Loneliness slowly drives me mad..." replied the duke, rubbing his forehead hard against his clenched fist, on which he rested his sore head.

"It is understandable. When we are completely alone, our peace of mind is often ruined by bad thoughts," Ausencio noted.

"I have learned to live with my thoughts. Recently, however, I happen to see different things and people, and I don't know anymore whether they belong to reality or if they are merely figments of my imagination..."

"Is your ducal majesty having nightmares again?"

"Tonight I went to the chapel. I was going to stand there for a moment and pray for my wife's soul and..." The duke stopped the story in mid-sentence, then drank the contents of his cup.

"Maybe he really didn't kill her and he himself fell innocent victim to some terrible intrigue or... but this cup... he must have known," Ausencio wondered, silently watching his master, who had just placed the empty vessel on the table. Only now did he see the ruthless gleam in his eyes. "An old calculating hypocrite..." Ausencio flinched. Suddenly he felt very cold.

"I, too, shudder at the mere mention of what I saw there..." said the duke, noticing a sudden twitch that passed over the servant's body.

He filled the cup full again, then drank out the entire contents within just a minute.

"Has this dreadful specter once again come to your majesty?" Ausencio asked after a pause.

"Not the same one," replied the duke. "But you are partially right. It was also a ghost from the past. He flashed before my eyes as I approached the chapel. A scary, stooped figure in a monk's habit..."

"I wonder what Iduna will say to all this..." thought Ausencio. But he dared not ask about anything more, so as not to arouse the duke's suspicions.

Chapter 14

Shadows of madness

August's efforts to restore Count de Aciago's health had brought the desired effect. The broken collarbone healed remarkably quickly, without any complications. After a very short period of convalescence, the count recovered fully. He ordered Blanca to return to the matrimonial bedroom. She accepted the order with pretended calmness, cursing her fate in her head, as well as the day when doctor Nacht appeared in the Palacio Aciago.

As he watched the count recover, as a result of his efforts, August also hated himself more and more. The more he saw Blanca, whom he loved with a feeling that was getting more possessive and fanatical with every moment, the more he sank into dark melancholy. It not only consumed his soul, but also slowly weakened his body, showing itself on his paler and more sunken face. But August didn't care about it at all.

The gloomy mood of the medic, who at the count's request took up residence in the Palacio Aciago, did not go unnoticed by his patient and employer.

"You haven't been quite yourself lately, my friend," he said to August as the guest appeared at the dining room right on time, at nine o'clock at night.

"Don't worry about my health, count. Indeed, I've been a little unwell lately, but luckily it's not anything serious."

"You look like a ghost."

"Thank you for such a nice compliment," August replied playfully. His pale lips curved into a forced smile. "To be completely honest with you, the climate here is not the best for me."

"A matter of getting used to it," said the count, lifting a silver goblet. "To the health of my savior!"

"To my patient's health!" August politely reciprocated the toast.

Blanca demanded that no dinner be brought to her. Like the thought of sharing the bed with the count, the idea of sitting at the table with him disgusted her. In order to avoid spending the night in the chamber, she decided to sneak out of the palace before her husband would go to bed. She knew the consequences of this decision, but was convinced that she had nothing to lose. She intended to spend as much time as possible with César before the count would take her freedom forever.

Not only did she subconsciously suspect that this day would come sooner or later, she even speculated where the Count de Aciago was going to imprison her. Whenever she looked from the distance at the lonely Gothic tower near the palace, she was terrified. She was also worried about the north facing, uninhabited part of the mansion, where the count used to detain those household members who opposed his orders or carried them out too carelessly.

She was also disturbed by the behavior of August, in whose general mood and external appearance she noticed a significant change. He wandered like a ghost through the shadowy corridors of the Palacio Aciago, gloomily following her with his pale eyes, with which he seemed to register every move of the object of his adoration. More and more often she supposed that the medic was looking for opportunities in which there would be a greater likelihood of meeting her by accident.

She knew, however, that Count de Aciago had a special esteem for this man, speaking of him in no other way than as his "savior" and "close friend." So she suspected that August might be spying on her actions at the behest of her husband. She had no idea how much he hated the count and himself for saving his life, or that it happened the very moment he first saw her.

Blanca's dislike of August was also fueled by the fact that he was obviously competing with César, being an illegitimate, but still the firstborn son of the duke. Recognizing his heroic determination to carry out his plans - both noble and perfidious - she suspected that in the fight for his rights, he would stop at nothing. What she hadn't realized, however, was that August loved her much more than he hated his father.

She left the palace as usual, through a side exit, to spare her eyes the blinding light of the candlesticks in the hall. Nor did she want to attract the attention of the doorkeepers who would immediately report everything to the Count. So, taking advantage of the fact that the latter was occupied with a lively conversation with August, she went downstairs, opened the narrow gate, and then disappeared into the forest wilderness, shrouded in darkness.

When the supper was over, the count retired. Not finding his wife in the bedroom, he became very angry. He called Andrés over and ordered him to go search for Blanca. The boy still remembered with horror his trip to the Hanged Men's Cemetery, so at first he wanted to excuse himself with an imaginary health indisposition, but the mission of following the actions of a woman whom he desired and at the same time passionately hated, attracted him much more than the terrifying vision of a dark forest.

"Take care that she doesn't notice you. Only in this way will we know the whole truth," the count ordered.

"Of course, count. This time I will do better than last time," Andrés assured him.

"Let's forget about what happened. What is important is that I am in good health," replied the count with apparent generosity. "Now go to the woods and try to find out where she is. It is an easy task, as there are only three traveled paths."

"Yes, sir. I'm not coming back until I find out where your wife is."

"That's what I like! As soon as you come back, come to see me and tell me everything."

"Of course, Count!"

Andrés thought with delight that he would kill two birds with one stone: first, he would discover the secret of Blanca's night walks in the woods, and second, he would avenge his disappointed love for his mistress. Additionally, he will buy into the favors of Count de Aciago. Satisfied with this prospect, he hurriedly headed for the winding stairs. There he unexpectedly met Jaime, who was just returning from the stables.

"Where are we going at such an inhuman hour?" The old man asked.

"I have received a confidential assignment from the count."

"I wonder what it is."

"As I mentioned, the assignment is confidential. So I'm afraid, old man, that I can't reveal the details to you."

Jaime guessed it all right away. He also knew that the young man would carry out his mission very diligently. Knowing the superstitious nature of the boy, as well as the unlimited possibilities of his vivid imagination, he decided to slightly thwart his plans. For he had the silent hope that he would either completely discourage him from obeying the count's command, or plant a seed of fear in his soul that would sprout much faster than Andrés could harm Blanca.

To this end, he used an old legend that Valerio, his late predecessor, had once told him.

"That's so unkind of our count..." he said, lowering his voice theatrically.

"Why do you think so, Jaime? Did you do something wrong again and fear punishment?" Andrés replied maliciously.

"None of these things. It's just that fear overwhelms me at the thought of this night expedition you go to…" Jaime worriedly scratched his chin.

"I don't think I need to fear anything."

"I don't recognize you. Ever since you came here, you have always been terrified of the night, you almost died of fear after the last quest for the mandrake, and here suddenly you go tonight into the darkness with truly Herculean bravado… I did not expect this from you!" Jaime provoked deftly.

"The Hanged Men's Cemetery is a terrible place, full of pirates and thieves. Besides, on my last trip, I got terribly sick because of that damn weed. It makes me shiver at the thought of the malicious little devil who killed my grandmother's first husband. But the Viciosa area is completely safe. There are neither bandits nor wolves there. Even the countess goes there after all and somehow she is still alive, even though she wanders through this forest like a ghost almost every night."

"You seem to be reading my mind…"

"What do you mean?"

"Funny… From what you're saying, it seems that the only ghost in this forest is actually our good lady… You have no idea what's lurking in those old stumps…"

"What are you talking about?" Andrés asked, slightly losing his confidence.

Seeing the young man's wide, terrified eyes, Jaime realized that he had done his job. He stroked his chin in silence for a moment.

"Jaime, please, what do you mean?" Andrés repeated his question.

He was getting more and more nervous.

"I feel obliged to warn you before it is too late," the old man began, lowering his voice. "The danger that awaits you in this part of the forest is deadly, but very elusive. In addition, it only threatens men who venture into those areas after dark. The countess is a woman, so she can walk with impunity. Remember that horrible incident of the count?"

"How could I forget about it? It's all the damn horse's doing. Blue is useless, it is afraid of its own shadow. Had the count chosen Pino, he would have certainly avoided the accident. It is a pity that the stupid beast did not end up in the slaughterhouse as it deserved!"

"Let's not talk about horses now, because that is not the point," said Jaime firmly. "It's not about the horse, but the shadows that scared it."

"What shadows? What are you talking about?" Andrés turned pale.

"Long ago, when our country was under Roman rule, some of the forest near Viciosa was inhabited by druids. Once upon a time they came into conflict with a centurion who ordered the cutting of ancient oaks which they considered sacred. When the priests protested this insult, threatening the Romans with a curse, the cruel centurion, ignoring their warnings, gave his men a signal to attack. Armed to the teeth, they attacked the helpless druids and massacred them with their swords. A terrible incident took place shortly after. One evening, when the soldiers went to the forest for firewood, a collective madness fell upon them. In a fit of terrible, suicidal fury, the Romans, along with the ruthless centurion, threw themselves on their own swords and died in agony. The only one who survived was a young legionnaire. From the very beginning, he was against the cutting of oaks, and was the only one who did not take part in it, nor did he participate in the cruel slaughter of druids. It is known from his account that while the other Romans were busy chopping wood, the forest suddenly swarmed with shadows resembling hooded Celtic priests. The soldiers lost their minds at the sight of them. At first they were foaming from their mouths and laughing madly, raving as if in a delirium. Then the mirth gave way to mournful solemnity, and the men, one by one, knelt on the ground, swaying in the wind like reeds, then drew their swords and aimed their blades at their breasts. When the centurion ordered the attack, all the soldiers, including him, took their own lives."

Andrés was deathly pale. With trembling hands he ran his hand through his hair and looked at Jaime with eyes unconscious with fear.

"Maybe it was a one-time act of revenge?" he stuttered.

"Unfortunately no," Jaime replied, "there have been more cases like this. Not so long ago, a peasant who ventured into those regions to pick some herbs, also went mad and hanged himself on an old oak tree. Another time, two French monks on their way to your homeland [16] climbed onto a lonely rock and jumped down heads first. They both died on the spot."

"Why has this cruel man sent me there, condemning me to certain death?" Andrés exclaimed.

"Most likely he has no idea about all this. After all, he fell victim to these shadows himself. This time they attacked not himself, but poor Blue, who went mad. When their victim travels through the forest on horseback, they scare the horse."

"Jaime, go in my stead!" Andrés pleaded.

"No way. I warned you because it is my duty. But I don't like you that much that I would give my life for you. You have to face it yourself. However, if you see any shadow, run away and don't look back."

"That's what I will do. Thank you for the advice, old man," the boy replied, patting Jaime on the shoulder in a friendly manner.

Saying this, he went out, closing the gate behind him. At the sight of the knotty trunks and the branches moved by the wind, he felt he was losing the use of his legs. "Just don't faint again!" He ordered himself, feeling dizzy. "Don't let yourself make a fool of yourself again, like you did then, with that weed! If something seems suspicious to you, you will run away as fast as possible, but for now, try to complete the task entrusted to you, because you will certainly not regret it. You have to be brave!"

He walked briskly down the main path without looking sideways. Every now and then the silence was broken by the screams of birds and the buzzing of insects. Andrés's heart sped rapidly at the sound of them. An icy sweat beaded his forehead thickly. When a picturesque clearing appeared before the eyes of the scared servant, he looked around and was terrified at the sight of broad oaks growing around it. He stood as if paralyzed, watching for a path Blanca might take.

The only path was very narrow and looked to be not frequented. The branches of the bushes overgrowing it swayed in the breeze, as did the corps of Roman soldiers mesmerized by druid spirits that Jaime had talked about. "This path is leading nowhere," he thought. "I have nothing to look for here. I'm coming back home!"

After he had already turned on his heel, determined to end his mission, the sounds of footsteps from the other end of the clearing reached his ears, a noise like the rustle of clothes, followed by the sound of human voices. One belonged to a man and the other to a woman. He paused motionlessly, listening. He couldn't understand the content of the conversation, but he recognized Blanca's voice right away. "So, that's the secret our lady keeps!" - he thought and, encouraged by the discovery, decided to find out who the stranger was.

The voices came from the right side, from behind four characteristically fused oak trunks. Andrés ran across the clearing very quickly and hid behind the trees. Straight ahead was the mouth of the cave, in front of which stood Blanca and a large, dark-haired man with noble features, dressed in a black cape. The conversation ceased. For a long moment the lovers stared at each other, holding hands and giving each other more and more passionate kisses, then they disappeared into the depths of the cave.

Overjoyed with this discovery, and feeling a foretaste of a sweet revenge, Andrés forgot about the shadows of the druids. He left his hiding place carefully, then set off on his way back. "Finally, I will be able to repay her for this lofty contempt," he thought with satisfaction. "The count will get furious and then he will take care not only of his saintly wife, but also of her lover. Knowing my master's character, I bet neither of them will live too long!"

Suddenly his heart stopped. A long black shadow stretched across the path where the moonlight fell.

"Mother of God, save me!" He groaned, stiffening all over his body. He stared in horror at the shadow, which was shaped like a human figure. However, when he realized that it came from an oblong boulder standing next to the path, he breathed a sigh of relief and continued on his way, counting down the hours till he would tell Count de Aciago about everything.

16   The fragment talks about pilgrims to Santiago de Compostela.

Chapter 15

Almas errantes

As soon as the downpour stopped and the sun began to sink westward, Brother Lisandro left the monastery walls and set off for nearby Valsombra. Many years had passed since the terrible crime he once committed, but he was still haunted by the image of the innocent victim of his ruse. The more he realized that he was nearing his death, the more he was haunted by the memory of that terrible day, when the blade of his vengeance, instead of stabbing whom it was aimed at, suddenly turned against the person from whom he had experienced nothing but goodness.

The cool autumn wind whipped his slumped back mercilessly, causing him unspeakable pain. Under the influence of autumn moisture, the huge tubers covering the monk's entire body became extremely vulnerable. Brother Lisandro, however, welcomed all these sufferings, treating the gusts of wind that lashed him as well-deserved flogging, and the painful eruptions on his skin - like a penitential hair shirt.

Located almost ten kilometers from Valsombra, Monasterio de Almas Errantes, or Monastery of the Wandering Souls, hosted twelve monks, each of whom, having changed his real name to a religious one, repented of his past sins. Among the most mysterious inhabitants of the rundown, neglected thirteenth-century monastery was its prior, Father Roland, the oldest of the monks, who had come all the way from Ireland.

No one knew the man's story, but it was suspected that it was as dark as his sullen, sunken face that resembled a skull covered with thin parchment. The other monks treated him with almost superstitious fear, despite the fact that each of them hid some terrible secret from the past. Due to his repulsive appearance, mysterious character and the suspicion that in his youth he earned a living as a mercenary murderer, he quickly earned the nickname *padre Roland de la Muerte* - meaning "Father Roland of Death".

One of the monks who did not fear the sinister prior was Brother Lisandro. Moreover, he sensed a soul mate in the gloomy Irishman. Father Roland, on the other hand, liked him because of his disability and disgusting appearance, which made the other monks, convinced that the terrible disease was contagious, avoid his company. This way, a kind of friendship developed between the two.

Father Roland was the only one to know his friend's terrible secret. Knowing how much he was suffering from remorse, he allowed him to say prayers at the tomb of Duchess Teresa. Although a strict rule prohibited monks from leaving the monastery walls, on All Saints Day in 1791, the prior granted Brother Lisandro a special dispensation that allowed him to go outside when he wished, after sunset.

Since receiving this dispensation, the crippled monk had not missed any opportunity to take advantage of it. Every day, right after the end of Vespers, he set off on a lonely journey to Valsombra, to stop for a moment at the small chapel of the Castro family and pray in silence for the soul of the tragically deceased Duchess Teresa. After having said the prayers, he looked around and discreetly slipped out of the garden, in order to return to the monastery before midnight.

That day, believing that the rainy weather forced all the inhabitants of the residence to stay inside the building, Brother Lisandro decided to honor the deceased in a special way. Reaching the garden, he saw that there was no living soul in it. So he decided that the time was right. As he approached the chapel, he took out a heavily rusted key from a cavernous pocket of his habit. After several unsuccessful attempts, the old lock finally gave up and Brother Lisandro went inside.

On both sides of the altar with an old blackened painting in its central part, stood storied racks, densely filled with long candles. Both the painting and the candlesticks were covered with a thick layer of dust, which indicated that the chapel had not been attended for a very long time. "Next time I'll clean up," Brother Lisandro promised himself, then took out a tinder and lit one candle with it, and with it all the others.

The chapel lit up like a flaming torch in the evening darkness. Brother Lisandro knelt before the altar. "Please forgive me!" he whispered. Two tears flowed from under his deformed eyelids, moistening his lumps-covered cheeks. Suddenly he heard footsteps in the distance. A shudder of terror ran through his body. For he recognized the gait, the sound of which, years ago, filled him with both terror and hatred.

"I must get out of here," he thought, then slipped out of the chapel with incredible agility, closing the door behind him. "Let them burn all night." Slipping under the fence, he saw the familiar figure of the duke out of the corner of his eye. Once he was outside the gate, at a safe distance, he paused to look at his former tormentor from afar. "Perhaps this is the last time I see him..." he thought.

But the duke was not the same man he had feared so much years ago. His steps were unsteady. Walking seemed difficult for him. When he reached the chapel portal, he paused, backed away, then took two steps forward as if he was about to lose his balance. Then he pulled the door knob. Unable to open the locked door, he knelt on the stone step and rested his head on the iron grate. A sudden sob shook his back.

Brother Lisandro watched this scene for a moment, deep in his thoughts, then set off on his way back. Instinctively, he glanced toward the gypsy camp that loomed on the horizon on the right side of the road. "Poor Alicia... she still can't forget what he did to her," he thought, remembering his old friend and companion in misery. "Maybe it wouldn't have happened had it not been for me..."

He remembered to this day how, during that memorable party, when the duke decided to make him the laughingstock of all the invited guests, Alicia raised her black eyebrows in an expression of tragic helplessness, kissed him on the forehead, and then ran out from the ballroom, throwing the rose that adorned her hair on the ground. He also remembered that when the Duke of Valsombra also left the hall shortly after her disappearance, he guessed that something terrible had happened.

The party was over, and Brother Lisandro, then known as Serafín, ran as fast as he could to the third floor of the palace, to the unused room where Alicia often spent her free time, practicing dancing figures. As he reached the door, his heart leapt in his chest. He knocked timidly, but no one answered. When he pressed the door knob and looked inside the room, he saw his friend lying motionless on the floor.

The tousled black curls strewn across the pale floor resembled a herd of snakes, writhing around Medusa's head. They partially covered the face and the exposed breast that rose and fell sharply.

"Alicia, what happened?" Serafín cried, kneeling beside her and brushing a strand of hair from her forehead.

"Thank you for coming," she replied.

Her aquamarine eyes, which till now had radiated joy and warmth, showed anger and hatred.

"I'll kill him," she said through gritted teeth.

"No. I will kill him for you," Serafín replied.

That afternoon he saw his friend for the last time. The next day she disappeared without a trace. Soon after, Serafín went for help to Iduna, whom he had been visiting for some time. The potions she prepared soothed the pain caused by the blisters on his body. She also liked to get him to confide. During one of these conversation, he told her how mean the duke was to him.

He also mentioned by the way Alicia, even though he had promised not to reveal her secret to anyone. But he felt instinctively that Iduna, who, as he noticed, hated the duke as passionately as he did, probably had been harmed by him in the same way as his friend. He remembered that as soon as his story was finished, she brought from the depths of her cave a small flask with some kind of tincture, dark brown in color and sweetly smelling, instructing him to mix the liquid with wine.

All these years, Serafín was sure Alicia was alive and was still planning her revenge. Sometimes it even seemed to him that in some incomprehensible way he sensed her presence in Valsombra. However, he did not believe in the revelations of Roberto, who just the day before poisoning the duchess told him that his friend, having nowhere to go after leaving the palace, joined the gypsies camp and became the wife of one of them.

He believed this unbelievably sounding story only after many years, when he met Alicia by chance during one of his penitential visits to the duke's ancestral chapel. He had just finished praying and was walking towards the exit, when suddenly he noticed a woman dressed in gypsy clothes, slipping out of the palace through the back entrance. He waited for her to leave the garden, then started toward her.

"Do you recognize me?" He asked, coming closer to her.

The woman turned her head. It was indeed Alicia. She brightened at the sight of his disfigured face, then threw herself on his neck.

"Serafín! How are you, dear old friend!" she exclaimed.

"So it's true what Roberto said that you have a Gypsy husband?"

Alicia grew sad.

"My husband died two months ago in San Sebastián. It was then that I realized it was time to go back and complete the plan I had put off during his lifetime. But now that Camil is no longer alive, I have returned here with our son. I see you've become a monk."

"I am repenting for the terrible act I have committed. Do you remember the oath I took to you that afternoon?"

"You have not kept your word..."

"I have. Unfortunately, I did not foresee one thing: the duke realized that he had been given poisoned wine. He looked carefully at the goblet, then held it out to the Duchess. I have no idea how he could have known the drink was poisoned... He was drinking from the same cup as usual..."

"The one he inherited from his father?"

"Yes... This iridescent glass seems to have some special properties."

"What do you mean?"

"When I was pouring the wine, I noticed that in contact with the drink, the vessel changed color slightly. But I didn't think it had anything to do with poison. But when the duke took the goblet in his hand, he immediately offered it to his wife, who still could not decide which type of wine to choose."

"Are you trying to say...?"

"... that by wanting to poison the duke, I made it easier for him to get rid of his wife," finished Brother Lisandro.

"And I was just..." Alicia began, but her voice stuck in her throat. She hid her face in her hands.

"What happened, Alicia?" Brother Lisandro asked.

"I just tried to poison him!" she exclaimed. "Unfortunately, I did not realize that everything would be wasted by this damned cup! I spotted the moment when a young maid, who was preparing dinner for the duke, left the kitchen for a moment, and then I crept inside. There was a tray on the table with a decorative decanter and this large glass goblet... I recognized it, so I was sure that I would poison the duke without putting anyone else in danger..."

"The duke will surely detect the poison the moment it enters the chalice with the wine, and it changes color."

"Are you saying that our tormentor is untouchable because of this cup?"

"Not exactly."

"What do you mean?"

"He has many enemies. He is a cruel, ruthless man, hated by half of Valsombra. Duchess Teresa died because of my fault."

"Not yours, his own."

"On the one hand, yes, but perhaps the Duchess would still be alive if it weren't for me. Punishing him is no longer up to us..."

"You sound like a goddamn monk!" Alicia exclaimed indignantly, then burst into tears as she ran towards the camp.

Since then, Brother Lisandro never saw his companion in misery again. Despite the fact that he had not forgotten the harm they had both suffered from the duke, he was glad his friend had failed to kill him. "Lord, thank you for keeping her from this madness," he sighed. "This road leads nowhere. It is enough that I have to live with the stigma of the murderer of innocent Duchess Teresa." He followed Alicia with his eyes, then headed towards   the   convent.

Chapter 16

Solanum lethale

César studied sleeping Blanca's face, lit by the faint moonlight streaming inside the cave.

"If only I knew what makes you have to live in the dark..." he sighed, looking at the eyes moving under the eyelids. "Perhaps Aitor will read something in these learned books that he studies so passionately..."

It was already dawn. Blanca's eyelids twitched slightly. As they slowly rose, they revealed large, glistening pupils framed by a barely visible dark gray fringe. "Something is causing the pupils to dilate!" César thought. "But what could it be?!" At the same moment Blanca looked at him, stroking his swarthy cheek with her almost transparent hand.

"I hate goodbyes... They are like small, malicious demons who take away the joy of meeting people..." she said.

"Nobody likes them. But let's not let them poison a single second," replied César.

"You're right. Let's spite them then," said Blanca, then threw her arms around his neck, drawing him to her.

The heavy, shiny locks of César's hair got out from under a wide silk ribbon, holding it back. Mingled with the loose, untamed strands of Blanca's hair, scattered on a makeshift cape bed, they created amazing patterns. The entwined bodies of the lovers melted into one, inseparable form.

When it was time to part, César waited as usual for Blanca to be at a safe distance, then followed her. "This is ridiculous," he thought. "I never worry about her at night, but only during the day..." When her petite figure in a light-colored dress disappeared behind the narrow gate for servants, he gazed thoughtfully at the massive, gloomy shape of the Palacio Aciago for a moment longer.

Then his attention was drawn to a detail he had not noticed before. Behind the palace, hidden in a forest thicket, stood a lonely, unattached Gothic tower. It was a remnant of an already nonexistent thirteenth-century building, erected for defensive purposes by the ancestors of The Count de Aciago. César estimated that it is located a dozen meters from the palace. "Knowing this cruel man, he must imprison people in it," he thought unexpectedly.

This bizarre reflection on the character of the count gave rise to further considerations. "What if he is the one who gives Blanca some substance that causes photophobia? Maybe this monster is poisoning her with something..." The very thought that Blanca's mysterious illness might be the result of an intrigue of her husband, overwhelmed with morbid jealousy, made shiver run down César's spine.

It was already daylight when he returned to the castle. Already from a distance, he saw the huge figure of Aitor raking the dead leaves that had completely covered the small stone courtyard during the night.

"Hello, my friend," he said.

"Hello, lord," the giant struggled to hold back from giving him a low bow.

"Remember when you once said that knowledge in the field of toxicology might be useful to us one day?" César asked, knowing there was no time to lose.

Aitor raised his eyebrows, surprised by the question.

"I remember, my lord. I hope none of your friends has been poisoned."

"Unfortunately, I suspect that may be the case. The case concerns a person close to me."

"Yes?"

"I hope you can keep a secret. I trust you enough that I am willing to entrust you with a very delicate, personal secret. However, you must swear that you will not reveal it to anyone. Someone's life is at stake."

"I swear by all things holy."

"The person concerned is Blanca, wife of the Count de Aciago."

"That cruel man the locals fear so much?"

"That one. She suffers from a mysterious disease which causes a severe photophobia due to much dilated pupils. This limits her life to such an extent that she can neither be in the sun nor in lit rooms. So after dark, she walks in the woods, because it is the only time when she is able to leave the darkened office where she stays during the day."

"A strange thing," Aitor got thoughtful.

"I know. I need your help and I believe you will be able to solve this mystery."

"That's not why I said it was strange. The thing is that some time ago I met a young woman here, who went for a night walk in the woods and then got lost. She seemed to avoid the light. When I looked at her surreptitiously, her eyes seemed to be missing irises. But later I realized that she might just have severely dilated pupils..."

"Do you remember what she looked like?"

"She was exceptionally beautiful. She had a very fair complexion and long dark brown hair that was tied up carelessly. I also remember a dark green scarf..."

"So it was Blanca. I met her under similar circumstances as you did. At first she did not want to reveal her name to me, so as not to put me in danger."

"Everything looks like that's her. It was night so I offered to walk her home, but she didn't want me to. God knows what kind of evil prowls this forest after dark! After all, the famous Hanged Men's Cemetery is teeming with pirates. I tried to convince her, but she refused categorically. She said she couldn't tell me where she came from. I respected that and did not follow her. I just didn't dare. Then I felt uncomfortable, as I realized that by following the stranger's wishes, I might have exposed her to some kind of misfortune..."

"Don't blame yourself, Aitor. It doesn't matter now."

"A stone fell off my chest when I learned that no one was hurt because of my stupidity."

"Your stupidity is nothing compared to the cruelty of Count de Aciago," César replied playfully, placing a friendly hand on his mighty shoulder. "When she finally revealed to me that she was Ramón Suárez's wife, I understood her fears. My person is not important here, however. I suspect that her husband or some other madman is systematically poisoning her, perhaps to restrict her freedom."

"It's very likely. Dilated pupils are a classic symptom of poisoning. Something even worse crossed my mind..."

"What do you mean?"

"That she tried to poison herself."

"It is impossible. I don't know a creature who loves life more than Blanca. She would sooner challenge you to a duel than hurt herself," César joked. "She might possibly poison herself by accident, but it's not very likely. This has been going on for a long time," he added, becoming more serious. "Please find out what poison causes dilation of irises and photophobia."

"Who will finish the raking?" Aitor worried, looking at the piles of leaves neatly stacked against the wall.

"Don't worry about that anymore. The leaves are not important. Go to the library and do the research. No matter how long it takes, I'll take care of the rest."

"In that case, I'm getting to work right now."

"Very good. I owe you, Aitor." The giant nodded, then headed for the library.

"I remember reading about photophobia somewhere..." he thought as he flipped through manuscripts and printed books dealing with poisonous plants. Suddenly he remembered his conversation with César about the belladonna. "These berries had similar properties..." he thought. After a few hours, he managed to find several descriptions of it in various works, in which it appeared under the name *solanum lethale*, and the latest classification in the Spanish translation of Linnaeus, recently brought by Lord Ravendale from Madrid [17]. Having read in one of those books that the deadly poisonous belladonna, administered in sufficiently small doses, does not kill, but causes, among other things, pallor, pupil dilation and severe photophobia, and therefore all the symptoms that occurred in Blanca, he immediately went to César's office to share this knowledge with him. It was already late, so Aitor decided to act immediately, suspecting that his master would soon leave the castle to meet his beloved.

César was just getting ready to leave when someone knocked on the door.

"Come in, it's open," he said.

Aitor appeared in the doorway, holding several books under his arm, some thick and some thin.

"Lord, I think I found what we were looking for," he said triumphantly.

"Really?" César was surprised.

"Do you remember our conversation about the belladonna?"

"Of course, it wasn't that long ago that I would have time to forget. However, from what I understand, this plant kills instantly..."

"Yes, but if only a small dose is consumed, it only causes mild poisoning, which is manifested by dilated pupils, photophobia and pallor... In some people it also causes increased pulse rate and various other symptoms."

César remembered that Blanca's heart always beat steadily but unnaturally quickly. Until now, he had believed it was due to fear or intense agitation. Now he understood that in all likelihood, Aitor had just discovered the source of his beloved's mysterious illness. "Everything fits!" he thought.

"My dear Aitor, I don't even know how to thank you! Your knowledge is invaluable!" he cried, then gripped the servant's huge hand tightly.

"Someone is probably putting poison to the wine. As far as I know, in the old days this concoction was used not only as a murder weapon but also as an aphrodisiac."

"Count de Aciago is capable of anything. Surely you've heard about his preferences... I very much hope that Blanca will come to the appointed place tonight and I will be able to warn her."

Saying this, he hugged Aitor, then headed for the cave to wait for his beloved. The night was unusually rainy, just as it was when they introduced themselves to each other in the clearing. The reddish moon was either shyly peeking out from behind the curtain of the gloomy storm clouds, or it was hiding behind it, leaving the forest in almost total darkness. A strong wind jerked a strand of César's hair from under the ribbon.

The bare boughs of the four oaks stared gloomily at the angry sky while the fallen leaves danced in the wind like Menadas. Taking refuge from the ever stronger gusts at the mouth of the cave, César watched this amazing spectacle. At one point it reminded him of an old fresco, depicting the dance of death, which he had seen many years ago in the crypt of the ancestral chapel in Valsombra, on the day of his mother's funeral.

Several hours passed, but Blanca did not come. "Something must have happened," thought César anxiously. "She used to come here every night, even before we met. She read books, walked, watched night animals... Perhaps someone found out about our meetings and informed her husband?" The very thought that Count de Aciago might find out about everything, filled his heart with dread. He knew the tales of Ramón Suárez's vengeful character well enough, and knew what he would be capable of, if he found out that he had been cheated on.

As he remembered one of those stories, a nervous twitch ran up his temple. It happened a few years ago. Count de Aciago hired a new gardener then, whose main task was to cultivate his favorite roses. At first, the man performed the work entrusted to him very conscientiously. However, as he began to receive enthusiastic praise, he lost his old zeal and soon the roses began to fade away. The angry count ordered him to be locked in the Gothic tower as a punishment. He entrusted the care of the prisoner to a servant who brought him water and biscuits three times a day. Less than a week later, the man was found dead. This story was once told to César by his aunt Eugenia, mother of Carmen Jiménez y Castro. She argued that the gardener had committed suicide not out of despair, as the punishment was to last only ten days, but out of fear.

As legend had it, the tower was haunted by the ghosts of Ramón's ancestor, the infamous Balduino, and his beloved cousin Isabel. It was the place of this couple's love trysts. According to Aunt Eugenia, these meetings were to take place in the exact same room where Count de Aciago had imprisoned the lazy gardener. Apparently, whoever met the ghosts of Balduino and Isabel, walking around the tight cells holding hands, would die immediately, unable to withstand their terrible sight.

"With a man like Ramón in power, you don't need ghosts or ghouls to die of fear!" César thought. "In addition, this tower looks very unfriendly. I don't even want to think about the conditions there." At the same moment he realized that since the count had already imprisoned someone in this awful place, he might as well have placed his own wife there.

"I have no time to waste!" - he said, then went towards the Palacio Aciago. When he was halfway there, a storm broke out. Deafened by the loud howl of the gale, he could no longer hear his own thoughts. Taking care not to be crushed by falling branches, he looked up every now and then at the treetops swaying in a maddened trance.

When he finally got there, the gale eased a little. There was a faint light in one of the windows of the count's residence. César walked around the enormous structure, then headed towards the Gothic tower. Plunged in darkness, it seemed uninhabited. The gargoyles with grotesquely twisted faces, protruding from the upper part of the wall, were carved so perfectly that they gave the impression that they were about to come to life, frozen for a moment only to confuse the viewer.

César decided the tower was empty and turned back. Passing the gloomy, dark mass of the Palacio Aciago, he instinctively looked towards the room where the light had previously been on. The dull glow was still radiating from the towering window. For a brief moment, it seemed to him that he saw someone's shadow on the wall, but it was so faint that it was impossible to tell who it might have belonged to.

17 *Parte prática de botánica del Cabellero Cárlos Linneo, que comprehende las clases, órdenes, géneros, especies y variedades de las plantas...* translated by Antonio Paláu y Verdéra.

Chapter 17

A lonely tower

A ndrés informed Count de Aciago of his discovery on the same night that he saw Blanca and César disappear together into the depths of the cave. As soon as he discovered the secret of his mistress, he immediately set off on his way back. He walked through the forest with his heart in his mouth, seeing in almost all shadows the malevolent ghosts of the murdered druids that old Jaime had warned him about.

After he finally reached the courtyard of the palace, he was exhausted but happy. "I did not expect fate to be so generous to me!" he rejoiced in spirit. "At last I will be able to get my revenge on her, and in addition I will gain the count's favor. One trip to the forest brought me two benefits." Having thought about this, he quickened his pace and almost ran to his master's office.

The door was wide open. The count was sitting at his desk, busy organizing his correspondence.

"Andrés! I have been waiting all night for your return!" he called, seeing the servant enter the room without knocking.

"Good evening, my lord. I know everything, but it's not good news…" Andrés replied with mock concern.

"Sit down and tell me!" The count ordered, pointing to an armchair in the window recess. He filled two large glasses with delicious sweet wine, handed one to Andrés and placed his personal one on the desk.

"Count, I don't know where to begin, so I'll tell you everything in order."

"Fine."

"As soon as I received the order to go in search, I left the palace. I chose the main path, because it seemed unlikely that your spouse, considering her illness and weakness, would take the risk of following one of the side paths, completely overgrown with weeds. This way I got to a clearing surrounded by old trees. Not seeing a soul, and having no idea which way to go, I paused to gather my thoughts. Suddenly I heard a conversation. One of the voices belonged to a man, and in the other I recognized your spouse right away; they came from the side of four oaks, with characteristic trunks joined together. I moved closer as silently as possible. Then a small cave appeared before my eyes, at the mouth of which I saw the countess in the company of this man."

"What did he look like?" Interrupted the count. The huge, deep purple veins in his temples swelled as if they were about to burst. Even from a distance, one could see the blood pulsing within them.

"He was tall and proportionally built. I remember his long, jet black hair, tied low with a silk ribbon, and his characteristic profile. It's interesting, but his face was a bit like the one of your doctor... He was dressed in a dark cape and a black triangular hat. I had the impression that he was a highborn man."

Count de Aciago thought for a minute.

"I know only one person who would fit that description. This is César Castro y de Abaroa, Marquis de Viciosa. The same one who is said to be involved in some dangerous political affairs. Mario told me that at the Duke de Valsombra's ball, he had seen him in the company of Lord Ravendale, the same one who is wanted in England for his revolutionary sympathies.

"Maybe it can be used against him..." Andrés suggested. "Friendship with a man of this kind certainly is not something to be proud of."

"This is true. You are one devious man, but your mission is completed for today. Deliberating about politics is not the task of the service. Go to bed!" the count snapped.

"Good night, count," Andrés said, leaving.

The count replied with a nod of his head.

After returning to the palace, Blanca, instead of going to the chamber, went directly to the study, where the bed and her personal belongings still were. In the early morning she heard a loud knock on the door. She froze. A strange feeling made her suspect her husband was outside the door. She walked slowly to the door and turned the key in the lock. As she had expected, her eyes saw the massive figure of Count de Aciago. Terrible anger was beaming from his eyes.

"I suppose you can guess what I'm here for," he said in a low voice.

"I changed my mind. I'm not going back to the bedroom. I'm staying here," she replied.

"I can guess why you're not going back there. Surely you prefer César's company to mine. I heard you have good time together," replied the Count sarcastically.

At the sound of these words, and at the sight of Blanca's husband's hateful gaze, she felt an overwhelming weakness.

"Who told you such things?" she asked, gasping for breath.

"It's not your business. Answer the question for me: are you ready to deny these revelations?" replied the Count.

Blanca didn't say a word. For she was not sure whether these were really revelations based on empty speculations, or whether the count had been following her personally. So she decided that it would be wise to remain silent, as she neither intended to deny César, nor to harm him and herself, by answering the accusation in the affirmative. She stared silently at the count with her great pupils. At one point the world swirled before her eyes and she fell to the floor.

She woke up in a small room with a pungent musty smell. A very narrow, long and tightly barred window, thickly covered with dirty cobwebs, and raw walls made of massive stone blocks, indicated that she was inside the gothic tower, about which she had heard all kind of terrible stories. "So my worst fears came true..." she thought as she looked around the small cell. "Now I can only wait for death..."

The sun was heading west. As the reddish beam burst into the room through the narrow window, Blanca narrowed her eyes and turned to face the wall. As she stared resignedly at the gray stones, she noticed that some of them had traces of dried blood on them. "So Jaime was telling the truth when he claimed that Ramón, like his father and grandfather, tortured people here..."

As the sun's rays faded and the cell became dark, Blanca thought of César. "I would be leaving the palace by this time. And soon I would reach our clearing..." she sighed. She imagined César waiting for her, leaning against one of the four oaks, watching the clouds slowly glide across the face of the moon, wondering why she has not appeared at the appointed place yet.

These thoughts made her eyes brim with tears that began to run profusely down her pale cheeks. "When I was saying goodbye to you, I didn't think we would see each other for the last time... I hope you can figure out the reason for my disappearance."

Her contemplation was suddenly interrupted by a piercing squeal that came from just beyond the head of the bed on which she rested. When she turned her head and looked in that direction, she saw a huge rat staring at her with obvious curiosity.

"As soon as I get something to eat, I'll share it with you," she said. "You first. I'll save two-thirds of my meal. If you don't die, it will mean that I can eat my portion without fear. What do you say?"

The animal seemed to understand her words, for it immediately ran to the corner and disappeared into the depths of the opening in the stone wall.

At the same moment there was a click of a key in the lock. Her heart stopped for a moment. She got up from the mattress, smoothing her gown. She looked fearfully at the steel door, which slowly swung open to reveal August's pale, sunken face.

"Doctor Nacht, I didn't think you would get involved in all this," she said reproachfully.

"My lady, how unfairly you judge me," he replied.

"You are my husband's friend, aren't you?"

"I'm his doctor, but that doesn't mean I'm on his side. I secretly got a backup copy of the tower keys. I've come to warn you."

"Warn me?"

"The count was trying to keep your disappearance a secret. However, it did not escape my attention. I suspected something bad had happened. Your husband trusts me, so I decided to get information from him about what happened to you. However, it was not as easy as I expected."

"That's very kind of you, doctor Nacht. I didn't suppose you were concerned about my safety so much."

"I would give my life for you," August said, then knelt down and kissed her icy cold hand.

His pale eyes stared at her with an expression of mad adoration. Blanca withdrew her hand gently.

"At first the count did not want to reveal your whereabouts. So I had no choice but to resort to a little trick and use the benefits of medicine in a completely different matter. I managed to catch the moment when Jaime set the table. On the pretext that I wanted an extra set of cutlery, I sent him to the kitchen. Meanwhile, I added a little bit of mandrake root tincture left over from your husband's surgery to the decanter with tempranillo. I asked for water for myself, excusing myself with a severe headache, which I would rather not make worse by drinking wine before going to bed. Soon the count became more open to honest conversation. He told me that he had decided to put you in this tower because of the alleged adultery. Just think of the terrible consequences of a morbid jealousy!"

Blanca swallowed hard.

"The count has also revealed to me a secret that will help you regain your health in a few days," August continued.

"How is this possible?" Blanca interrupted.

"When he drank the third goblet of wine, I provoked him to confide by hitting his weak spot."

"What do you mean?"

"I said that I would never want to marry a woman who is so difficult to temper. When the count heard these words, glad that I share his position on marriage, he got up from the table, then staggered over and hugged me."

"I hope you only expressed that opinion for the sake of your clever trick," Blanca said.

"Of course! In his place, I would be your devoted servant... But returning to the whole matter, provoked in this way, the count told me how he is restricting your freedom. He does it with the help of poison, which the cook adds to the wine on his orders. Now he will probably be adding it to the water. Old Juan is fully trusted by the count, having served his father from his earliest years. In the past, he has helped him eliminate few inconvenient people."

"A poison?!" Blanca interrupted. Her eyebrows shot up in utmost surprise.

"Yes. It is juice from the fruit of a plant called belladonna. Usually, consumption of this substance causes almost immediate death, however, when given in very small doses, it causes pupil dilation and photophobia."

Blanca looked at him in disbelief.

"I know it all sounds like a fantastic story," August said. "But if you allow yourself to help me, I will make the daylight enjoyable for you again."

"I guess it's no longer necessary now… Knowing Ramón, I'll never leave this place."

"If you keep drinking the poisoned water, you will eventually die. I'll get you out of here, even if I have to pay for it with my own life. I swear by my mother's memory."

"You are a good man, doctor Nacht."

"I am not helping you out of kindness, but because I love you."

She didn't answer.

"Although the count has not allowed me to visit you, I will personally bring you fresh water. You're not in any danger on my part."

"Thank you!" she rejoiced. "May the fate reward you for this sacrifice?"

"May it be so," August replied, looking into her eyes.

"Certainly it will be so," she replied with a friendly smile.

He bowed low, then left, locking the door behind him. Blanca couldn't get her thoughts together. On the one hand, she feared August, seeing his infatuation and determination, and realizing that he was a very dangerous man. On the other hand, she was tormented by the awareness that, after regaining her health and possibly leaving her prison, she would have to decisively push away the one to whom she owed her return to the world of the living.

Having turned the key in the door to the cell, August stood by it for a moment longer, mesmerized by the sight of his beloved. As he descended the steep, winding stairs to the bottom of the tower, he leaned back against the cold, damp wall.

"Certainly it will be so," he repeated Blanca's last words like the echo. "Certainly it will be so…"

Chapter 18

A sleepless night

Meanwhile, Count de Aciago was wondering how he could get rid of César once and for all. He knew that any attempt to harm him through the Inquisition, would most likely not bring the desired effect, as his brother, Cardinal Suárez, has been a good friend of Duke de Valsombra for a long time. Despite his involvement in politics, Mario certainly would not hurt the son of one of his closest friends.

After much thought, the count came to the conclusion that the only and surest way to eliminate César would be to kill him in a duel. This kind of vengeance would also give him the greatest pleasure, for the hated opponent would disappear forever from his sight. Additionally, César's death would cause Blanca's suffering, which he cared about no less than about killing the man with whom she had cheated on him.

Contrary to August's fears, the Count planned to keep his wife alive while making her existence as intolerable as possible. He knew that sooner or later, the time would come when she would die by her own hand, as did several of the tower's previous inhabitants. He was also aware that the grief caused by the death of her beloved would significantly accelerate this decision. "Nobody lasted in this tower for more than a month," he thought with satisfaction.

Sitting down comfortably in the armchair, he sipped his favorite sweet wine and imagined how the blade of his so far infallible sword hits César right in the heart, and then the bloody stain formed around the wound expands rapidly, covering the opponent's entire chest. He awaited with even greater delight for the moment when he would personally bring the news of his victory to his unfaithful wife.

A knock on the door snatched him from his blissful reverie. It was Andrés.

"Count, I brought the correspondence," he said, pointing to the silver tray in his left hand.

"Thank you very much. It's good that you are here. Leave the letters on the desk and saddle me a good horse. I'll need it tomorrow morning. Blue is a bit erratic, so pick one that can be relied on. This is an urgent matter."

"Yes, sir," Andrés replied obediently.

The supper time came. The count arrived at the dining room on time. When he came, August was waiting for him. Jaime bustled around the table.

"Juan has already prepared a meal for the countess," he said.

"Perfect. Tell Marta to carry it to her."

"I'm on my way."

August instinctively looked back at Jaime. The man immediately left the room to pass the order. Aged but still in perfect health, Marta still served Ramón's father and was the only person among all the servants who was not afraid to enter the tower after dark. As loyal as the cook Juan, and as ruthless as he was, she enjoyed the unwavering trust of her master.

The count and August ate their supper in silence, then retired, each to their own chamber. Neither of them slept that night. The count counted down the hours until morning, when he would go to neighboring Viciosa to challenge César to a duel.

"These are your last moments, Cesar Castro," he said. "Make the best of them, because you will be joining your mother tomorrow."

Meanwhile, August secretly went to the tower to bring Blanca water. When she heard the lock click, recognizing the medic's footsteps, she pretended to be asleep. As silently as he could, August set the vessel down on the stone floor, then carefully went downstairs. With the second of the two spare keys he had stolen from Pilar's cell the previous day, he closed the wooden gate of the tower and headed for his chamber.

"I have to go to Iduna. Surely she will advise me on how I can win this angel's heart..." he thought, then hurriedly prepared everything he needed for the road. The dull, quivering light of the candle dying on the table, made his shadow blurred and indistinct. He was not also recognized by César, who was just passing Palacio Aciago on his way back to his castle.

August went to the stable, saddled his horse, and then rushed east to meet his unfailing friend. Remembering the horrible procession he had seen in the woods when he had ridden to the Count of Valsombra the previous time, he tried to go as fast as he could to avoid a similar encounter. The night was unusually clear. The bright moonlight, falling on the forest road, made it bright and safe.

At one point the horse neighed anxiously and stopped, digging its hoof in the ground.

"Don't be afraid, they're just forest scares," August tried to calm the animal by patting it on its back.

As he looked around, he realized that he was in the same exact place where he had seen the macabre retinue not so long ago. He trembled all over his body. He sat still for a moment, listening and watching out for the ghastly procession. The forest, however, was gripped by a night lethargy. Finally, he managed to convince the horse that they were in no danger and could go on. The horse snorted and took off.

When he got there, he found Iduna sitting on the mattress, lost in thoughts.

"Hello, Iduna!"

"I knew you would come, son."

She walked over to August and as soon as he dismounted the horse, whom he tied to the oak trunk, she wrapped her thin arms tightly around him.

He sensed that she wasn't in the best mood.

"I saw you in a dream," she said. There was worry in her eyes.

"I guess it wasn't a good dream."

"Very bad one."

"Tell me."

"If you really want..."

"Your dreams never lie. You said it yourself."

"That's true," she said, eyeing him sharply. "I dreamed that while walking through the forest, you met a beautiful angel on your way, from whom a bright light shone. He smiled at you. As you tried to approach him, he disappeared, the earth parted under your feet and a terrible tornado-like whirlwind dragged you into the abyss."

"This dream is true indeed. It perfectly illustrates the terrible torment I am now going through..."

"You fell in love unhappily. I don't ask with whom."

"She is the wife of Count de Aciago, who hired me as his personal doctor. She really looks like an angel."

Iduna looked at him darkly.

"Forget her or she will bring misfortune upon you. This is your angel of death."

"How can this wonderful, noble being bring misfortune?"

"We agree, my son that my dreams never lie. Right, Álvaro?"

The falcon made a few low sounds, then unfolded its strong wings in turn, one at a time. August admired this beautiful creature, whose wise eyes seemed to understand perfectly every word they said.

"Álvaro agrees with me," said Iduna. The bird confirmed with a soft, long squeal.

"Iduna, is there any way to avoid this imminent misfortune? I will not stop loving her even when my heart stops beating."

"You'll never get reciprocity."

"Is that why this angel disappeared?"

"That is exactly why."

August's eyes darkened. He turned his back to Iduna, who approached him and put her hand on his back.

"You are very much like your mother in some ways," she said.

"What do you mean?"

"Like her, you are easily deluded. If you want something badly, you are deceived by illusory hope, even if the case is lost from the beginning. It's a trap."

"Do you know any miracle cure, anything that would help me get her reciprocity?"

"There is no such measure. The only cure for your misfortune is willpower. If you want to live, you have to let go of this obsession."

"I am not able to. Promise me you'll be with me when my time comes."

"I promise you, son," Iduna whispered, her voice breaking. "I promise."

"I have to get back to the Palacio Aciago now," August said, then untied the horse from the tree.

"Remember: you have to forget about her. You have your whole long life ahead of you!" Iduna repeated.

But she knew August would not listen. He kissed her goodbye, then got on his horse and rode away without looking back. All the way back he thought about the conversation with Iduna and the valuable but impossible advice she had given him. He also imagined himself as he stands at the top of the stairs in the Gothic tower, Blanca smiles at him, and in the same second the stone steps suddenly collapse under his feet, creating a powerful whirlpool that pulls him into the dark abyss.

When he got to the Palacio Aciago, it was already daylight. In the stables, he met Andrés bustling around a white horse. "Is the count going somewhere with a visit?" he thought. "It must be urgent if he had his horse saddled first thing in the morning." On his way to the dining room, he met the count, who was just leaving the palace. He was dressed in an elegant light blue frock coat, trimmed with silver thread. "I wonder where he is going in such a festive outfit..."

Before going to bed, August directed his steps towards the kitchen, where he prepared a jug with fresh water. Making sure no one could see him, he went to the Gothic tower to change the supposedly poisoned water for safe one. As he walked up the stairs, Blanca recognized his steps. "It's unbearable!" she thought. "I let him save myself, meanwhile he suffers more and more. The suffering I cause hurts me even more than my own misfortune..."

At the sight of August's deathly pale face, even whiter than her own, she was overwhelmed by fear. Meanwhile, he placed the vessel on the ground, then looked at her adoringly with his light blue eyes, whose intense color highlighted the darker and darker bruises caused by insomnia.

"Are you feeling well, doctor Nacht?" she asked.

"I was called to a patient at night. Bullet wound, a nasty thing," he lied, not wanting to worry her. "I am going to go get some sleep now."

At that moment Blanca realized that for the first time in months, the morning sun shining through the window did not hurt her.

"It's amazing!" she exclaimed. "I think I'm starting to see better."

August looked into her eyes, delighted to see that the pupils had contracted to reveal gray-blue irises.

"Your pupils started to function properly. You'll be completely healed soon!" he confirmed.

In a fit of spontaneous joy, Blanca grasped his hand in both her hands and squeezed it tightly.

"Doctor Nacht, I don't know how to thank you!" she whispered.

August stood motionless, gazing into her eyes with silent delight. She was still holding his hand.

"Countess, I lived for this moment," he said. "Your recovery is the greatest gift for me."

"Take care of yourself, doctor," she replied. "Your health is also very important to me."

She released his hand.

"Close the window just in case," August said. "Marta cannot find out that you are recovering."

"Of course! How careless I am. After all, I could have put you in a lot of trouble, because at the news that I am starting to see normally, Ramón would launch an investigation to find out who was replacing the poisoned water with fresh one."

"I don't care about myself. I have only you on my mind," August replied, picking up the water jug Marta had left behind.

"I did not expect to have such a friend in you."

"I'd do anything for you."

Saying goodbye with these words, he bowed low and left the cell.

Chapter 19

The Stigma

The count reached Viciosa without any problems. When he saw César's castle, covered with all the colors of autumn, his heart beat faster. "Soon now," he thought. He was minutes away from the confrontation. "I wonder what is in the western part," he wondered as he stared at the wing of the building, plunged in the twilight. At that moment, he saw a red-haired giant who had just emerged from an uninhabited part of the castle.

"Honorable sir, how can I help you?" Aitor asked, bowing politely.

"Please tell your lord that the Count de Aciago is waiting for him in the courtyard," the count ordered.

After a short while, César appeared inside the enormous gate. "You probably know what brings me here."

"I can guess," he replied, looking the count straight in the eye with a confident gaze. "Tell me what happened to the Countess de Aciago."

He knew perfectly well that Blanca was alive and was almost sure that she was in the Gothic tower, for he had sent Aitor out at dawn to scout. The servant, seeing Marta walking towards the gloomy building, carrying a tray of meager breakfast, guessed everything at once and immediately shared this observation with his master. César, however, could not help humiliating the count by directly asking about his wife.

Without a word, the count threw down a gauntlet at his feet. César bent down and picked it up, thereby accepting the challenge. There was an imperturbable calm on his face.

"Swords?" He asked.

"Swords. *A la primera sangre* [18]."

The count was so sure of his victory that he intended to additionally humiliate his rival by killing him immediately in a conventional match to the first blood.

"Please indicate a time and place," César ordered, eyeing him defiantly.

"Today at noon."

"Agreed. I will be waiting in the courtyard with my second."

The count tugged at the reins ostentatiously. The big white horse reared in a spectacular way, waving its hooves in the air just above César's head. But the man did not budge. The corners of his mouth curved slightly in an ironic smile.

"See you at noon!" he shouted, turning back, then slowly returned to the castle.

The horse shook its mane, snorted, and then dropped its hooves to the ground. The angry gaze of his rival followed César to the castle gate.

On the way back to the palace, the count realized that he had no second. After a moment's thought, his choice fell on August. "Doctor Nacht will be perfect. I hope he will, otherwise I will have to appoint someone from the service. I would not, however, bear such a disgrace! He has to agree!" he thought. When he reached Palacio Aciago, his first steps were towards August's chamber. The door was wide open, so he entered without knocking.

He found him at his desk, carefully studying the work of Carlos Musitano.

"My dear doctor Nacht," began the count.

August turned his head sharply. Absorbed in reading, he did not notice that someone was in the room.

"How are you, count!" he replied.

"I came to ask you for a favor..."

"I hope I can do it to you."

"This case is a matter of a very delicate nature. Recently, I had a personal conflict with the Marquis de Viciosa. This man insulted me in a very severe way, so I had no choice but to demand justice. This morning I challenged him to a duel. He accepted my gauntlet and we set an hour: noon. We will fight traditionally, with swords, to the first blood."

August's eyes widened. He couldn't say a word.

"Everything happened so fast that I didn't even have time to appoint a second..." continued the count.

"First, he locks his wife in this terrible tower, and then challenges my brother to a duel. Why him? Could this usurper have something to do with my beloved?" August wondered frantically, immediately putting together the events of the last few days into a logical whole. "Has fate mocked me twice?"

"My dear friend, are you all right? You look like you've seen a ghost!" the count cried.

"I am perfectly fine, count."

"You don't know the Marquis de Viciosa, do you? I hope he's not your acquaintance or friend, otherwise I would be in trouble."

"On the contrary. César is one of my greatest enemies. I would be glad to do you this favor."

"Great. We leave at half past eleven. I am going to order the carriage to be ready for us. I'm not going to walk through the forest on foot."

"It would be a pathetic sight, you wading through the brushwood, dressed up like this," thought August.

"How do you know César, doctor?"

"Like you, I am connected to him by a personal conflict. An old family history. However, I'd rather not talk about it."

"I understand you perfectly, doctor Nacht. If this is a difficult subject, I will never mention it again."

"I'll see you in the hall at half past twelve. I'll be on time, maybe even a little ahead of time."

"Great. I will probably also come ahead of time. I can't wait to drown the sword in his chest."

"Neither can I." August replied unexpectedly.

They shook hands, then the count left the room. August remained alone, overwhelmed by the storm of thoughts. His eyes turned somber. "This fool is sure to lose. The collarbone is just beginning to heal and he still has unhealed dislocations. He shouldn't fight in this state... Sooner or later I will have to fight my brother personally," he thought. "I've suffered enough from this impudent usurper!"

The appointed time has come. August and the count appeared in the hall almost simultaneously. There was an elegant carriage, drawn by two black and roan horses, in the courtyard. Like the count, and perhaps even more than him, August was eager to see the blood of his hated brother. "Perhaps luck will smile at me soon..." flashed through his mind. "If César disappears from the horizon, removing this pompous fool will go smoothly."

They arrived on time. As soon as the carriage stopped in front of Castillo de Viciosa, César appeared in the courtyard, accompanied by a tall, handsome man who seemed to be a foreigner.

"Well, well! Lord Ravendale himself!" The count whispered.

Seeing August, César paled slightly.

"Welcome to Viciosa," he said, reaching his hand out to his brother. The man shook his hand stiffly, at the same time giving him an icy look. Hate radiated from August's pale eyes.

"Count, this is my second, Lord Harold Ravendale."

The Englishman greeted the Count with his usual polite smile.

"It just so happens that Lord Ravendale has just come to visit me," César said.

"I got caught up in the middle of it like a rat in a trap!" Lord Ravendale joked.

"I have already agreed with Count de Aciago that we will fight to the first blood," César reminded.

Lord Ravendale nodded to the boy standing to one side, who was holding a roll of velvet containing two identical swords. He pushed the cloth away and walked over to the count.

"Please choose one of them," he said.

The count looked carefully at both of the swords, then selected the one closest to him.

"Time to begin," said Lord Ravendale.

The opponents looked at each other. When their swords crossed for the first time, August's heart began to beat like crazy. The clash of the arms echoed tremendously in his burning brain, drowning out the rush of thoughts. He stared at the fighters as if hypnotized. "I don't know anymore for which of the two I wish death more..." he thought, puffing up his nostrils.

In the same second, the blade of César's sword grazed the count's left shoulder. The latter, however, disregarding the self-imposed principle *a la primera sangre*, and ignoring the warning signals given by the seconds, furiously attacked the enemy, trying to kill him. Then César cut his right cheek with one swift movement of his sword. Blood spurted profusely from a rather deep wound, and the count fell unconscious to the ground.

August, who had prudently taken basic wound care supplies with him, immediately took care of his patient, forgetting the whole conflict for a moment.

"I'm sorry it ended this way," Lord Ravendale commented. "Hope the scar won't be too visible."

César looked at his friend meaningfully.

"*You old hypocrite!* [19]" he whispered.

Lord Ravendale barely suppressed a smile.

"I'll do my best, though I can't guarantee anything," August said.

"I hope he will have a stigma for the rest of his life," César replied, wiping his forehead with a handkerchief, then headed towards the castle.

When the count regained consciousness, he got into the carriage with August's help. He was furious. "I came to finish him once and for all, and instead he made a laughing stock of me!" - he thought.

"Give me the mandragora," he said to August.

The pain was getting excruciating.

"Unfortunately, I don't have it with me. As soon as we get home, I'll take care of you properly. Please don't say anything now."

The count clenched his hand and, in helpless anger, slapped his fist on the edge of the carriage window with all his might.

"I came here to kill him…" he said through his teeth, pressing the handkerchief tightly against the wound that was still bleeding heavily.

"I don't know why you got into conflict with César, but I sincerely feel sorry for you that it turned out that way. Believe me, count, I hoped even more than you that the Marquis de Viciosa would lose this duel," August said.

"Thank you, doctor Nacht," replied the Count.

August silently stared out the window at the passing trees. The almost complete certainty that his rival was none other than César, not only did not change his feelings for Blanca in any way, but - on the contrary - even fueled them. In addition, it also strengthened his intention of eliminating his brother, who he thought stood in the way of his happiness again.

18 Spanish *To the first blood.*

19 Ang.   *You*   *old*   *hypocrite!*

Chapter 20

Digitalis grandiflora

Count de Aciago's cheek was cut quite deep. August disinfected and sutured the wound as best he could. Although he genuinely hated his patient and cursed himself for saving his life, he performed the procedure with extreme care and attention. When he performed his medical duties, the Hippocratic Oath was an absolute sanctity for him. On the other hand, when he carried out informal, discreet assignments, the exact reverse of this ancient formula automatically became his rule, though he never turned against his former patients. In the case of the count, however, he had given up all scruples. He only waited for the right moment to skillfully eliminate him from the game, and free Blanca from him.

Nevertheless, from the moment he realized that the hated brother once again stood in the way of his happiness, this time depriving him of his beloved woman, he decided to deal with him at all costs. He was sure that César would gladly accept the challenge to the duel. As an excellent swordsman, he was not afraid to face him in open combat. He just waited for the opportunity to come.

In the evening, he discreetly went down to the kitchen, as usual, and picked up a jug of clean water. Then, taking care not to be noticed by Marta or anyone else from the service, he went to the tower.

He found Blanca standing by the window. Deafened by the howling of the autumn wind, she hadn't even heard his footsteps. He decided to withhold the news of the morning duel from her, for he had the quiet hope that in time she would forget about César, due to the long separation.

He did not know, however, that the sight of his own face, so much like his brother's, only fueled her longing.

"Good evening, countess!" He said, setting the vessel on the floor.

"My good doctor Nacht, nice to see you again!" Blanca greeted him. "You have no idea how grateful I am to you. I didn't think that even though I am trapped in this terrible place, I would enjoy my regained vision so much."

August kissed her hand.

"If only I could die knowing that this would make you happy, I wouldn't hesitate for a second."

"I assure you that your death would cause me great sorrow. So please don't even think about this nonsense," she replied.

"I'll live for you then," he declared.

Blanca saw a gloomy melancholy in his gaze. He stood in the doorway a moment longer, looking at her face adoringly, then bowed almost to the ground, took the poisoned water and closed the cell door behind him. As soon as he got outside, he saw a human figure in the distance. A big man, about his height, wearing a black cape and a black triangular hat, approached the tower. "César…" August thought. He felt an unpleasant tug in his heart. "So it's true…" He paused, watching the intruder.

Blanca was just standing by the narrow window, staring at the starry sky and listening to the calls of the forest birds.

"The forest looks just like it did then…" she sighed to herself.

Then, hearing someone's footsteps by the tower, she instinctively looked down. César appeared before her eyes. The window was quite high, which made it impossible to exchange words, especially since the night was quite windy. So she outlined

in the air: "Te echo de menos" [20]. August did not see it, he
stopped around the corner of the tower, watching the whole scene,
but the face of César, who had read the message, lit up. "Soon,"
he replied in the same way. August and Blanca read his message
simultaneously.

August, with a lump in his throat, decoded the next love
confessions César was drawing in the air. His blue eyes became
glassy, and his entire body went deathly numb. "It's as if he was
sucking my whole life out of me..." he thought. He chose to
remain hidden until the lovers said goodbye. He didn't want
Blanca to witness the unpleasant confrontation of the brothers.

The sound of neighing horses broke him out of his somber
reverie. In the distance, he saw an elegant carriage rapidly
approaching the Palacio Aciago. When it stopped in the
courtyard, a man got out and started running towards the palace.
He was let in immediately. August poured the poisoned water on
the grass, then, carefully returning to the palace through the side
entrance, made his first steps towards the kitchen, where he left
the empty vessel. Then he went upstairs.

When he reached the vicinity of the hall, he accidentally
overheard Count de Aciago talking to the messenger.

"Is it serious?" the count asked. He was clearly upset.

"I'm afraid so. This morning the cardinal felt unwell. He is
getting worse with every hour."

"Where's doctor Nacht?" The count cried.

Hearing these words, August himself appeared in the hall.

"I was just nearby," he said, "and I heard that I am needed.
Has someone gotten sick?"

"Cardinal Suárez. This morning he felt very bad. Only you,
doctor Nacht, can help His Excellency. You saved his life once
already."

"If the condition is so serious, we don't have a second to
spare," August replied, then ran to his chamber, where he got all

the medicines he needed. After saying goodbye to the count, he followed the messenger to the carriage.

"I understand we're going to his Excellency's palace?" he asked.

"Yes, doctor," replied the messenger.

Cardinal Suárez lived in a stately palace near Oviedo. Like his brother, he liked luxury and glamour. Almost every piece of furniture in the residence was adorned with gilding and ornaments, and the interiors were decorated in accordance with the latest fashion. The palace, however, did not enjoy a very good reputation. Since the time a blind girl drowned in the garden pond, strange stories have been circulating around the area, as is usually the case in similar situations. When they got there, a stout woman ran out to meet them.

"Doctor Nacht, just in time!" she exclaimed.

"Cristina, take the doctor to the cardinal," ordered the messenger.

"I know the way," August replied, then walked briskly toward the gate.

The cardinal was deathly pale. A slight smile appeared on his face at the sight of August.

"Why is everything around so blue?" he whispered with difficulty.

August frowned. He sat down on the edge of the bed and squeezed the patient's wrist.

"The pulse is erratic," he said. "And then there's color vision... His Excellency sees everything in blue. This is a classic symptom of poisoning with *digitalis grandiflora*, commonly known as digitalis."

"Poisoning?" Father Pedro, who had been watching over the cardinal's bed, was surprised.

"Yes, sir," August confirmed.

"How is that possible, doctor?"

"I know what I'm saying. I have already dealt with a similar case in Venice. Someone was trying to poison a patrician. The symptoms were identical. Unfortunately, there is no effective antidote for digitalis. It all depends on the general condition of the body and the dose of the poison. I am optimistic, for his Excellency has so far enjoyed perfect health."

"Who would poison me?" the cardinal coughed up.

"I have my suspicions..." Cristina said suddenly.

"Tell me!" he ordered.

"I have warned your Excellency about Julia more than once!"

"Who is Julia?" August asked.

"She's His Excellency's cook," Father Pedro explained. "His Excellency loves the dishes she prepares and is not going to send her back, even though this woman is completely crazy," he added in a whisper.

"Julia lost her daughter ten years ago," said Cristina. "Since then, she is no longer herself. His Excellency felt sick after she brought him breakfast. For several days she had been walking very depressed, it was sad to see her like this... But who would have thought that she was capable of murder?"

"Losing a child is a terrible tragedy," said August.

He remembered Iduna.

"Poor woman. But I know her and I know what she is capable of. She had threatened more than once that she would avenge her daughter's death," Cristina remembered.

"I have nothing to do with this!" exclaimed the agitated cardinal.

"It was an unfortunate accident," said Cristina. "Please follow me, doctor. I'll tell you everything."

They left the bedroom together.

"Julia was in the garden with her daughter that day," Cristina began. "She had a day off then. She was playing with the little one at the pool. Sofía, because that was the girl's name, was blind from birth, so she could easily hurt herself. She had to be watched constantly. It so happened that a bishop suddenly came to the palace and he had to be offered some food. The cardinal ordered Julia to prepare dinner. She agreed, asking his Excellence to let her take her daughter with herself. His Excellency assured her that he would send Jorge to look after the girl. However, he forgot to fulfill his promise and Sofia was left alone unattended. She accidentally slipped and fell into the pool. The reservoir is quite deep, so the girl drowned almost immediately. When his Excellency belatedly remembered her and ordered Jorge to go to the garden, he found her body in the pool. Today is the exact anniversary of this event..."

"She did well," August thought after hearing the story about the cook. "This whole family are nasty, soulless egoists. It is a pity that she did not manage to carry out her revenge all the way to the end..."

"From that moment on," Cristina continued, "the ghost of this little girl haunts his Excellency's garden. Nobody dares to be there at noon, as this is the time when Sofia drowned. Those who saw the apparition, said that it was slowly emerging from the pool and..."

"These are just stories, Cristina," August interrupted. "Such things only happen in the human imagination. I myself have recently experienced a very strange hallucination. After a very exhausting visit to one of my patients, during which I accidentally inhaled a very potent substance, I received an urgent call. As I was driving through the forest, I saw a macabre retinue..."

He didn't finish the sentence, because Cristina suddenly turned pale and covered her mouth with her hand.

"Cristina? Are you okay?" August asked.

"Doctor Nacht, what you saw bodes misfortune for you..." she stammered.

"These Spaniards are so superstitious!" August sighed. "We are at the end of the eighteenth century, and you still believe in the old quirks."

"Have you seen the retinue of figures dressed in white tunics, carrying torches of burning bones?" the woman asked, ignoring the sarcastic comment.

"Exactly..." August confirmed, raising his eyebrows in surprise. "I admit that due to extreme exhaustion and intoxication with this drug, I was deceived by my own eyes, and furthermore, I infected my horse with this fear, to the point that the poor animal was sweating with blood."

Cristina crossed herself.

"I will pray for you, doctor Nacht," she whispered.

The poison did not bring the expected effect and the cardinal survived. August watched him all night. Meanwhile, Father Pedro ordered to find Julia. But no one had seen her in the palace since breakfast. When everyone, including the cardinal himself, started thinking that the woman had fled to avoid punishment, the gardener ran to the palace, out of breath.

"Julia is dead!" he exclaimed.

The cook's body lay in an inconspicuous place, near the pond. Her wide open eyes and mouth froze in horror, as if she had seen something terrible. August stated that she died suddenly, finding an attack of apoplexy as the cause of death.

20 Spanish   *I*   *miss*   *you.*

Chapter 21

Castillo de Viciosa

While August was riding to the cardinal's palace, César strolled alone in the woods, recalling the moments spent with Blanca and wondering how he could free her from the terrible prison in which she had been locked up by her husband. It was not without pleasure that he thought of the scar, with which the blade of his sword had forever marked the Count de Aciago's face. "Now, every time he looks in the mirror, he will remember me fondly," he thought. There was a slight smile of satisfaction on his face. When he was in the clearing where he met Blanca, he stopped and looked around. The forest lay in dead silence, broken from time to time by the voices of night birds and the rustle of leaves blown by the wind. César looked up at the starry sky and saw massive clouds approaching at a rapid pace from the north. The pale moonlight framed his statuesque face in a bluish glow, making him look like the stone gods in the duke's garden in Valsombra.

He lay down on the grass littered with dry leaves and closed his eyes.

"I'll get you back soon, dearest," he thought. He imagined that the strands of his own hair, which brushed his forehead in the wind, belonged to Blanca. At one point, these dreams became so similar to reality, that it seemed to him that his beloved was indeed sitting next to him and leaning over his face.

As the clouds completely covered the moon and the wind tugged hard against the mighty branches of the ancient oaks, César opened his eyes. His daydreaming was over. He was all alone, having the ominous howl of the approaching gale as his only companion. He rose from the ground, brushed the leaves off his cloak, and then walked briskly towards the castle. He barely had time to get home before the downpour began.

In the hall he was greeted by Aitor, who was just leaving the east wing to retire to his chamber in the western part of the building.

"Just in time, my lord," he said.

"Heaven seems to be angry with this cruel man," César said. "It's weird... I have a feeling that I'm going to release her soon."

"Lord... I have an idea..." Aitor began.

"Tell me what you came up with."

"The conditions in this tower are terrible. Countess de Aciago will not survive the winter. There is only one way to save her from death. I don't know if you'll like my plan."

"It depends what the plan is like."

"It's a bit weird, your..."

"No titles!"

"I'm so sorry. We have to get her out of there at any cost."

"How?"

"I considered various options. I could easily deal with the wooden gate. However, it is difficult to say what the interior door is made of."

"Unfortunately, we do not know that. It can be reinforced with steel, as is often the case with defensive structures."

"That's the thing. We have to get there without using force."

"So what are you suggesting?"

"My plan is as follows. Gangs of pirates roam in the vicinity of Palacio Aciago, especially at the Hanged Men's Cemetery. I will dress as one of them and wait near the tower for the old woman who brings the countess's meals. I will cover her mouth to keep her from screaming, then put a dagger to her throat and order to open the door. I'll make up some story to make it all sound credible."

"This plan is completely insane... but brilliant!" César called.

"I could do it even this morning. The old woman will most likely be there at dawn," Aitor suggested.

"The sooner the better, I think," César agreed with him.

"It's a bit naive, but good from a practical point of view. Staging a kidnapping by pirates, we will gain time. After all, such a scenario is quite likely - these robbers often kidnap people, especially women. In any case, Count de Aciago will not be sure whether his wife was actually kidnapped for ransom by the thugs, or whether she was insidiously freed out of the prison by us. All I have to do is dress up well and darken my hair. The later they figure out the truth, the better."

"I could lend you my old clothes, but I'm sure they won't fit you," César joked.

"One shoulder of mine would fill your entire frock coat," Aitor laughed. "I have an old red vest in my chest. It will be perfect for the disguise. All I need to do is brush my hair and beard with charcoal to at least disguise the characteristic color."

"Great. I did not expect that we could achieve the goal in such a comical way, and, to be honest, deep down I was already beginning to count on a miracle... But as usual, you thought about everything."

"I can't bear the thought that this fragile being has been doomed to live in a place that would be a school of survival even for me," Aitor replied. "Besides, I care about your happiness more than my own. Without your Ma... without you, I would have remained an illiterate lumberjack for the rest of my life."

"You are a good and wise man, Aitor. You deserve what you have and more," said César.

At dawn, Aitor, quite convincingly disguised as a pirate and armed with a dagger and a revolver, set off towards the Palacio

Aciago. Upon reaching his destination, he hid in the bushes around the corner of the Gothic tower. As he had expected, when the night darkness began to give way to the gray dawn, Marta's squat, slightly angular silhouette appeared on the horizon. Instinctively, Aitor placed his massive hand on the butt of his revolver, then reached for the dagger.

As the maid was near the door, he jumped out of the bushes in a flash, then covered her mouth with his massive hand while holding the dagger to her throat. Marta dropped the meal tray.

"Do what I tell you, or I'll gut you like a fish," he whispered in her ear.

The woman nodded several times.

"If you say a word, I'll feed all the foxes at the Hanged Men's Cemetery with your carcass!"

Marta nodded obediently again, and Aitor uncovered her lips.

"Open up!" he ordered.

Trembling with fear, she produced the key, then, after several unsuccessful attempts to put it in the lock, opened the gate.

"We're going inside!" Aitor ordered. "You first. They reached the top of the spiral staircase. "Good thing that I didn't try to break through the gate myself. Now I would be as helpless as a child!" - Aitor sighed inwardly at the sight of the steel door leading to the cell. Marta turned the key in the lock and they went inside. Blanca just woke up. At the sight of the enormous figure of the servant, whom she immediately recognized, and the terrified face of Marta, she understood immediately that the longed-for day of regaining freedom had come.

Seeing Aitor's grotesque disguise, she immediately realized that she had to participate in the whole farce to make it as credible as possible. "How ingenious César is! He disguised his servant as a pirate to get me out of here. I can't ruin it. I will make Marta believe that I was kidnapped by pirates so that she would not guess the truth," she decided. She stepped back, pretending to be mortally terrified, then closed her eyes and fell to the ground in a faked fainting.

Aitor admired the spectacle she performed so spontaneously.

"Let's go!" he ordered, putting the dagger to Marta's throat again.

Then, without any effort, he lifted Blanca from the mattress. When they were downstairs, he looked at the terrified Marta, then at the door. The woman understood the order and obediently turned the key in the lock.

"Remember the foxes. They look hungry lately, and they won't turn down a little meat. You are to act as if nothing has happened. Otherwise you know what awaits you. I have my people in this palace," he threatened.

Marta was deathly pale and trembled all over her body.

"I won't say anything! I swear at all the saints! I'll do what you want, just spare my life!" she promised, shaking her head grotesquely.

"That's what I like!" replied Aitor, then disappeared with Blanca in the forest wilderness.

After they got some distance away, he stopped and looked back. There was complete silence in the forest.

"Put me down," Blanca asked. "There's no one on the horizon. Marta is completely soulless, but at the same time, quite cowardly. She will certainly follow your instructions very diligently," she added, unable to contain a laugh.

"Countess, I must admit you played your part very convincingly," Aitor replied, setting her down on the ground. "It is as if you were privy to our plot!"

Soon they reached the clearing. Blanca smiled to herself at the sight of the four fused oaks, behind which there was the cave. "How different this place looks during the day. It is just as beautiful, but it seems to lack this magical aura…" As she looked around and saw the towers of Castillo de Viciosa on the horizon, her heart beat faster.

"We're almost there," Aitor said.

"I know where we are. I know these areas like the back of my hand," she replied, looking thoughtfully at the leafless crowns of old trees.

When they reached the castle, Blanca's eyes fell on the building's east wing, where, as she remembered from her first conversation with Aitor, César resided. Recognizing the impudent grapevine, bursting into his bedroom with arrogant nonchalance, she remembered the moment when she discovered with horror that the mysterious stranger she had recently met and kissed in the clearing, was not just anybody, but the Marquis de Viciosa himself.

They arrived at the courtyard. Thousands of multi-colored leaves danced in the air, lifted by the cool northern wind. Aitor opened the gate. They entered a large hall that seemed untouched for centuries. A massive ten-armed chandelier, made of black steel, hung from the stone vault. Large candles burned on its arms. Two sets of huge stone stairs led to the two wings of the castle.

"Please follow me," Aitor said. "My master is probably expecting us upstairs."

Blanca looked in all directions, admiring the monumental structure of the building. Following the giant, she remembered the moment Aitor had offered to introduce her to his master. When they reached the top of the stairs, she saw a rather narrow corridor ending with a soaring stone vault, from which iron lanterns, attached on solid chains, hung every dozen or so meters, apparently dating back to the Middle Ages, just like the chandelier in the hall.

Blanca looked impatiently at the narrow pointed doors leading to the individual chambers. Finally Aitor stopped at one of them.

"Here!" he announced, then pressed the handle.

They found themselves in a large room, unlike the rest of the mansion, decorated in a contemporary style, which, however, did not conflict with the Gothic majesty of the building, but harmonized with it beautifully. An exquisitely crafted crystal chandelier hung from the cross-ribbed vault, and the entire interior exhibited a cool, restrained elegance.

There was no one in the chamber.

"My lord must have gone out onto the terrace," Aitor said, pointing to the narrow, soaring door ahead.

At the same time, César appeared in it. He looked at Blanca in disbelief, wondering if the beautiful figure standing in front of him was merely the product of his mind, exhausted by all-night's worries, or whether he really had the cause of his worries before him.

Aitor bowed and left the room, but César didn't even notice. He did not dare to take a single step, staring at Blanca with great disbelief and, at the same time, with the utmost adoration. Instead of empty black pupils, shining gray-blue eyes stared at him. As she came closer and threw her arms around his neck, he realized that this was not an illusion, but that his most unreal dream had really come true.

Chapter 22

Papaver somniferum

From the very morning Iduna felt anxious. At night, she thought she heard the distant cry of little Yurde amid the howling of the wind. She was not sure, however, whether she really heard the child's voice or whether her senses had failed her, troubled by long-term suffering. Her uneasiness infected Álvar, who occasionally flapped his wings nervously, making long, alarming squeaks.

Iduna was worried about August. She was still thinking about their last meeting. She remembered with worry his thin, cadaver-pale face, and the absent gaze of deeply shaded bright eyes. "What have you got caught into, my son?" She sighed at the thought of the unhappy love of the medic, which awoke the worst possible premonitions in her. "Oh, how I would like to protect you from this…"

Another matter was on her mind as well, namely the recent attempt to poison the duke. At first she suspected this was August, who she knew was planning to take revenge on his cruel father by using poison. However, when he made an unexpected visit to her, she understood that his mind, so far absorbed in the desire for revenge, was now completely overcome by an entirely different, debilitating passion. Thus she did not even ask him about anything, as she considered it obvious that, contrary to appearances, it was not August who was behind the attack on the duke's life.

She was broken out of her reverie by the sound of familiar footsteps, getting closer with each passing second.

"Ausencio!" she exclaimed when she saw her young friend.

"Iduna, you look worried. Is something bothering you?" The boy wanted to know, anxiously looking at her sullen face.

"The older I am, the more the cold bothers me. That's all," she lied.

Iduna actually loved the cool fall-winter weather. On the other hand, she hated the summer heat, which had a weakening effect on her.

"A stone fell off my chest," replied Ausencio.

"I am not used to having others worry about me. Usually, it's me to find answers for people's worries," she said.

"I have come to share with you a story that may sound quite unbelievable..." began Ausencio.

"Yes...?" Iduna picked up with interest.

"There was an incident recently that greatly upset my master. If I had to rely solely on His Majesty's account, I don't know if I could believe it. However, it just so happens that I saw it all from the window..."

"What happened?"

"Do you remember that terrible downpour?"

"Of course, that was about two or three days ago."

"In the evening, His Majesty went to the family chapel, where Duchess Teresa was buried. I watched from the library window as he left the palace walking there. Suddenly I noticed that there was a very strange figure hanging around the chapel: a hooded monk in a black habit. A cripple."

"Was he very short and hunchbacked?"

"It is difficult for me to determine his height, because I watched everything from above. However, he seemed to be quite short and very hunched. I noticed his hand - it was very strange, it seemed to me it was covered with some terrible growths..."

Iduna looked at him piercingly. "Serafín," she thought. "So I was right to think that the last attempt on this cruel man's life was not the work of August, but of someone else entirely..."

"When my master was a few dozen steps from the chapel, the monk suddenly took out a key from his habit pocket, with which he opened the door without any problem. He must have lit all the candles, so after a while the whole building was filled with light. It looked amazing! At the sight of the glow emanating from the chapel, His Ducal Majesty paused for a moment. He saw the intruder, who quickly left the garden and disappeared into the darkness. His Majesty looked terrified..."

Iduna listened with increasing curiosity.

"Later I saw my lord kneeling on the steps of the chapel. He looked as if he was about to die himself. I was about to go out to get him, but eventually he returned to the palace on his own," continued Ausencio.

"It's very strange indeed..." commented Iduna." Serafin as a monk... I wonder if it's just a disguise, or maybe he really decided to atone for a tragic mistake..." she thought.

"Since then, his Ducal Majesty has not been himself... He sleeps in a brightly lit room, with the door open, as if he was terrified of the darkness. Yesterday he spoke again of the nightmares I have already told you about. I don't know what this horrible hunchbacked monk has to do with all this..." Ausencio wondered.

"Certainly a lot..." Iduna replied thoughtfully.

"He calls for me or Roberto all the time. This is slowly becoming unbearable. Roberto says his Majesty is going mad. Since these nightmares have tormented him, not only does he sleep in the brightly lit bedroom, but he orders us to burn lights throughout the palace. He claims that the ghost of the deceased duchess appears in different places, driving him slowly insane."

"He is tormented by remorse..."

"Last night, the duke had us light candles, even in the corridors. This makes it very difficult to fall asleep. Roberto and Inés somehow cope with the light coming into their rooms, but I can't sleep at all. Do you know any remedy that would help me sleep?"

"All I can think of is opium. Old Iñigo, who introduced me to the secrets of herbalism, successfully healed with it a young man who, like you, suffered from insomnia. I have tried it on myself before, as well as other remedies of this kind. Sometimes I cannot live without it myself..."

"I will be grateful to you with all my heart."

Iduna disappeared in the depths of the cave for a moment, then returned with a small purse containing some dark powder.

"Here's your medicine. But you have to be very careful with it," she warned. "If you use this remedy too often, there will come a point where you will become its slave. It happened to this young man whom Iñigo had cured of insomnia. He developed a taste for his medicine to such an extent, that in time he learned to prepare a poppy seed decoction himself."

"I will be careful, I promise," Ausencio assured her.

"It's a must."

"There is something else..."

"Tell me."

"This crippled monk is not the only bizarre figure recently seen in the palace in Valsombra..."

"Who else appeared there?"

"Rodrigo, his Majesty's cook, remembered that a Gypsy woman was walking around the garden on the day someone put arsenic in the wine..."

"Probably Alicia," thought Iduna.

"How old could this woman be?" she asked curiously.

"From what Rodrigo said, she might be about fifty..." Ausencio replied. "Why do you ask?"

"Just curious," she replied with a slight smile.

She wisely decided to keep the story of Serafín and Alicia to herself. For she did not trust Ausencio enough to tell him that the poison that killed the Duchess de Valsombra came from herself.

"Rodrigo claims that this gypsy girl once served in a palace."

"Why does he think so?"

"Apparently he recognized her features."

"Did he say anything else? For example, what was her name?"

"He said nothing like that, but he got dreamy remembering her former beauty. Apparently, she is the beauty with whom the duke himself was in love..."

"So that's Alicia for sure!" Iduna thought. "Now I know who treated Martín with arsenic. What a brave woman!"

"Inés asked Roberto to tell our master about it, but he refused. He must have had great affection for this woman. He also obligated all of us to remain silent."

"Since she was so beautiful, perhaps he was not indifferent to her charms himself," Iduna remarked.

"In Valsombra, very close to the palace, there is a gypsy camp. If Roberto had told His Majesty about everything, this woman would have been doomed. By wanting to protect her, the old good man recklessly exposes us all to mortal danger..."

"I don't think she is a threat to anyone but the duke," Iduna reassured him. "This looks like a personal story from many years ago. I would bet my life that you can sleep peacefully. This woman was clearly trying to get revenge on the duke for something."

"If it is as you say, my master must have hurt her a lot."

"It certainly was so. Let's remember that this man gave his own wife a cup with poison..."

Ausencio got gloomy.

"Who knows how many people have suffered because of him..." he sighed. "My master can be very ruthless."

"We'll probably never know that..." Iduna replied. "One thing I am sure: despite the fact that he is ruthless, the remorse will eventually drive him mad."

"I think it already did. His majesty is acting more and more disturbingly. He does everything not to think about the recurring nightmarish visions. Recently, for example, out of nowhere, he decided to organize a great fox hunting."

When Iduna heard the word 'hunting', an icy shiver ran down her spine. At the memory of the moment when the duke's dogs dug their fangs into Yurde's small, defenseless body, her eyes darkened. "Now I know, son, why I heard your voice at night... Those damned hunts!" she thought.

"Iduna, are you well?" Ausencio asked, looking at her gloomy face with worry.

"Don't worry about me, Ausencio. This is a momentary weakness. Remember I'm not that young anymore!" she joked.

"Apparently the duke has already sent out invitations. Roberto told me he had ordered the Count de Aciago to be notified, among others."

At the mention of the latter, Iduna's thoughts immediately turned to August. "If only I could, I would annihilate that damned witch!" She thought hatefully of Blanca. "I feel that because of her I am going to mourn the death of my son for the second time..." At that moment, August's sunken face appeared before her eyes. At the same time, Yurde's childish laughter echoed in her head, mixed with the mournful howl of the wind. "Soon   now..."

Chapter 23

The Pirate

As soon as Cardinal Suárez began to regain his strength, August, finding that his patient's life was no longer in danger, decided to return to the Palacio Aciago immediately. As his blue eyelids drooped heavily, he could see Blanca's porcelain face in front of him. "Mein Engel..." [21] - he thought of her adoringly, looking forward to the moment when he would return to the Gothic tower.

He was exhausted. The trip back to Pueblo Aciago severely strained his weakened strength. A few sleepless nights made him daydream while riding through the forest. It seemed to him that he saw figures in white tunics on either side of the path overgrown with nettles, very much like the ones he had seen in the woods when he first went to the Count de Aciago.

The words of terrified Cristina, explaining the meaning of that vision, were still ringing in his ears. Although immune to all superstitions by nature, August somehow could not forget about it. He was also worried about the behavior of the horse, which, like on that fateful night, stopped from time to time, snorting nervously and hitting the hard ground with his hoof.

When he finally got to the Palacio Aciago, he entrusted Adrian to care for the animal as tired as himself, and went straight to his chamber. As soon as he closed the door behind him, he threw himself on the bed, and fell into a deep sleep almost in the same second. The disturbing visions that arose in his mind, however, prevented him from having any rest.

For he dreamed that he was walking through a dark forest similar to the one in Viciosa, where Iduna lived. A fair-haired boy led him by the hand, singing a funny, childish song in a sweet voice:

Little thrush, tiny thrush,
all speckled...

The child's hand was blue and icy. Every now and then the little boy looked at August and smiled amiably at him. When they reached the lake that looked very much like Claro del Agua, the boy suddenly disappeared. August looked around but couldn't see him anywhere. All he could hear was his singing, mixed with laughter. A dense fog lay over the lake.

It was only Jaime's and Andrés' raised voices that woke him, and the sound of quick, nervous footsteps in the corridor. He rubbed his eyes and sat on the edge of the bed, listening. The conversation between the servants seemed very agitated. August did not understand much of this tense exchange. However, the single words he managed to pick up, made him alert.

He went out into the corridor. He was going to get Blanca water as soon as possible, since it was already past six in the morning. However, feeling that the lively conversation had a lot to do with her person, he decided to ask the servants.

"Has something happened that I should know about?" He asked.

"It doesn't concern you directly, but it is so serious that everyone should find out as soon as possible. The Countess de Aciago has disappeared during the night," Jaime spoke up first.

"How come disappeared?!" August felt the ground fall out from underneath his feet. "What could have happened to her?"

"Nobody knows that, doctor," Andrés replied.

"Who told you?"

"When Marta went to bring her food, the Countess de Aciago was not in her cell, as if she had evaporated. The door and entrance gate were still reportedly locked with all locks," Jaime reported.

"Impossible," thought August. "There are only two sets of tower keys. One of them is with Marta, the other with me. Marta never leaves her keys and is completely loyal to the count. So there is only one logical explanation: someone had seriously scared her and persuaded her to give out the countess. The old woman is hiding something, but soon the madman will make her tell what really happened. He can do it, and if not, I know how to help him. But meanwhile, before anyone realizes that I have taken the spare set of keys, I have to drop it back."

"Have you notified the count?" He asked the servants.

"He doesn't know anything yet," Andrés replied.

"So what are you waiting for?" August rebuked them both.

"Doctor Nacht is right," Jaime said. "We have no time to waste!"

The servants went to the Count de Aciago's chamber, meanwhile August quickly ran down the stairs, then, taking advantage of Pilar's momentary absence, slipped imperceptibly into the storage room where he left his keys. As he returned upstairs, the figure of the count appeared before his eyes. His face was purple, and the veins in his temples and neck swelled as if they were about to explode.

"Bring that old hustler here right now! I'll get the whole truth out of her!" He threatened as he grabbed Andrés by the lapels of his livery. "If that goddamn bitch isn't found by tonight, I wouldn't want to be in the skin of either of you!" He drawled through his teeth.

"Count, we will do everything in our power," said Andrés, frightened.

"Very good. Otherwise you know what awaits you!" The count replied, pushing the boy away with such force that he almost lost his balance. "Bring me Marta! Immediately!" He ordered in a raised voice.

Andrés and Jaime ran down the stairs, passing August on the way.

"Count, I heard what happened..." he began. "If I could do anything..."

"So those old fools have notified you first and not me?" The count interrupted him. "What's that supposed to mean?" He exclaimed, then started coughing with a dry, wheezing cough.

"Calm down, this cough sounds very bad," August said firmly. "I would give my own life to free the Countess de Aciago, or at least find out where she is. Let me question Marta."

The Count nodded in agreement, then took a deep breath and instinctively rubbed his neck.

Just then, Jaime appeared on the stairs, leading Marta with him. She looked scared.

"You old stupid woman!" The count shouted. Another disturbing whistle came from his chest.

"My lord..." Marta began.

August looked at her searchingly. He sensed that the woman was hiding something.

"My Lord... I know who kidnapped your wife..." she stammered.

"What?!" The count cried, rushing over to the maid and grabbing her by the throat. "You hid the truth?"

"Count, Marta is clearly afraid of someone," said August. "Let's allow her to speak first, then we will know what to do."

"Our lady was kidnapped by pirates..." Marta said in a barely audible voice.

"What the hell? Pirates?! Have you completely lost your mind?" The Count interrupted abruptly.

"Go on," August ordered.

The Count de Aciago was gripped by a wheezing cough again.

"When in the morning I went to the tower as usual, to bring the Countess breakfast, a huge man suddenly jumped from behind the corner. I knew from his clothes that he was a pirate. There are plenty of them hanging around this area... Under the threat of death, he ordered me to lead him to the cell, so I understood that I had no choice but to fulfill his demand. When we got upstairs, my lady passed out from fear. The pirate carried her out of the cell effortlessly. He ordered me to lock the door. When we went outside, he also instructed me to close the gate and go to the palace, without telling anyone. He threatened that if I say a single word, he would feed my carcass to the hungry foxes that prowl at the Hanged Men's Cemetery. I was scared to death, that's why..."

"That's why you hid the truth from your master!" Interrupted the enraged count. "You old idiot!"

"There's something amiss with all this..." August interjected. "If the lady were indeed kidnapped by pirates, they would have probably demanded a ransom. This alleged pirate told Marta to be silent instead, as if he were trying to buy some time. It's highly suspicious..."

"What do you mean, doctor Nacht?" The count cried, gasping for breath.

"Pirates usually kidnap people, especially the rich, to extort large sums of money, jewels, or some other goods from their relatives. No pirate would make Marta keep quiet, but rather order her to tell you the amount of the ransom requested. I personally think this man was lying."

"What are you getting at, doctor?" The count wanted to know.

"Marta, could you describe what this pirate looked like? Maybe it will give us a hint...?" August turned to the maid.

"I won't forget this monster for the rest of my life! He was of superhuman height. I've never seen such a huge man before! And his wild, terrifying face, hands like pincers... He will haunt my dreams for the rest of my life!"

"Thank you, Marta," August replied. "Count, I think I know who kidnapped your wife," he added, not hiding his satisfaction.

"Meaning?"

"Do you remember that giant who was hanging around in the courtyard of the Palacio Viciosa? The alleged pirate is none other than César Castro's servant!"

"Are you saying that the whole kidnapping was orchestrated by the Marquis de Viciosa?" The count cried.

"Most likely."

August remembered the moment he saw César near the Gothic tower. Just like then, his heart tightened and his body began to go numb. The lofty figure of his brother, so much like his own, appeared before him vividly. He remembered clearly the love confessions he made in the air. At the mere mention of them, he felt an icy stab in his heart.

"The Marquis de Viciosa must have found out somehow that you imprisoned your wife in the Gothic tower," he said. "He must have sent his servant there to free her. I am almost certain that the countess is now in Viciosa, or possibly on her way to France."

At these words, Count de Aciago's face suddenly darkened, taking on a bluish purple color. He raised both hands to his neck as if trying to loosen the invisible noose tightening around it. Unable to free himself from his death grip, he staggered, then fell to the floor. August ran to save him. The count was unconscious. There was a terrible whistle coming from his chest for a moment longer, and then there was dead silence.

August grabbed his wrist to measure the pulse, but after a moment nodded his head and put the already dead hand down.

"I'm afraid there is nothing else I can do for him anymore, unfortunately," he said.

"Holy Mother!" Marta stammered.

Jaime and Andrés stared in disbelief at the body of their master, whose fury had frightened them endlessly just a few minutes ago. Marta knelt down beside him and burst out into a sudden sob. August's pale blue eyes stared for a long moment at the barely scarred wound that disfigured Count de Aciago's now dead face. "You will not deal so easily with me..." he addressed César in his thoughts.

21 German   *My*   *angel.*

Chapter 24

The Challenge

The golden light of the afternoon sun illuminated Blanca's dark auburn hair, giving it an intense autumn hue. When she slowly opened her eyes and saw César beside her, she did not quite believe yet that she had regained both her health and her freedom almost simultaneously. Although she was aware that Count de Aciago might imprison her again, she decided not to think about it and to enjoy the present moment, even if it was to last only until evening.

For neither she nor César knew that Ramón Suárez had been dead for ten hours. Nor were they aware that the ruse invented by Aitor had been discovered so quickly, or that August was planning to arrive at Viciosa soon. He was only stopped from arriving immediately by the necessary activities related to the preparations for the funeral of the Count de Aciago and the visit of the deceased's brother, Cardinal Mario Suárez.

Blanca couldn't take her eyes off César. At last, she could fully enjoy seeing him. Thinking that at any moment they would be separated again, perhaps for longer or even forever, she decided to remember every little detail of his face. "When Ramón throws me into that terrible tower again, at least I will be staring at you whenever I close my eyes... And no one will ever be able to deprive me of that again!"

César pulled her to himself, then for a long moment his lips pressed into her mouth. Soft light played on their skin and hair, creating a beautiful, golden, black and chestnut stained glass, as if the sun itself had decided to celebrate their regained happiness together with them. "Nobody and nothing will take you away from me. Even if I have to pay for it with my own life!" he promised in his thoughts.

At the same time, Mario Suárez's gilded carriage stopped in the courtyard of the Palacio Aciago. The cardinal, still slightly weak after his recent illness, but already healthy and dressed as impeccably as always, slowly got out of the carriage. He came alone, accompanied by a coachman and a servant, refusing the proposition of Father Pedro, who offered to keep him company on this sad journey. He wanted to say goodbye to his brother alone.

Mario Suárez's only human instinct was the strong bond he had with Ramón. While the loss of both parents and the recent illness of their sister did not arouse any emotions in him, at the news of his brother's death his stone face twitched, and his narrow eyes filled to the brim with sincere tears. However, he quickly managed to overcome his sadness, and even the sight of the count's stiff, purple body did not disturb him.

After greeting the cardinal, who gave all the necessary instructions to the service, August walked down to the courtyard, from where he went straight to the stables. Having saddled his horse, he headed for Viciosa. "Time to face the usurper who tries to deprive me of everything I love. One of us will have to step aside forever…" he thought, and then galloped in the direction he had chosen.

The sun was already heading west. A huge cinnabar disc shone from behind the black trunks of the trees. Seeing this, August remembered the words of Iduna, who had once warned him against *sol rojo*, saying that it was a bad omen. "Red sun always brings blood and misfortune," she said then. August thought for a moment.

"Even if I had to bleed to death - in the end I will die for you, my love! I will offer you a sacrifice of this miserable life," he said to himself.

At the same time, a red beam fell on his chest, resembling an open wound.

"Forgive me, Iduna," he whispered.

The horse snorted nervously. August stroked his mane, then signaled him to move forward.

The forest was slowly hiding in darkness. The figure of the rider racing through the shadowy forest looked unreal. The pale, fair-haired man on a gray horse looked more like a northern god of vengeance than a human being. The towers of Castillo de Viciosa loomed on the horizon. August's heart sank at the sight. "If he doesn't accept the challenge voluntarily, he will have to do it out of necessity," he thought.

It was night by the time he reached Viciosa. There was not a living soul in the castle courtyard. The eastern part of the magnificent Gothic structure was covered in a gloomy shroud of darkness, and the last dark red rays of sunlight reflected in the panes of the west-facing windows. As August instinctively looked in that direction, the sinister fiery glow fell on his face again.

Blanca went to the window to feast her eyes on the familiar sight of the night forest that was the setting for her secret encounters with César. Suddenly she noticed a figure of a fair-haired rider in the courtyard. An icy chill ran down her spine. She backed away in horror.

"What scared you so much, my love?" César asked, coming up to her and putting his arm around her.

"Look out the window. Someone's standing in the courtyard," whispered Blanca. "I guess it's..."

"It's my brother," interrupted César. "I knew that this comic ruse that Aitor and I came up with wouldn't have a long future.

However, it got the job done and that was what we wanted. The count probably figured it out and sent August for you."

"He's probably still ashamed of the scar Aitor told me about."

"Certainly. He will carry this mark for the rest of his life."

"Don't let them imprison me. I would sooner kill myself than return with him to the Palacio Aciago," Blanca called.

"Don't be afraid. I will rather die than let them take you. I'll go downstairs and find out what he wants."

Saying this, he placed a long kiss on her lips and immediately left the chamber. Blanca went to the window again. Her heart was pounding like mad. She watched in horror as August's horse hit the ground over and over with its hoof. She knew that the animal's behavior reflected its master's state of mind. "Poor madman... I owe him the recovery, but now I will have to wish him death. This is unbearable!" - she thought.

After a while César appeared in the courtyard. He walked slowly, confidently. Blanca's heart froze. Instinctively, she brought her hand to her mouth and bit her index finger painfully. As hypnotized, she stared at two very similar men, differing only in color. August was sitting the whole time on his horse, which was still shifting from hoof to hoof.

When Blanca saw that there was a conversation going on between the brothers, she discreetly opened the window, hoping that she could pick up at least a single fragment of the sentences. Unfortunately, the height at which she was standing did not allow it, and furthermore, they spoke very quietly. She could only distinguish between August's distinctive German accent and César's elegant *castellano* [22]. Afraid that the guest would notice her face in the window, she moved away from the glass.

Exactly at the same moment, August threw down a leather gauntlet at his brother's feet. César picked it up with a sardonic smile, then headed for the palace. August, meanwhile, rushed back. Blanca stayed by the window, nervously playing with the strands of her loose hair. Her heart was still pounding madly in her chest, and her body was overwhelmed by weakness.

When César returned to the chamber, she was close to fainting. How great was her surprise when she saw the satisfaction on his face.

"I have good news," he said at the doorstep, "if it is appropriate to say so, of course."

"What do you mean?" Blanca asked.

"The Count de Aciago is dead," declared César.

His innate manners urged him to be serious, though his soul glowed.

"How is this possible? This man enjoyed Herculean strength and iron health! He only got sick as a result of fights and accidents."

"Turns out he wasn't as healthy as you think. He had suffered from asthma for years. When they realized that my servant had kidnapped you, he suffered a violent attack that resulted in suffocation. There was no way to save him."

Blanca stared at César, not knowing what to say. It was not proper for her to show her joy for the death of her husband, and besides, she still had the thrown gauntlet before her eyes.

"I saw from the window that..." she began.

"He challenged me to a duel. Over you."

"To the first blood?"

"To the death."

Blanca's big eyes turned glassy and motionless.

"It's terrible!" She exclaimed.

She walked over to the bed and sat on the edge.

"This man is crazy. At first, I feared him even more than my husband. And yet it was him who saved my life. He discovered that the count ordered to give me a poison that caused my photophobia. He brought me fresh water every day, and that's the only reason why I finally regained my sight..."

"Don't beat yourself up. He helped you because he is head over heels in love with you. Otherwise, he would have poisoned you personally without blinking an eye," César replied.

"Why do you say such things?" Blanca asked, frowning.

"This man has two faces. He is ready to give his own life for those he loves. He is also undoubtedly one of the greatest medics that Italy, and probably Spain, has ever seen. However, his dark side is terrifying. Harold Ravendale recently met a Venetian whose father was killed by August. This man followed him all the way here to take revenge..."

At these words, Blanca paled.

"How do you know it's your brother who is behind the murder?"

"Apparently, the man's wife commissioned it to August. Soon after, however, she became seriously ill herself, and when she knew that her end was near, she told her son the whole truth. The case is improvable, a word against word. Officially, the patrician died of natural causes, which was confirmed by two famous doctors. However, his son is now in Viciosa, ready to fight to the death. If August comes out of our duel alive, the next one will be waiting for him and he will surely lose that one. Besides, my brother seems to be sick..."

"He looks like his own shadow..."

"Lord Ravendale told me that this Venetian is an excellent swordsman."

"When will you fight?" Blanca asked.

"Tomorrow at noon."

"In the courtyard?"

"Yes, my lady" César smiled and kissed her forehead.

"I'll go with you."

"Are you sure you want to look at this?"

"I have to be there. Otherwise I will die."

"I'll write to Lord Ravendale. He will be my second also this time. Poor Harold, I'm dragging him into my quarrels again," said César.

He went to the desk and immediately began writing a letter to his English friend.

"August will probably come with one of the servants," Blanca said, then fell silent in a melancholic reverie. The mere thought of having to look at Andrés' insolent smile again filled her with disgust. "If only he would come with that good old Jaime!" She sighed inwardly.

She got up and went to the window, from which she looked thoughtfully at the forest, immersed in the night silence. The figures of her deceased father, Count de Aciago, Marta, Andrés, Jaime and finally August, flashed before her eyes. As she remembered his almost white hair, a deathly pale face, and blue eyelids from under which his light blue eyes looked at her in fanatical adoration, a shiver of terror ran down her entire body.

That night was the longest one in her life. She stared until the morning at sleeping César, whose statuesque face was illuminated by the faint light of the waning moon. His chest rose and fell in slow motion, unlike her heart, pounding like a wild bird trapped by hunters. For a moment she imagined herself staring at his lifeless face. Superimposed on this terrible vision was the memory of August's face, which always seemed to her to be tainted with the stigma of death.

22 Spanish *Castilian*; the name of the standard Spanish.

Chapter 25

Light in the dark

Despite his progressing illness, brother Lisandro regularly visited the Castro family chapel. Each time his trips to Valsombra cost him more and more effort, but despite the terrible pain consuming his body, the monk did not miss a single opportunity to visit Duchess Teresa's tomb. However, he no longer lit candles, so as not to attract the attention of the duke or other inhabitants of the residence, but rather he quietly sneaked into the gothic building, where for a long moment he begged the soul of the deceased for forgiveness.

Eventually, he managed to catch a time of day when he was almost absolutely sure, or at least it seemed so to him, that no one in the household would see him. But he was wrong. Since the last chance meeting in the garden, the Duke of Valsombra stood every day by the west window of the library at the same time that he saw his ex-servant near the chapel by accident last time.

Not sure whether what he saw that day was a ghostly apparition, a figment of his own imagination, or a reality, he decided with his typical stubbornness to find it out empirically. He had been recently increasingly tormented by terrifying visions of his late wife, who now appeared at different times of the day and night, gradually driving him insane.

The duke's fear of the ghost that harassed him, quickly turned into an obsession. From the moment he thought he had seen Duchess Teresa in his study one evening, he had all rooms in the palace lit after dark. He slept in a lit room, calling from time to time for one of the servants.

The sight of the distorted figure in the garden was no less torture to him than the nightmares that plagued him. Every time the figure of a stooped monk appeared at the threshold of the chapel, his pulse sped up rapidly and streams of icy sweat poured over his body. For he had not supposed that Serafin was visiting his wife's grave merely to beg her forgiveness. Rather, he thought he was doing it to drive him insane.

Unlike the duke, who was terrified by the ghost of the murdered duchess, Brother Lisandro deliberately evoked the image of her gentle, absent face. Whenever he returned to the chapel, he dreamed of receiving any sign of forgiveness from her. In vain. The figure of an angel looked down gloomily, while the dark, soaring structure exuded a repulsive chill and the acrid scent of damp candles.

The closer Brother Lisandro was to his death, the more vivid and intrusive became the memories of that fateful evening, when the object of his revenge turned into an accomplice of a random, unplanned, but horrible crime. The duchess was one of those people who, apart from Alicia and little César at the time, always defended the derided and scorned cripple.

That day, after the Vespers were finished, Brother Lisandro left the monastery as usual and went to Valsombra. Despite sudden worsening of the weather and the terrible pain that intensified during the rain, the monk slowly and unevenly trudged in the chosen direction. The icy rain lashed his disfigured, stooped body like harsh whips.

It was almost winter already. From time to time the frosty air was torn apart by the calls of the hawks and the gloomy croaking of ravens. Brother Lisandro paused for a moment to catch his breath. He felt his legs failing to obey him. When he looked down, he shuddered. Some growths on his feet swelled, turning a deep reddish-brown color. The pain grew more and more excruciating, but the monk squeezed his eyes shut, took a deep breath, and continued on.

When he reached the place where he met Alicia, he looked towards the Gypsy camp. But he didn't notice a single wagon. The field was empty, except abandoned dishes and rags lying here and there. Brother Lisandro sighed heavily. He remembered the last conversation with his old friend and companion in misery. Her resigned and terribly sad face flashed before his eyes as if alive. "Be well, Alicia! May God guide you."

Pulling the hood over his head, he headed towards the palace, which was clearly visible from this distance. He noticed from far away already that all the chandeliers on the ground floor were lit. He paused for a moment, his eyes wide in astonishment. Soon the windows on the first and second floors also shone with brilliant light. From a distance, the palace looked like a huge flaming torch.

Brother Lisandro cautiously walked past the fence and slipped into the chapel. The unbearable smell of mold and damp wax hit his nostrils. The monotonous sound of heavy raindrops bouncing off the stone walls, combined with the whistling of the wind, the rustling of fallen leaves and the squeaking screams of gulls, perfectly reflected the melancholic mood of Valsombra.

Inside the palace there was a turmoil. At the duke's orders, lights were lit throughout the building. At the same time, feverish preparations for the hunt were underway, in which the most important people in Cantabria and Asturias were to participate. A table for guests had already been prepared in the dining room. However, some of the most distinguished were not destined to reach Valsombra. For one unopened invitation to the hunt was still on a table in one of the chambers of the Palacio Aciago, and the other - in the library of Castillo de Viciosa.

The duke had no idea about the death of Count de Aciago yet, but he did take into account that his son would not come, and he sent him an invitation just pro forma, knowing well César's deep and incomprehensible aversion to hunting, which he considered a manifestation of bottomless stupidity and barbarism. Lord Ravendale, on the contrary, loved to hunt. Unfortunately, a few days after receiving the invitation from the duke, the servant delivered him a letter from César, informing him about the duel. It was supposed to take place the next day around noon, exactly at the time of the hunting.

Opening the letter from his friend, Lord Ravendale sighed heavily. "He must really love this Blanca if he will fight for her a second time..." - he thought. As he read the end of the message in which César mentioned that the duel would be fought to the death, his initial disappointment with his inability to participate in a fox hunt gave way to deep concern.

He immediately notified the duke of his planned absence, excusing himself vaguely by "sudden circumstances of a private nature." However, he sent a messenger at nine o'clock in the evening, so before the latter could reach Valsombra from the Bárcena Menor, a little to the west, where Lord resided, an elegant table setting had already been prepared also for him. Though the Duke had little liking for Lord Ravendale, he highly appreciated his excellent knowledge of the hunting art.

Discreetly leaving the chapel, Brother Lisandro looked towards the palace. The nervous steps and the raised voices of the servants coming from there were in stark contrast to the tranquility in the garden and in the chapel. The statues of the ancient deities seemed to be in a deep sleep, similar to the one that held the bodies lying in the ancestral chapel like a shroud.

Brother Lisandro looked one last time at the gloomy figure of an angel, towering over the Gothic mausoleum, then started on his way back. It was almost midnight when he reached the convent. Father Roland was the only monk who still had not gone to bed yet. Brother Lisandro found him deep in thoughts, wandering around the cloisters like a ghost. After exchanging the usual greeting with the prior, he hobbled towards his cell.

After he extinguished the candle, he struggled to stretch his legs on the hard bunk, gritting his teeth hard because of the pain piercing through his body. For a few minutes he stared at the plume of smoke escaping from the blown candle, which formed fantastic shapes in the air, now birds with trailing tails, now grotesque gargoyles, and now serpentine tangles.

The smell of damp wax brought back a gloomy memory of the chapel in Valsombra. Brother Lisandro's eyes filled with tears.

"I have so little time left..." he sighed.

At the same moment he noticed a faint light near the window, similar to that produced by fireflies.

"Have I gone crazy?" He said to himself, his eyes widening. "It is not the season for fireflies!"

He raised himself on one elbow, watching the strange phenomenon with interest. He wasn't sure if what he was seeing was a reality or a daydream. The light shone brighter with each passing second. The initially faint and shapeless spot of brightness became more and more distinct, over time forming an elongated form that slightly resembled a human figure. Brother Lisandro got up from the bunk.

Gradually, a head, hands and a shape of a woman's dress emerged from the luminous mass. After a moment of staring at the increasingly clear face of the phantom, the monk recognized the familiar features. The initially motionless lips curved into a gentle smile. The figure approached Brother Lisandro, who stood petrified. She held out a hand of light to him. The monk stepped back in horror.

"Don't torment yourself, Serafín," said the apparition.

"My lady!" He gasped, trying to kneel down.

As enchanted, he stared at the luminous figure that drifted in the air just above the floor.

"I couldn't watch your suffering. I hold no grudge against you, Serafín…" she said.

Tears filled Brother Lisandro's eyes to the brim, and ran down profusely along his horribly misshapen cheeks, making their way through the growths covering them.

"I beg your forgiveness…" whispered the monk.

"You do not need to. It's late. Go to bed. We'll meet soon…" she added, then dispersed in the cool air.

Brother Lisandro stood still for a very long time, looking straight ahead and smiling through his tears.

When in the morning he did not come to the chapel or the refectory, the other monks began to worry. During the modest breakfast, they looked at the empty chair and then at each other. Father Roland was the only one to remain imperturbable silence, staring glumly at Brother Lisandro's place. As soon as the meal time was over, he immediately went to his cell.

The monk's body was lying on the floor. His face, which had showed a gloomy melancholy during his life, beamed now. His open eyes were still turned toward the window. Brother Lisandro died smiling.

"Goodbye, my friend," Father Roland said, his voice breaking, then closed his eyes with one movement of his hand. "Lucky you, Lisandro. Your sin has been forgiven."

Chapter 26

The Hunt

The night before the hunt was unusually quiet. For the first time in a long time, the duke slept the entire seven hours undisturbed. Not only was he not tormented by the visions of his deceased wife, but he dreamed of nothing at all, which for a man as imaginative as Martín Castro was really unusual. He woke up early in the morning, well rested and ready to receive the distinguished guests who were about to come to the palace in Valsombra.

After an overnight downpour, the sun finally shone over Cantabria. "It's time to end this madness! To think that I let my own fantasy put a spell on me!" The duke thought, looking out the window at the garden, bathed in autumn hues of red and gold. "Let it be time for laughter and pleasure now! I'm not going to torture myself for one more moment. Soon the fear will give way to fun!"

The duke smiled with satisfaction at the sight of the first carriage that entered the courtyard. As more carriages appeared on the horizon, Roberto entered the bedroom with a silver tray with two letters on it. The first was from Harold Ravendale. The duke frowned at the mere sight of his sophisticated italics. "Idiot!" - he muttered under his breath, opening the letter and guessing its contents.

The second envelope bore a cardinal's seal.

"Mario Suárez is not coming? How is that possible?!" The duke was surprised.

Having torn the lacquer apart with abrupt move, he began to read. Suddenly, he paled.

"Lord, is everything all right?" Roberto asked.

"How is this possible?" The duke could not believe it. "This man was an example of health!"

"Has something bad happened?"

"Count de Aciago died of asthma two days ago... The funeral will take place on Saturday... For obvious reasons the cardinal will not come either."

However, it was not so much the news of the count's death that upset the duke, as the other messages contained in the priest's letter. Namely, he mentioned a "brilliant medic" who made every effort to save his brother. *Despite the fact that the health of my beloved Ramón has been supervised for some time by doctor August Nacht, an excellent physician, and also my protégé...* - he wrote.

"*My protégé,*" the duke repeated aloud. "So this man, who came out of nowhere, bought into the favors of Cardinal Suárez! Well well!" He exclaimed, then slammed his fist on the desk with all his might, knocking over the inkpot.

Roberto grabbed the object at the last moment, saving the pile of notes and unfinished correspondence lying on the table from being spilled with ink.

"Like mother like son!" Cried the duke. "He can ensnare everyone! With me though, he will have an uphill battle, I know all about these tricks!"

"Dear Lord, is the hunt still going to happen in light of this unfortunate circumstance?" Roberto asked timidly.

"Of course! I am not going to give up the pleasure I have been waiting for so long just because Ramón Suárez has chosen this moment to die!" Replied the duke, glaring at him furiously. "To hell with that fool and his asthma! And I invited Ravendale only out of courtesy, so I'm not going to lament over his absence either. I'll be down in the hall soon."

The flattering mention of August upset the duke so much, that he went downstairs with Roberto to greet the first guests without reading the end of the letter that he abandoned casually on his desk. Therefore, he did not have time to learn the second part of the letter, in which the cardinal explained the cause of his brother's sudden death in his typically diplomatic way.

Soon after the duke left, Ausencio appeared in the bedroom to do the daily cleaning. Noticing the two pages lying on the desk, neatly written in elegant script, he could not resist the urge to read them. *I really do not know, my dear friend, in what words I should put this delicate and at the same time painful matter in order to spare you humiliation,* the cardinal wrote. - *According to the reports of the household, the death took place shortly after my dearest and greatly missed brother learned about the sudden disappearance of the Countess de Aciago, who, according to one of the servants, was kidnapped by pirates marauding in the area. Our invaluable doctor Nacht, however, questioned the maid carefully and on the basis of her testimony, he was able to conclude that the alleged pirate was in fact the servant of the Marquis de Viciosa, that is, your son, César. This shocking news left my brother, who had been struggling with asthma for years, to suffer a fatal attack.*

"Well, I wonder what Iduna will say to all this..." Ausencio said to himself. "I'm sure the whole thing will interest her very much, especially since it directly concerns my master's son..."

At the sound of footsteps, he quickly put the letter back on the desk and went back to work. Inés entered the room.

"I bring you good news," she said, jumping up and down with joy. "The duke just told me to tell everyone that we have a night off! Only Ricardo and Juan stay, because they have to take care of the animals."

"Great!" Ausencio rejoiced. "I already missed Iduna and Álvaro and our conversations... I will finally bring my friend a delicious story," he planned the coming meeting in his mind.

Having served his guests with a wonderful breakfast, the duke ordered to prepare a dozen sizeable pointers and to saddle the horses. When everything was ready, the hunters went into the forest together with the beaters. The free wing of the hunt, scheduled to be manned by Lord Ravendale, ultimately went to the husband of the Duke's cousin Eugenia, Count Juan Jiménez y Molina.

Iduna heard the barking dogs from afar. At this sound, her heart contracted in her breast to the size of a walnut, and her fists clenched like the claws of a bird of prey. Sensing her tension, Álvaro, who was just resting on a branch of an old oak tree, spread his massive wings and made a series of high-pitched sounds. Iduna stretched out her arm and the bird flew down on it with his usual caution.

Stroking and kissing the falcon's wing, she listened to the ever louder howling of the pointers. She closed her eyes, and then the scene from years ago, when two pointers caught up with Yurde lying on the ground, played back in her mind. Again she saw the gray dog grab the boy by the neck, while the other, brownish in color, sank its teeth into his thigh, snarling furiously and biting deeper and deeper into the body with every split second.

The child's piercing scream sounded in Iduna's ears with the same intensity as it did then, merging with a warning squeal of Álvaro, who suddenly bounced off her shoulder and flew up in the air.

"What annoyed you so much, birdie?" She asked.

As if in response, Álvaro flew to the rock, the same rock under which Yurde had died. A shiver ran up Iduna's spine. The bird tilted its head to one side. His big, glistening eye stared at the guardian with a strange seriousness.

Moments later, a frightened fox ran past the mouth of the cave, and a few steps behind it - four pointers of Duke de Valsombra followed. At the sight of their shiny hair, their muscular paws and their open, panting mouths, Iduna felt blood in her throat. "So Ausencio was right... He has indeed arranged a fox hunt! How I would like Martín to be in the game's place..." Álvaro, as if reading her mind, let out a long series of squeaks again, then flew up onto his branch.

"Surprise!" A cheerful, youthful voice said suddenly in the distance.

Iduna looked around. Ausencio emerged from behind a broad beech tree behind her.

"Ausencio! It's great that you visited me on this day. I hate these hunts more than anything else in the world! They make me feel depressed."

"And I love them more than anyone else, because his majesty always allows us to leave the palace then. I associate hunting with freedom."

"I, with death..." whispered Iduna. But let's not talk about unpleasant matters. Let's go to the cave!"

Once inside her rock kingdom, Ausencio made himself comfortable on a pile of skins.

"I'd like to thank you for the medicine," he said.

"Did it help?" Iduna asked.

"Greatly! I hope I no longer need it, since my master has announced that he is doing better. I also learned a very interesting story today by accident," he announced.

Iduna looked at him out of the corner of her eye, simultaneously filling a wooden bowl with hazelnuts.

"When I came to the duke's chamber to tidy up a bit, I noticed that there was an open letter on the desk. It came from Cardinal Suárez..."

"He's a very unpleasant man... And so is his brother."

"The brother is exactly what the letter was about."

"Really?" Iduna perked up.

"It turns out that he died a few days ago. He is said to have been killed by a severe asthma attack."

Iduna's eyes widened.

"Tell me everything!" She exclaimed.

"I will summarize what I read there."

"I can't wait!"

'The cardinal wrote something like this: his brother's wife was secretly kidnapped by a man who was initially thought to be a pirate. When her disappearance was discovered, the Count de Aciago was immediately notified about everything. There was also a doctor in the palace with a foreign-sounding name, and it was him who concluded that the kidnapper was not a pirate, but a servant of the Marquis de Viciosa, that is, my master's son. Apparently he met this man..."

Iduna turned pale. "Poor August... The last time I saw him, he looked sick in body and soul. Knowing his insane determination, he will follow this woman anywhere, even to hell..."

"When the medic shared his observations with the Count de Aciago," continued Ausencio, "he suddenly felt unwell and died..."

"Do you know anything more?" Iduna asked.

"Unfortunately, I had to stop reading because I heard Inés's steps, she came to announce that the duke had given us the afternoon off. She stayed in the chamber to help clean up, and we left the palace together. The letter is still on the desk..."

"It's a pity..." Iduna sighed.

"August will probably try to fight for her..." she pondered. "He hates César as much as he hates his father. Not only the revenge plan we had taken failed because of this witch, but to make things worse, she also ran away with his own brother. I know August and I know that he will do his best to retake her, especially since César stood in his way once again... Meanwhile, he looks like a ghost of himself. If he is going to fight like this, the malicious fate will also deprive me of my adoptive son…"

"I wonder if my master intends to react to this somehow…" Ausencio asked after a long silence.

"I do not think so. Despite their differences, he will not start a war with his son. César is an adult, he has a title and a large property. He lives in isolation and does not care about anyone's favors. His father cannot force him to do anything. But he will certainly be furious with the scandal that will make him personally a laughing stock. Martín is an old, vain hypocrite. Everything is supposed to look nice on the outside…" - Iduna replied bitterly.

There was a long silence. Ausencio stared at the greenish growth covering the ceiling of the cave. Then a furious barking of the duke's pointers and the pitiful whimper of a fox came from a distance. At this sound, Iduna's face twitched. She slowly rose from her seat and walked closer to the mouth of the cave. She crossed her arms over her chest and bit her lip.

"They already got it…" she sighed.

A sudden gust of cold, late autumn wind filled the grotto with a sullen, low-pitched howl, which mingled with the sharp barking of the dogs. The fox could be no longer heard. Ausencio realized it was time for him to go back.

Chapter 27

La Lavandera

The thought of the next day's duel with his brother filled August with supernatural energy. He spent the night in a strange, half-asleep state, interwoven with distant memories of his early childhood and the pictures from the recent past. Blurred views of Venice, plunged in the morning lethargy, above which a thick, bluish vapor hung, passed before his half-open eyes. As soon as the familiar landscape dissolved into a fog, August thought that he was in the theater, where, sitting on the lap of an old matron, he was watching his mother on stage, playing the role of a mythical heroin. The words of the famous aria she sang then, echoed in his brain as if he were hearing them here and now:

> *Che fiero momento!*
> *Che barbara sorte!*
> *Passar dalla morte*
> *A tanto dolor!*
> *Avvezza al contento*
> *D'un placido oblio,*
> *Fra queste tempeste*
> *Si perde il mio cor [23].*

After she sang the last word, the stage was covered within a minute with flowers and ribbons. Some of them stuck to Dorothea Nacht's golden hair, making her look even more like the dying Eurydice. It was her last performance.

For a moment August thought he could see his mother's face close to him, as if woven from rays of light. She was young again, as on the day of her great triumph during the performance of *Orpheus and Eurydice*. She looked at her son with that gentle smile that even her illness did not take away from her. It only faded from her face once and for all the day Martín turned them both away.

Due to the sleepy fluidity that overwhelmed August's mind, Dorothea Nacht's radiant face was transformed into the snow-white face of Blanca. Light blue, serene eyes in a golden frame turned into gray eyes, filled with melancholy, with slightly dark circles and dark, almost black eyebrows, while the delicate, fawn hair took on an intense, dark chestnut color.

August opened his eyes. He got up from the bed and went to the window. Drawing the curtains aside, he paused for a long moment, staring at the forest, immersed in the night silence. He opened the window and inhaled the cool air.

"We will see tomorrow if I lost both of them..." he said to himself.

He listened to the gloomy howl of the wind. He thought he could hear fragments of words and conversations from the past in the mass of uncoordinated whistles and groans, but he was unable to put them together in a whole.

At the same time, César was deep asleep. It was not, however, a peaceful sleep, but something like deathly lethargy. Despite the fact that his chest rose and fell rhythmically, creating an appearance of undisturbed peace, he dreamed that he was deep underground, in the crypt of the ancestral chapel in Valsombra, gasping for breath and aspiring into his nostrils every gulp of stale air sucked from empty eye sockets and lung cavities of his ancestors.

The awful feeling disappeared with the coming of the dawn.

As César gradually awoke from his sleep, it seemed to him that the stone gate above his head was suddenly sliding aside, opening a way outside for him. When he slowly opened his eyes, he saw Blanca's face above him. She stared at him silently for a moment, then greeted him with a long kiss.

August greeted dawn, leaning against the stone sill of his chamber window. Wiping the cold sweat off his forehead with the sleeve of his shirt, he ran a hand through his hair, then walked over to the mirror. Frowning, as if in slight disbelief, he stretched the trembling hand towards the mirror. The man on the other side of the glass made the same move. August stared at the palms of their hands joined together in an identical gesture.

He stood there for several minutes, breathing deeply. The world swirled in front of his eyes. Gray light slowly filled the room. When Jaime arrived, carrying lavender soap and clear water, August did not even notice his arrival. Even though the previous day he had agreed with the old servant that he would be his second, August decided to reach the place of the duel alone.

He was still standing motionless before the mirror in front of a pale, fair-haired man with a sullen look and a thin face.

"Good morning, Doctor Nacht," Jaime said. "Can I help you with anything?"

"No thanks," August replied. "Put down what you brought and leave."

"When are we setting off?"

"I'll go first, you will follow me. The duel begins at noon."

"I understand, doctor. I'll be on time," said the servant, and left the room.

"He looks like a ghost of himself," thought Jaime. "If I ran into him in the dark, I'd be scared!"

August's unnatural pallor and the melancholy that emanated from his entire person, caught the eyes of all the household members. Cardinal Suárez also noticed a change in the medic's appearance and behavior. When he arrived at Palacio Aciago after his brother's death, August came to greet him. Upon seeing him, the Cardinal asked if he was ill by any chance.

He was right. August had completely neglected his own health, dividing his time between visits to patients, remembrance of his recently deceased mother and, above all, reflecting on his unrequited love. Not for one minute did he not think about Blanca or return to the happiest moments of his life when he visited her in the Gothic tower in secret from everybody, including the Count de Aciago himself.

Finally, the long-awaited day had come when he had to overcome his own weakness and face César, whom he considered to be the embodiment of his fate of eternal rejection by people closest to him. He stretched his right arm out in a fencing stance. The weakened tendons trembled under the sudden tension, and the hand, clenched around the handle of the invisible sword, opened. The whole world swirled before his eyes again.

As he stared at his fossilized, sweaty fingers with child-like helplessness, suddenly his mother's words, which she often repeated to him in moments of doubt, echoed in his ears: *Sei ein Mann!* [24] He repeated this command aloud several times, walking around the chamber, all elements of which seemed to drift and ripple in the thin air, as if Palacio Aciago had somehow strangely moved into a red-hot desert.

Within one brief moment the weakness subsided. August washed himself in a flash, donned a clean shirt, a blue frock coat, and carefully arranged his fair hair, which he tied back with a blue ribbon. After eating a modest breakfast in the dining room, he ordered Jaime to saddle the gray horse.

He jumped into the saddle in one springy motion, stroked the animal's neck, and started toward Viciosa.

Faint rays of sunlight shone through the pearly clouds, falling on the knotty trunks of ancient oaks and the smooth, delicate bark of beech trees. August felt like in the old days again: strong, confident in victory, full of contempt for the weakness that had been in full control of him just an hour ago. "*Sei ein Mann!*" He mentally ordered himself one last time, then he galloped forward.

Suddenly, the entire forest was covered by a thick, milky fog. The horse neighed and shook its mane.

"*Still!* [25]" August whispered, stroking the clearly nervous animal.

Wandering almost blindly, he rode a small stretch of road forward. But when he heard the murmur of a stream nearby, he stopped. For he realized that he had unknowingly left the path and was now by the Arroyo Oculto stream, the same one by which the Count de Aciago had suffered a serious accident.

It was easy for August to identify the place, for he remembered that not so long ago, Jaime had told him about the only creek in this part of the forest. "There is no other possibility," he thought. "If I remember correctly, the Arroyo Oculto runs by the César's Castle." He also remembered that Jaime had mentioned an old, disused mill, seen from Viciosa. He decided then, that instead of turning back to the path and risking falling off his horse, he would follow the creek.

After he had ridden quite a distance, his attention was unexpectedly drawn to a moving dark shape that he saw from the corner of his eye on the other side of the stream. At that moment, the horse began to snort nervously, and his sides became damp with sweat. August stopped. He saw the figure of an aged woman, wearing a long coat with a hood.

She was kneeling by the water, in which she was washing some rags. As August looked at her hands, he flinched. Frighteningly thin hands moved slowly in the sluggish, Acheront-like currents of the Arroyo Oculto. The bony fingers, covered with gray-brown skin and ending with long claws, did not belong to a living person: there was a clear mark of death visible on them.

The horse neighed again and reared up, hooves kicking violently in the air. August could barely control it. The washerwoman did not seem to notice anything. She was still kneeling by the water, repeating the same monotonous moves. When August looked at her hands again, he swallowed instinctively. The rag she was washing was all bloody. The stream waters were gradually turning reddish.

August was close to fainting. His weakness, just overcome by willpower, was making itself felt again. A bead of cold sweat appeared on his forehead, and his hands felt damp and limp.

"*Sei ein Mann!*" He said loudly, through his teeth.

Hearing those words that he spoke himself, made him feel a little better again. He gripped the reins tightly and looked at the washerwoman with courage.

The woman raised her head slightly. The face was still invisible, hidden under the huge black hood. "I'm not leaving this place until I find out who she is!" August decided. "Only a miserable coward would run away in fear at the sight of a helpless old woman..." The fog had already cleared, and the abandoned old mill Jaime had talked about, appeared in the distance. Seeing that he was already very close to Viciosa, he resolved to wait patiently for the stranger to reveal her face.

As the black hood rose a little again, August's heart began to beat faster. He looked at the water and found with horror that the entire stream had turned intense crimson. Then the woman raised her head in one sharp movement. From under the hood peeked out the most monstrous and disgusting face August had seen in his entire life. It was a hideous skull covered in the remains of decaying skin. The lower jaw hung loosely on scraps of tendons, and a piercing scream rose from a cavernous, black and toothless throat. Its terrible echo carried throughout the forest, scaring off the birds sleeping on the old branches, which soared into the air as if stricken by sudden madness. August felt his head spin. With the last of his strength he embraced the horse's neck. The animal stood as if paralyzed.

"*Sei ein Mann!*" He whispered, his voice breaking.

When he came to his senses after a moment of a total numbness, he no longer dared to look towards the other side of the stream. He repeated his mother's command once more, then gently but firmly tugged the reins, and set off towards Viciosa, not looking back and leaving the monstrous vision behind, in the darkness of the forest. Dorothea's words worked like a magic spell on him, and he soon regained his will to fight.

At the sight of the gothic towers and fortifications of Castillo de Viciosa, he felt a surge of almost superhuman strength. In one second, he forgot about the sinister apparition, turning his thoughts to Blanca.

"I will get you back soon, my love," he sighed. Her figure and the porcelain-like face with melancholic gray eyes appeared before his eyes again. In his mind, she smiled at him again, as she did when they last saw each other in the gloomy tower.

Ominous, graphite clouds came from the direction of the mountains, completely obscuring the sky, and separating the sun from the world like a heavy curtain. The towers of the castle plunged into gloomy darkness, and the vines, tightly overgrowing the building, took on the same blood red color as the Arroyo Oculto stream. At this sight, an icy chill ran down August's back.

It was almost noon when he reached Castillo de Viciosa. Jaime was already waiting there. César and Lord Ravendale were already in the castle courtyard. Suddenly, August saw the figure of Blanca, clad in the same light-colored dress she wore the last time he came to visit her in the Gothic tower. He felt his heart sink into darkness.

"*Sei ein Mann!*" He said to himself.

23 Fragment of the libretto of the Eurydice's aria from the opera *Orpheus and Eurydice* by Ch. W. Gluck.

24 German *Be a man!*

25 German   *Quiet!*

Chapter 28

The diamond ring

Before the jaws of the pointers closed on the throat of the helpless fox in a death grip, the Duke of Valsombra separated from his companions. There was a strange sound that seemed to come from the side of the marshes deep in the forest, and resembled a distant child's laugh, interspersed with crying and interrupted by brief moments of silence. The duke paused to listen.

"First, I was tormented by these terrible phantoms, now I hear voices that do not exist... Am I losing my mind in my old age?" He wondered. The sounds, however, were so clear that the horse heard them as well. The duke was relieved to see the animal showing signs of distress. "At least I know I'm not crazy... But I have to find the source of these sounds," he decided.

He tugged the reins in a fast move and squeezed the horse's sides with the spurs. However, it was the first time in his life that the animal did not obey his master's command. So the duke stuck his spurs with all his might, thinking that by doing this, he would force the animal to obey. When that didn't work, he whipped it several times. In response, the horse pushed its front hooves to the ground and began to kick its hind legs menacingly, trying to throw the rider off.

When the duke realized that for some unknown reason, the heretofore obedient steed had become reneged, and that it would be impossible to make him obey the command, he jumped off the saddle and, leaving the animal behind, started in the direction of the voice. Curiosity was one of those passions, alongside a love of glamor and feminine charms, which Martín Castro could never control.

The sun in turn looked out from behind the clouds or was hiding behind a pearly-gray screen, like a teasing child playing hide and seek. Despite the illusion that the voice was coming from nearby, the duke realized that it would take him at least an hour to discover its source. However, he decided to find out where this strange sound came from at all costs.

After a while, he forgot about the ongoing hunting, especially since neither the calls of hunters nor the barking of cheerful dogs could be heard in the place he had reached on foot. In an instant, the capricious nature made him abandon the entertainment, though he had been completely absorbed in it until now, in order to solve a riddle that unexpectedly caught his attention.

The child's laughter sometimes turned into loud sobs, then suddenly stopped to turn into a melodious song. "What the hell is all this supposed to mean?" The duke thought, looking around. The voice seemed to either carry high above the leafless treetops or come from beneath the ground. The duke wasn't sure what to do, and as he was about to turn back towards the palace, a sound suddenly rang out right next to him, as if the invisible little boy was singing a song especially for him.

"Where are you?" He asked. "And who are you? I swear I won't hurt you. I also had a son your age once..."

In response, he heard bursts of pearly laughter, as if his words clearly amused the child.

"Whoever you are, what do you want from me?"

There was dead silence for several long minutes, but then the child's voice could be heard again. This time it was a laughter mixed with sad, tearful tones. It was coming from the far end of the forest.

Without hesitating any longer, the duke walked in that direction. However, each time he thought he had arrived at the mysterious child's whereabouts, the voice would come from farther away. He followed it like a guide until he finally reached the deepest, swampy part of the forest, the subject of many stories that circulated in the area, ranging from completely fantastic to sounding quite probable. None of the locals dared to enter those areas for fear of the ghosts of mushroom pickers and hunters who never came back from there. Others attributed these disappearances to the vengeful action of sirens, who allegedly lured lonely travelers with their singing, and then dragged them into the swampy abyss. Some villagers talked about a mysterious beast that supposedly devoured people alive.

The cause of the unexplained disappearances, however, was much more prosaic and completely natural. Well, in the center of this infamous part of the forest, there was a small clearing that was filled with a deadly quagmire. At first glance, this place seemed completely safe, because the swamp, tightly covered with light green plants, looked like solid ground. The unfortunate people who ventured into these areas in search of mushrooms, berries and other forest treasures, or in pursuit of spooky game, when succumbed to the deceptive nature, died within a few moments in the muddy depths. As soon as the dense swamp engulfed the already motionless tips of their fingers, protruding above the surface like the ends of dead branches, the aquamarine cover instantly closed over them like the liquid lid of an ancient tomb.

Unaware of the quagmire, the duke continued tirelessly ahead, sinking almost ankle-deep in the thick mud and not noticing the passage of time. It was already noon.

When he reached the edge of the clearing, the sight of huge dragonflies with metallic green abdomens and glass wings, dancing above it, made him somewhat suspicious, but he did not suspect that there was a deadly danger lurking under the picturesque, aquamarine carpet.

The child's voice grew louder and seemed to come from the very center of the quagmire, and more precisely from some point in the air just above it. At first, a cheerful laugh interwoven with the quiet humming of verses of always the same song, turned over time into a series of sad sighs, and finally into a dramatic, excruciating lament. The pitiful sobs echoed off the reddish trunks of the pines surrounding the clearing.

"Who are you?" Cried the duke. "Answer me!"

In response, the invisible child cried out loud and uttered a few incomprehensible words.

"I do not understand!"

The child sobbed again, then suddenly laughed, filling the entire forest with a joyful voice.

"Have mercy on me! Who or what are you? Why are you tormenting me? What do you want from me?" Asked the duke, spreading his trembling arms helplessly.

An invisible being seemed to lure him into the clearing. This time, however, the voice came from just above the aquamarine surface. The duke looked at the dragonflies dancing in the air. His heart beat a little faster and beads of sweat appeared on his forehead. He took a couple of deep breaths, then took two steps forward.

The ground was quite soft, but felt reasonably solid. "Let's hope the grounds continues to be like this. I'm not leaving here until I know where the voice haunting me is coming from!" The duke decided, then took a few more steps. He noted with satisfaction that he was already very close to the source of the mysterious sounds. The silvery, childish voice took on the tone of a cheerful, chattering laughter again.

When the duke managed to make his way to the very center of the clearing, the mud had already covered his legs up to the middle of his thighs. The invisible being that lured him to this place laughed out loud just above his head, then fell silent for good. As the duke looked down, he realized with horror that he was almost waist deep in the mud.

"What harm have I done to you that you are punishing me in such a cruel way? Why are you tormenting me? Say who you are, or at least set me free from this hell!" He cried desperately.

But there was a deaf silence in the forest, broken only by the whirring of the wings of the huge dragonflies and the soft buzzing of mosquitoes.

The duke stared in horror at the gradually rising level of the mud absorbing him, when suddenly he heard a series of loud, prolonged squeaks above him. As he raised his head up, the majestic silhouette of a peregrine falcon appeared before his eyes. The bird made large circles in the air, observing the figure of an old man trapped in a quagmire from above. The man raised both his arms in a desperate gesture, as if he begged the falcon for help, driven by an irrational outburst of hope for salvation.

Suddenly the sky began to clear up. The afternoon sun peeked out shyly from behind a dense veil of white, gray and almost black clouds, quickly breaking free from its prison to fill the entire clearing with bright light in a triumphant gesture. The bright rays completely blinded the duke staring at the sky, at the same time diffracting in the mirror of the magnificent diamond ring that adorned the ring finger of his right hand.

The resulting beautiful rainbow caught the eye of the bird, which suddenly stopped in the air, staring at the unusual light phenomenon as if enchanted. The sun's rays, shimmering with all possible colors, played on the duke's frightened face and his desperately outstretched arms, jumping like mischievous imps on his forehead and eyelids.

The falcon watched the unusual phenomenon for a long time, then suddenly lowered its flight, heading towards the terrified old man, who was already up to his armpits under the aquamarine surface. At the sight of the outstretched claws of the bird, he instinctively closed his eyes, trying to protect his head with his arms. These, however, protruded over the surface of the swamp like dry branches, immobilized by thick mud.

"Spare me!" Cried the duke, opening his eyes one last time. In a split second, sharp claws dug into his eye sockets. The excruciating screams of the old man, dying in torment, filled the clearing. The falcon sitting on his head let out another series of long squeals, as if wanting to announce his triumph to the world. As the mud brushed his claws, he suddenly flew up, taking the diamond ring off the victim's finger in an agile movement of the curved beak.

In less than a minute, the quagmire swallowed the duke's hands, and the aquamarine lid was sealed irreversibly over his body. The bird hung in the air for a moment longer, as if it were amazed that the famous Martín Castro, whose life resembled an endless theater performance, had disappeared from the face of the earth so quickly and so imperceptibly.

After Ausencio left the cave and disappeared on the horizon, Iduna was left alone. She went outside and looked at the branch Álvaro usually sat on. She was surprised to see that it was empty.

"Álvaro! Where are you, birdie?" She exclaimed.

She looked around, but the falcon was nowhere to be seen. At the same time, she was overwhelmed by a feeling of strange peace and inner harmony. "Something extraordinary must have happened," she thought.

At the same moment, a string of squeaky tones reached her. The familiar sounds came from above, from behind her back.

When she turned her head, she saw a bird making a large circle in the air, its wings spread in the air. When he was dozen meters above the ground, she noticed that he was holding a small, shiny object in his beak.

"Álvaro! Where have you..." she began.

The falcon landed on an oak branch and Iduna's voice died on her lips.

She recognized the diamond ring of Duke de Valsombra.

"Where did you get it?" She asked.

The sight of the bird's bloody claws spoke for itself. The falcon let out a long squeal, then gingerly flied down onto Iduna's arm, brought his head closer to her forehead and plunged its beak into her hair. She kissed his gray wing. The profuse tears that ran down her cheeks, moistened the bird's silky feathers. While Álvaro combed the silvery strands of her hair with his beak, she twirled in the fingers of her right hand a magnificent ring, woven of the finest golden filigree surrounding a large diamond. She remembered the last time she had seen this gem up close, when Martín Castro's hand, decorated with it, closed her mouth, and the weight of his body pressed her to the damp ground.

She shivered at the mere memory of the scene. When Álvaro flew to his favorite oak, she headed towards Claro del Agua. Reaching the forest lake, she took off the ring that the falcon had brought her from her finger and threw it into the water with all her strength. The last afternoon sunbeam managed to split in the mirror surface of the diamond before the dark water engulfed the precious   gem.

Chapter 29

Little thrush...

Lord Ravendale arrived at Viciosa at a quarter to twelve. As soon as César saw his elegant carriage from the window, he beamed.

"Reliable as always!" He said appreciatively, then ran to the courtyard to greet his friend. Blanca followed him. That day, she decided not to leave his side, wanting to spend every second they had left with her beloved.

"What have you gotten yourself into again?" The Englishman asked, getting out of the carriage.

At the sight of Blanca, who appeared at the palace gate, he understood that the duel was inevitable. The letter from César was very short and gave no details, so Lord Ravendale thought that Count de Aciago would be on the other side again.

"I hope the count has learned enough after what has happened recently, and he will not try to bend the rules to suit his moods," he said.

"The Count de Aciago is dead," replied César.

"How come?"

"He died of an asthma attack a few days ago."

"So who are you going to duel with?"

"With my brother."

Lord Ravendale turned pale. Although he was privy to the secret of the kinship between César and August, he did not expect, however, that they would have to fight till death.

"Did I hear you right? August Nacht challenged you to a duel?"

"Yes, my dear Harold."

"I did not think that he had such esteem for Count de Aciago."

"It's not about the count," said Blanca. "I am the cause of this disaster. I pray that August will come to his senses and withdraw the challenge..."

"I don't think he will," said César. "He is extremely determined."

At the same moment, the silhouette of a rider on a black horse appeared at the edge of the forest.

"Jaime!" Blanca called.

"My lady," the servant greeted her.

"I guess you'll be the second for the other side," Lord Ravendale said to him with a friendly smile.

"Doctor Nacht made me his second," Jaime confirmed. "However, he did not want me to come with him. He was the first to leave, so I thought I'd find him here."

"We'll wait patiently," said Lord Ravendale.

"The doctor is extremely punctual. It worries me that he has not arrived yet ..." admitted the kind hearted servant. "I hope no misfortune happened to him..."

At that moment there was a rumble coming from the depths of the forest, and everyone saw the bright figure of August on a gray horse. He jumped off the saddle and greeted Lord Ravendale and César, giving them his icy, wet hand. At this sight, Blanca leaned against the cold stone wall. August's blue eyes, surrounded with dark circles, stared at her with an expression of somber melancholy.

The same boy who had assisted in the duel with Count de Aciago, emerged from the palace. He brought the same two swords, wrapped in velvet cloth.

"I understand that you gentlemen will fight to the death," Lord Ravendale said grimly.

"Yes, sir," Jaime replied for August.

"Doctor, pick your sword," the Englishman asked.

August walked over to the boy. He studied the arms for a moment. He chose the sword, whose blade reflected the sun. The boy handed the other one to his master. César stroked his head and then sent him back to the castle.

The brothers faced each other. They were so much alike, but they looked like two exact opposites. In the rays of the sun that had just flashed in the cleared sky, César's black hair, swarthy skin and dark clothes contrasted starkly with August's pale face, platinum hair, and light clothes. Blanca stared at them wide-eyed, digging her fingernails into both hands until the snow-white skin cracked and blood flowed, staining the dress.

"*Sei ein Mann!*" August ordered himself one last time. At the joint sign of both seconds, the brothers crossed their swords. August's hand trembled slightly. The clash of iron scared the flock of ravens sitting on the wide beech tree. As on command, the birds took flight at the same time. For a moment, their jagged wings dimmed the sun, and a loud croaking came from the dark throats.

"It must be a good omen…" Blanca thought, looking at the birds wings, then at César's hair and his coat of the same color. August's hand trembled again, this time a little stronger. He pulled himself together, however, and, looking deeply into his brother's eyes, took a sharp step forward, aiming the blade of his sword at his heart. The latter, however, quickly countered the attack.

César's blow proved well-aimed. A scarlet, vine-leaf-shaped stain appeared on August's chest, and began to gradually spread.

"Enough!" Lord Ravendale shouted.

August looked at his wound, then collapsed to the ground. Jaime and Lord Ravendale immediately ran to him. As a trickle of dark blood flowed from the corner of his mouth, the seconds looked at each other. César dropped his sword. For the first time in many years, his black eyes filled with tears.

August looked at Blanca one last time. Their eyes met. She couldn't say anything because the words caught in her throat. With horror and disbelief, she looked at his transparent face and bluish, slightly parted lips, from between which more and more blood was flowing.

"*Für dich, meine Liebe...* [26]" he choked, still staring at her with dimming eyes, and spitting out a stream of blood.

The image of her face gradually blurred before his eyes, merging with the melancholic, gentle face of Dorothea Nacht, which then turned into Iduna's dark, wrinkled face. It seemed to him that she said, "Sleep, son." The last, irregular beats of his own dying heart drowned out the words of his friend, which he managed to read from the movement of her lips.

A moment later, a terrifying whistle came out of August's breast. The whole body jerked violently, then let out its last breath. His eyes froze, still staring at Blanca. Lord Ravendale took off his hat.

"*Requiescat in pace* [27]," he said.

"Doctor…" Jaime muttered, his voice breaking.

Blanca slowly walked over to the dead man, then knelt beside him and closed his blue eyes with one move of her hand.

César was still standing in the same place, staring at the body of his brother whom he had killed himself. He couldn't move a single finger or say a single word. The rush of thoughts drove him into a deep trance, similar to a delirium. He still couldn't believe what had happened. He alternately imagined that he might be in August's place, and wanted to turn back time and not accept the challenge.

After a while, the terrible numbness passed. César took his black hat off his head, then walked over to August's body lying on the ground.

"Goodbye, brother," he said.

He hid his face in his hands for a moment, then turned toward the castle without a word. Blanca said goodbye to Jaime, then took Lord Ravendale's arm and followed César with him. Aitor, who was watching the duel from the window, went out into the courtyard and helped Jaime transport the deceased to one of the carriages in the coach house.

As soon as Iduna threw the ring of Duke de Valsombra into the lake, she heard Yurde's laughter, which after a while turned into soft singing:

Little thrush, tiny thrush,
all spotted...

At the sound of the child's song, her heart pounded, then shrank like a frightened weasel. The only living person she truly loved was August. So when the soul of her deceased son gave her a sign that someone dear to her was dying, she immediately guessed whose face would soon appear to her in the dark waters of the lake.

She knelt by the water, staring intently at the mirror surface. At the sight of the stirring water, her throat tightened and she felt a stab in her chest. After a while, a familiar, deathly pale face appeared in the depths, blue eyes peering out from sunken eye sockets. There was a trickle of blood between the lips, and the eyes grew cloudier and more absent with each passing second.

Suddenly, the blue lips moved as if they were going to say something with the last of their strength. Iduna did not know German language, but her natural intuition allowed her to guess the meaning of August's last words.

"Für dich, meine Liebe..."

Along with this unfinished sentence, a copious stream of blood flowed from the dying man's mouth. His eyes became completely cloudy and motionless.

"Sleep, son," whispered Iduna.

August wanted to answer, but the words died on his bluish lips. After a while, the water of the lake became cloudy and the pale face disappeared into a black vortex. Claro del Agua fell into a gloomy silence. The sun suddenly vanished behind a screen of dark graphite clouds. From the already leafless, spreading treetops, flocks of birds suddenly shot up and scattered across the sky.

Iduna knelt by the lake for a long time, staring blankly at its gloomy waters. She knew she would never see anyone's face again in the dark surface. She also realized that August's departure meant she wouldn't hear Yurde's laugh anytime soon. The sudden rush of longing for the boy overshadowed the despair over the loss of her adopted son, whom she had failed to save from himself.

All she wanted now was to rest next to her child in his damp grave, covered with the intensely green moss. She got up from her knees and looked at the sky. The first drops of winter rain fell on her wrinkled face, and quickly turned into a downpour. It seemed that the sky buckled under its own weight and fell to the ground, pushing the world into a sea of endless gray.

The long, silvery strands of Iduna's hair blended into one with the water streaming down them. Her majestic figure, standing on the shore of a choppy lake, resembled some ancient deity, or the embodiment of untamed nature. She stared straight at the sky with her black eyes under lowered eyebrows, as if giving a final challenge to the clouds, wind and sun.

26 German *For you, my love.*
27 Latin   *Rest*   *in*   *peace.*

Chapter 30

Angelo Florentini

Young Angelo Florentini spent many months searching for his father's murderer. 70-year-old Cosimo, one of the richest Venetian patricians, enjoyed excellent health despite his years. However, he never got the chance to live to even older age, as he fell victim to a perfidious plot that his wife had devised.

Twenty-five years younger than her husband, Domenica Florentini began an affair with a surgeon and astronomer, whom she planned to marry after Cosimo's death. Since it didn't look like the burly old man was going to leave the world of the living quickly, the impatient lovers decided to slay him insidiously. The only way to do it could be a poison that would leave no trace.

It so happened that the chosen one of Domenica had a close friend, who not only knew poisons very well, but also accepted discreet orders from influential citizens who wanted to get rid of inconvenient people. This man was a foreigner and had a seriously ill mother to support, a former opera singer. His name was August Nacht.

According to the plan, the old patrician was to die in his sleep, showing no disturbing signs, so it would seem that his life ended for the most natural causes. The only person who could cope with this difficult task was the eminently gifted doctor Nacht, known for the fact that, apart from his excellent knowledge, he also possessed extraordinary dexterity.

For a generous reward, he prepared poison, a little of which was enough to spike any dish or drink. After several hours, it caused drowsiness and then death. Following his instructions, Domenica put a few drops of this tasteless and odorless substance on the bottom of the goblet, from which her husband used to drink a small portion of dry wine just before going to bed.

The poison served its purpose perfectly and Cosimo Florentini went to eternal sleep. Domenica, pretending to be a despairing widow, and the unsuspecting only son of the deceased, Angelo, buried the old man with honors in the family crypt. After the mourning period was over, Domenica married her lover in Saint Mark's Cathedral. Her happiness did not last long, however, as she soon became seriously ill.

Neither her newly married husband, nor the excellent doctor Carlini, nor even August Nacht himself, famous for being able to cure even the most hopeless cases, could help her. Thinking that sudden illness was God's punishment for killing Cosimo, Domenica, consumed with strong remorse, decided to tell her son the whole truth. She died on the same day.

As soon as Angelo found out under what circumstances he lost his beloved father, he decided to avenge his death. However, August had left the Apennine Peninsula a few days earlier, and Don Severino, Domenica's husband, had an excellent reputation in Venice, and it was highly doubtful that he would ever be able to prove his involvement in poisoning Cosimo, let alone bring him to justice. Thus Angelo decided to take the matter into his own hands.

He immediately challenged to duel Don Severino, who, due to his lack of fencing skills, paid for it with his life. Then he decided to find August and deal with him as well. He left Venice almost the next day, heading west overland. He had learned from a reliable source that Spanish blood ran in the veins of *Il dottore della morte*, and that he left immediately after the death of his mother. Therefore, he established that the doctor could, with all probability, go to Spain.

The young Venetian had never left Italy in his life, so the journey to a distant country seemed endless to him. He had doubted many times that he would ever find the man who had prepared a lethal poison for his father. He knew August's face and asked about him almost everywhere, giving a fairly detailed description of him, but no one was able to give him any specific information.

He found the murderer's trail only on the French-Spanish border, where the owner of an inn, after hearing about a tall, fair-haired man speaking with a German accent, immediately remembered that a similar man had stayed there some two and a half weeks earlier. The conversation with the innkeeper poured hope in the heart of Angel, who was already beginning to doubt the sense of the whole undertaking.

The old man knew nothing except that he had been hosting a man, more or less fitting the description, who was traveling towards some town to the west of Santander. These scanty messages were more than enough for the young Venetian. Exhausted by the long journey, he decided to recover the lost energy in order to soon begin an intensive search for his father's murderer, now sure that he was going in the right direction.

He stayed in a small, picturesque village called Bárcena Menor. There was a small inn that belonged to a certain Atanasia Elguero. The entire first floor had been occupied for a long time by an English lord who had become so at home in this cozy place that he was not going to leave it any time soon. The little room in the attic was empty though.

After several weeks of fruitless searching, Angelo began to doubt again that he would ever find his father's murderer. The breakthrough came one evening, when an Englishman invited his young neighbor to the table during a supper. Lord Ravendale turned out to be fluent in Tuscan, so the conversation was smooth from the very beginning.

Angelo told his new friend the purpose of his trip to Cantabria as a secret. It happened just when August was staying in the residence of Count de Aciago, who imprisoned Blanca in the Gothic tower. Lord Ravendale was a discreet man by nature, but when he heard some things about August's past in Italy from Angel, he decided to inform César immediately. He was also impressed by the determination with which his young neighbor intended to avenge his father's death, so he decided to lead him on the German's trail.

When, following Lord Ravendale's instructions, Angelo finally arrived at the Palacio Aciago, ready to challenge Cosimo's murderer to a decisive duel, the funeral was underway in the Suárez family chapel. The cardinal, who considered August to be the closest friend of his deceased brother, and owed him his life himself, decided to bury him in the lowest part of the crypt, where the count had been recently laid.

Unaware of anything, Angelo wanted to come face to face with August as soon as possible. Unable to wait any longer for the opportune moment, he slipped imperceptibly inside the small Gothic structure, filled to the brim with mourners, and accosted Jaime, who was standing right at the entrance.

"Whose funeral is this?" He asked.

"It's a tragic story," replied the servant, his voice breaking. "We have only just buried Count de Aciago, and now we have to say goodbye to his friend."

"Who was this man?" Angelo kept asking.

"He was an outstanding doctor. He died in a duel…" Jaime's voice stuck in his throat.

"What's his name?"

"August Nacht."

Angelo felt his knees buckle.

"Who was he dueling with?"

"With the Marquis de Viciosa."

"What was it about?"

"It's a very complicated story."

"I knew this man. We are connected by an unsettled case from the past. I need to know the truth."

"Please follow me," Jaime said. "We'll go outside the chapel."

He took Angelo by the arm and led him out into the courtyard.

"It was about Countess de Aciago, Blanca Morales. Dr. Nacht was unhappily in love with her. I cannot reveal any details."

"So he died in a duel over a woman..." Angelo mused.

"Yes," Jaime said dryly. "If you allow me, I will return to the chapel now and say goodbye to the deceased."

Angelo's heart stopped for a moment. At first, stunned by the news of August's death, he was glad that the invisible hand of justice had reached his father's killer. But when he heard that the doctor had died in a duel over a woman, and thus realized that he would never be able to avenge Cosimo personally, as honor dictated him, he was overcome with despair. Jaime disappeared inside the chapel, and Angelo knelt on the damp stones.

"Tutto è perduto...[28]" he sighed.

He quickly got on his horse and left Pueblo Aciago, going in the direction of Bárcena Menor. He returned to the inn in the early morning. As soon as he returned to his attic room, he went to the window. The world was just waking up. A dense fog still hung over the picturesque landscape. Angelo put his hand on the hilt of the silver dagger he always carried with him. "I don't think I have any other choice... Enough of this comedy!" - he thought.

He slid a silver dagger with the initials C.F. engraved on it, a memento of his late father, out of its scabbard and placed it on the bed. For a long moment he stared intently at the noble, carved blade, reflecting the pale early morning light.

"Perdonami, mio caro padre! [29]" he said. He gripped the hilt of the dagger firmly, then he pushed it into his chest with all his might. Two large streams of dark blood flowed out from the wound and the half-open mouth.

Lord Ravendale, who had been struggling with insomnia for some time, was just standing by the window, staring out into the still asleep countryside. When he heard a groan above him and then the sound of a falling body, he immediately ran out of the bedroom and climbed into the attic. Angelo's room was open. The young Venetian was lying on the floor. He was unconscious but still alive.

Without wasting a moment, Lord Ravendale dragged his wounded friend up the stairs, then awakened Atanasia Elguero.

"I need a carriage. I know a man who can save him," he ordered.

The terrified woman nodded several times and ran to wake her servant. After a while, the vehicle was ready to go.

"We're going to Viciosa!" Lord Ravendale shouted.

When they reached Castillo de Viciosa, Aitor was just bustling about in the courtyard. Seeing the carriage of Lord Ravendale, who had just left the castle, he guessed that an urgent matter had brought him back.

"Your lordship!" He greeted the visitor.

"Aitor, it's great to see you here. I came just for you. I brought my injured friend!" Said the Englishman.

The giant raised his eyebrows in surprise.

"The Marquis de Viciosa once mentioned to me that you are passionate about medicine. He even said you sewed his hand together."

"This is true. Depends on the man's condition."

"He tried to commit suicide. The wound looks terrible."

"I've seen all kind of wounds before, my lordship. I'm not afraid of such sights," Aitor replied with his usual stoic calm. "I will do what I can, of course, as long as there is still anything to save..."

"Great. Now help me get him out of the carriage."

They placed the wounded Italian in the chamber where Lord Ravendale used to sleep, and which César had offered him many times. He, however, preferred a hundred times more to stay in his inn in Bárcena Menor.

Angelo's lips and eyelids were completely blue. He was breathing very unevenly. Aitor unbuttoned his shirt and examined the wound carefully.

"Luckily, he didn't hurt his heart. However, the injury is quite serious. First of all, we must thoroughly disinfect this wound," he said. "I'm going to prepare the appropriate mixtures."

His huge figure disappeared into the dark hall.

At the same moment Blanca appeared at the gate. At the sight of the bloodied man lying in the courtyard, she instinctively backed away.

"Who is this man?" She asked.

"He's my friend. Angelo Florentini is his name. He lives in the same inn as me in Bárcena Menor. He followed August all the way here from Venice."

"Is that the man you told César about?"

"That's him. Nacht was involved in poisoning his father. I don't usually get involved in such matters, but my conscience kept me from protecting a hired killer, who additionally posed a serious threat to my friend."

Blanca's face turned gray.

"I led him on August's trail and told him he was connected to Cardinal Suárez," continued Lord Ravendale. "Angelo was going to challenge his father's murderer to a duel. I don't know why he took his life, but I suspect it may have something to do with August's death."

"Perhaps he has come to the conclusion that a malicious fate has deprived him of the revenge he longed for..." Blanca replied.

"I suspect so. Where is César?"

"I'm concerned about his health. He only just recovered after this terrible duel, and now, suddenly, a messenger arrived... César left for Valsombra in the early morning to help in the search."

"What kind of search? What messenger?"

"Harold, haven't you heard anything? Duke de Valsombra disappeared while hunting. The horse returned to the palace alone. They are looking for him day and night. Despite the fact that César's relationship with his father is rather cold, he will do everything in his power to find him."

Just then, Aitor came running.

"Fortunately, I had a mandrake tincture ready. It is the best disinfectant."

"I remember August used it too..." Blanca remarked. "He healed Count de Aciago when he broke his collarbone. The wound was extremely nasty, but my husband survived and recovered quickly."

"It is an infallible medicine," said Lord Ravendale. "By the way, I'm amused by all the legends about the mandrake."

"Me too," Aitor added, wiping the wound with a piece of a clean cloth soaked in the tincture.

Angelo Florentini fortunately survived. He regained consciousness on the next day already, and the wound was not infected. At Lord Ravendale's request, he told Blanca personally about August and his secret profession, and about his father's death. She felt ashamed for not quite believing César when he mentioned the gifted medic's second, dark face.

Nevertheless, even though she was aware of how dangerous and ruthless August was, she also knew how strongly and unconditionally he could love. The memory of his pale, sunken face and the somber melancholy emanating from his pale blue eyes haunted her like a ghost. It was a long time before she could free herself from the gaze he gave her at the time of his death. „Murió por mi..."[30] she thought.

It was late afternoon. A violent gust of wind opened the half-closed window of the room where Angelo Florentini was recovering. A dozen blood-red leaves of a vine fell into the room and for a moment circled around the room in a crazy air vortex, then finally fell to the floor. Blanca's heart stopped for a moment.

28 Italian *All is lost...*
29 Italian *Forgive me, my dear father!*
30 Spanish   *He   died   because   of   me.*

Chapter 31

The Swamp

It was just before noon when César arrived at Valsombra. As he entered the long line of poplars leading directly to the duke residence, he looked out of the carriage window. The golden leaves lying at the foot of the bare trees resembled from a distance a magnificent carpet, stretching all the way to the gate of the palace. The intense color of this carpet harmonized and at the same time contrasted with the graphite clouds, gloomily hanging over Valsombra.

From behind this somber vault, the sun suddenly appeared, illuminating the magnificent structure in a spectacular way. The palace looked like it was on fire.

"It's a bad omen, my lord," said old Francisco. César didn't answer. Deep down, he had a similar conviction, though it was not due to superstition, but only because there was a rather low probability that the duke would be found safe and sound.

"If the horse came alone, it means something bad happened to the father. If he had been attacked by robbers, they would have stolen his horse first," he analyzed. Bright light reflecting in all the glass panes of the mansion blinded him, so he covered the window of the carriage. As the carriage was approaching the palace, one could see from the other window the ancestral chapel, with the majestic figure of a fierce angel of death towering over it, leaning on a sword illuminated by the sun.

Only now did César notice that the face of the statue was facing the windows of Duke de Valsombra's bedroom.

"As if it was waiting for this moment..." he said to himself. As the sun's rays fell on the angel's head, César thought he saw a certain change in the stern stony features. The statue's hitherto gloomy face seemed to suddenly soften. Moreover, one could even call it cheerful. "Am I going crazy, just like my father and brother?" César thought anxiously, carefully examining the sculpture, which until recently had been formidable.

When the black carriage finally stopped in the courtyard, Roberto ran out of the palace.

"My lord, when are we going?" He asked.

"Immediately!" César replied. "No traces?"

The old servant looked depressed.

"Nothing at all," he said.

"Have you tried searching with dogs?"

"No…"

"Father had two favorite ones."

"Indeed. He walked with them almost every day."

"We'll take them with us."

"I'll go get Ricardo. For some time now, the kennel and the stable have been under his care."

Roberto walked away quickly, leaving César alone with the coachman. After a while he returned with a tall young man who was leading two large pointers. He bowed almost to the ground. The animals looked at César distrustfully at first, but after a while they recognized him, breaking away from their guardian and wagging their tails happily.

"This is Luna," Ricardo said, stroking the face of the larger brown female, "and this is Estrella," he said, pointing to the second, slightly smaller, lighter colored one.

"I didn't even remember their names…" thought César. "Even though such names are not easy to forget!" When he realized how long he hadn't spoken to his father, and how laconic their last exchange was, he got cold. "He must have exchanged more words with my brother on his birthday than with me in his entire life... Isn't that funny?"

"My lord, are you ready?"

"Of course. Francisco, you are staying. I'll go with Roberto."

"Yes, my lord," replied the coachman.

Luna and Estrella obediently ran by their side, barely lifting their noses off the ground. When they led them to a distant part of the forest, César looked at the duke's servant in surprise.

"What could my father be doing here?" He asked.

"As far as I remember, there are swamps not far from here..." Roberto noticed quietly.

"If father has ventured into those areas, we'll never find him again. There's a quagmire over there."

"But the horse made it back safe."

"It looks like my father left it here, but why would he do it?"

"Perhaps he saw or heard something that made him continue on foot, leaving the horse behind..."

"But what could it be?" César frowned.

"Your father, your..."

"Please, Roberto, I hate all these silly titles."

"Your father hasn't been well lately."

"He's been sick for a long time."

"It's not about a disease. His Majesty had nightmares and bizarre visions. For the past few weeks, he slept with candles lit every night, but recently he had us put on lights throughout the palace as soon as it got dark. And his visits to the chapel..."

César looked at Roberto carefully.

"As if he was afraid of something... but what?"

"Exactly..."

"What were these visions you just mentioned?"

"Ausencio told me about it in secret... His Majesty saw his deceased wife, your mother.

César's face darkened.

"I remember dreaming of her too... When I was a little boy, I missed my mother very much. I visited her grave in the chapel every day and spent hours there, pleading with her in my thoughts to come and say goodbye to me. One night I had a dream that she had granted my request. But she was no longer the same as I remembered her... The nightmare dreams began to recur, until finally..."

"Until finally your father called Father Felipe," finished Roberto.

At the mere memory of the thin monk of superhuman strength, César felt his stomach tighten. The rickety figure of Father Felipe stood before his eyes as if alive.

"I still remember the substance he gave me to make me foam. In this way, the trickster simulated a possession by a demon."

"I wonder what happened to him."

"Apparently he became a prior."

"We were all scared of him!"

"Till this day, I sometimes dream about him at night..." César sighed. "Perhaps my father, when he dreamed about my mother, understood how wrong he was in attributing the nightmares to the actions of demons..."

"Your father didn't believe such things. It was his friend, Cardinal Suárez, who claimed that a demon had possessed you, and he brought his cousin to Valsombra. Your case brought him considerable publicity..."

"It looks like the entire Suárez family are maniacs obsessed with fame," César said. "But *de mortuis nil nisi bene* [31]," he added ironically.

Suddenly, Estrella started barking furiously. Luna immediately joined her, digging with her front paws through the muddy ground, from which she produced a silver-plated button. There was a coat of arms engraved on it, with the *MC* monogram in the center. César turned pale. He picked up the button, cleaned it with a handkerchief, and then put it in his jacket. The pointers, excited about the discovery, filled the forest with barking.

"We have the first trace!" César called. "Let's go!"

They followed the dogs that ran towards the swamps.

"That doesn't bode well, lord...." Roberto sighed.

"I am of the same opinion," replied César. "But I must know the truth."

"Me too - I have served His Majesty for over fifty years!"

Luna and Estrella led them to the edge of a circular, marshy clearing, covered with small aquamarine plants.

"A bog," said Roberto.

"That's what I was afraid of..."

At the same moment Luna ran to the old, half-withered oak, fiercely trying to leap up to its lowest limb.

"Luna!" César called. "Show me what you've found!"

The dog's barking turned to a pitiful whine. Estrella ran up the other side of the tree. As César and Roberto came closer, they saw the watch of the Duke de Valsombra, which strangely and inexplicably hung on the branch.

"How did it get here?" César asked, taking the watch off the branch.

Luna and Estrella continued sniffing, delving into the swamp. César decisively grabbed the collar of the first and then the other dog, saving them from certain death in the tricky waters of the quagmire.

"I think we already know how my father died..." he sighed.

"Please look at this," Roberto called.

His voice died on his lips, and his outstretched, trembling hand pointed toward the center of the quagmire.

As César looked in that direction, weakness overwhelmed him, and he almost let off his hands the two pointers, who, whimpering, still struggled to certain death, determined to get their master's body out of the watery grave. In the very middle of the aquamarine clearing, exactly where Álvaro had blinded Duke de Valsombra, before he sank forever into the abyss, the bloody stains were still visible, the relics of his recent agony.

31 Latin   *Of   the   dead,   [say]   nothing   but   good.*

Chapter 32

Taxus baccata

The pouring rain finally stopped. The sun was already heading west. Its great red disc peeked ominously from behind the trunks of ancient trees, as if the entire forest was about to burst into flames. Iduna stared at the blood-red reflections that danced like fireflies on the mirror-like surface of the lake. The light reflected also in her black eyes, making them look like flaming torches.

Deep in thoughts, she walked around the lake, carefully observing the water, and then headed towards Yurde's grave. Just behind the small grave there was a sprawling, several-hundred-year-old yew, whose branches resembled elongated human hands. Iduna loved the feel of the smooth bark of the old tree, and its soft, dark emerald needles. In the rays of the setting sun, the red fruit shone like precious stones, beautifully harmonizing with the deep hue of the leaves.

Iduna picked up a thin twig and began to tear off the delicate needles, one by one. When she had a dozen or so of them, she raised them all to her mouth, then carefully chewed and swallowed. She kissed the bare twig, then rolled up the sleeves of her dress and knelt by the toddler's grave.

"Soon now, son," she whispered.

In response, she heard the joyful laugh of a child. At the sound, her face lit up for the first time in almost forty years.

"We'll be together soon," she said with a smile. The voice drifting in the air began to get closer, as if the boy was greeting his mother. His silvery voice resounded above Claro del Agua again:

Little thrush, tiny thrush,
all spotted...

Iduna dug her bony fingers into the ground. Sharp chippings of lime and dried roots hurt her skin painfully. Her heart was already beating unevenly, and beads of cold sweat appeared on her forehead. Her wounded hands fiercely put apart large parts of the earth, throwing away stones. The blood that flowed profusely from them, mixed with the damp earth. Iduna's breathing grew shallow and hoarse.

"Thank you, my faithful friend!" she turned to the old yew, which towered majestically over the grave, guarding the remains of her child.

A strong wind moved the branches of the tree, which rustled softly, as if it wanted to answer.

"Soon, son..." she said with effort. "A few more moments and we will be together again..."

When the pit was about a cubit and a half deep, she felt dizzy. She wiped her forehead with her shoulder. The world was already getting dark before her eyes, upon which the curtain of darkness was slowly falling. The taste of poisonous needles was still in her mouth. With the last of her strength, she laid herself in the grave she dug, directly adjacent to the grave of little Yurde. His cheerful laughter was still ringing in her ears.

With her dying lips she sang the first bars of the child song about a thrush, which her son liked so much.

Little thrush, tiny thrush,
all spotted...

She remembered the next verses. She sang them ever softer and quieter, pouring earth over her numbing body with her weak hands.

> *It soared on its wings today*
> *Over the mountains, forests...*
> *It soared on its wings today*
> *Over meadows, fields...*

Eventually the tune died on her lips. Her wide open eyes stared fixedly into the billowing storm clouds.

The sky flashed with bright bluish light that illuminated the dead face. The lightning that reflected in her eyes made them look alive again for a moment. There was a thunder in the distance. A dull rumble echoed widely off the rocks and tree trunks as it circled Claro del Agua. The rain fell on the clearing again, washing away the earth and the clotting blood off Iduna's hands.

When Álvaro found his lady's body, he flew down to the grave. Sitting on her breasts, he tilted his head up, then let out a piercing scream. He stared at her stiff, motionless face for a long time, tilting his head from side to side. He finally settled on her shoulder and, as always, plunged his curved beak into the locks of gray hair, combing it strand by strand.

When César and Roberto returned from the forest, bringing sad news about the death of Duke de Valsombra, Ausencio decided to visit Iduna as soon as possible. It was late already and he had some essential work in the palace to do, while he had all the morning off. So he went to the forest first thing in the morning. Heavy graphite clouds still hung ominously over the whole Cantabria.

He had a strong sense of loss tormenting him inside, but he had no idea what was causing it. "My new master is famous for treating his service well. I shouldn't worry about my future, as the

Marquis de Viciosa will certainly take care of us. He came back safe from the quagmire, and Roberto is alright as well. And yet, ever since morning something has been bothering me... But what on earth is it?" He wondered.

At the sight of the familiar rock looming on the horizon, under which Iduna's grotto was located, he felt a sudden and incomprehensible surge of fear. He heard Álvaro squeal in the distance. He recognized his voice immediately, but noticed that it sounded slightly different than usual. As he got closer, he saw the falcon circling in the air. At the sight of Ausencio, the bird sat over the empty cave and let out a long sound from his chest.

Suddenly, he took off and flew to an oak tree, and from there to another tree, indicating to his visitor to follow him. A shiver ran up the boy's spine. "Something happened to her," he thought. Álvaro, meanwhile, flew from branch to branch, without losing sight of Ausencio. But when he finally understood that the young man was following him, he soared into the air and flew towards Claro del Agua.

"Maybe she is just sitting by that lake of hers again and talking to the ghosts... I wish it is so," thought Ausencio. When he reached the clearing, he looked around, but he could not see the familiar figure anywhere. Nor did anyone respond to his calls, which echoed back to him. "Where could she have gone?!" He wondered. He sensed however, that the day which he subconsciously feared very much, had come.

He looked up at the hawk, which was flying in wide circles over the clearing, occasionally letting out the same prolonged wail. Ausencio realized the bird was trying to attract his attention. When he looked in his direction, Álvaro flew to the side of the clearing, where Yurde's grave was at the foot of the ancient yew. With a loud, piercing scream, he sat down in a tree.

Ausencio headed that way. He walked reluctantly, as he sensed that his worst fears would soon be confirmed. When he noticed the freshly dug grave, he shuddered and stood still.

Álvaro started calling him again. After Ausencio got there, he froze motionless, staring wide-eyed at the fragment of the dress protruding from the grave, and at the stiff hand with spread fingers, covered with solidified blood mixed with the earth.

Iduna was still staring at the sky. Her face was serene.

"What have you done?" Ausencio exclaimed, as if he were counting on an answer.

Then he knelt by the grave and brushed thick tufts of gray hair away from her forehead, then took a handful of spilled dirt in both hands.

"What have you done?!" He repeated, sobbing.

He looked at his friend one last time, then closed her cloudy eyes with trembling fingers.

His tears mixed with the raindrops that began to fall abundantly on the blood and mud-covered dress of the deceased. He threw dirt over her face, then, as if in a mad trance, grasped more handfuls and hurled them into the grave until the body was no longer visible. He covered the grave with another layer of soil, and placed several dozen carefully selected large stones on top.

When he was done, Álvaro flew up, then for several long minutes made larger and smaller circles in the air, right above the graves of the mother and child.

"You are finally together..." Ausencio sighed, wiping tears and dirt from his face.

As soon as he spoke these words, the yew made a loud rustling noise, and the sun peeked out from behind a huge gloomy cloud, casting a bright light on the fresh grave.

"El sol de los muertos..." he said to himself.

The beam of blinding light first fell on Iduna's grave, and then enveloped the neighboring one, where her little son was resting.

"Be happy, wherever you are... Iduna, I will always remember you," Ausencio whispered, his voice breaking.

Two graves, bathed in sunlight, shone like a flaming torch against the gloomy darkness of the forest.

After a while the sun hid behind the black curtain of storm clouds again, covering the clearing with darkness. At the same time, a series of sharp squeals of the hawk pierced the deep silence. It was no longer that terrible, long lamentation, but something like a merry shout. Ausencio's eyes narrowed and he looked up. The bird made another long circle and then flew away. His noble silhouette grew smaller and smaller, till it finally disappeared on the horizon.

Ausencio was left alone in the clearing. He stared blankly at the two graves and at the majestic yew guarding them. Suddenly he noticed that one small twig was devoid of needles. He picked it up, then ran his fingers over the leafless bark. The wind blew more forcefully again, ruffling the curly hair of Ausencio, who was listening to the melodious murmur of the old tree.

For a very short moment it seemed to him that the noise of the coniferous twigs was forming words, as if the yew wanted to convey some message to him. Gradually the murmur turned to a whisper, then a humming. Two voices, the first, piercing and silvery, evidently belonging to a little boy, and the lower, clear alto, to a young woman, were singing a child song.

"Iduna?!" Ausencio exclaimed, looking around.

In response, he heard a double, cheerful laugh. After a while, the voices began to recede, until they were no longer audible.

Chapter 33

Sarabande

It was May 20, 1792. The earth, heated by the warm spring air, was covered with a marvelous cloak, woven from countless flowers.

The grapevines growing on Castillo de Viciosa had already sprouted new leaves, tinting the bleak wall of the old castle a vivid green color. Six months had passed since the death of Duke de Valsombra. Therefore, César and Blanca decided to publicly announce their engagement.

Lord Ravendale followed his friend's example. He also decided to get engaged to his younger cousin, although it was not without obstacles from her parents, who could not come to terms with the fact that their only daughter chose as her husband an eccentric, much older than herself, and with an adventurous past and controversial views. Lord Ravendale was the first to arrive at the castle, while Carmen and her mother Eugenia soon followed.

Blanca, wearing a dark green dress adorned with black lace, immediately became the center of attention of all the guests. Fresh forest flowers were woven into her elaborately pinned, partially loose hair. Against the background of the courtyard, bathed in greenery, and the decorations in the hall, which was adorned with deliciously fragrant lilies of the valley, she resembled the Greek Persephone or one of the Celtic goddesses.

Like his father, César was very fond of good music. He brought the best artists to the castle, the same ones who entertained the guests at the balls arranged by the duke. Apart from the orchestra, Carmen, whose greatest passion was playing the harpsichord and piano, was also to perform. Especially for her, Blanca had delivered from the Palacio Aciago her own instrument with a delicate but expressive sound, on which her young friend could play Scarlatti's sonatas and Handel's suites.

Around noon, Aitor, who had been studying medicine at the University of Salamanca for two months, arrived at Viciosa. One of his first patients, Angelo Florentini, showed up next. The Venetian was still in Spain, but moved from the inn in Bárcena Menor to Castillo de Viciosa. César, with whom he was bound by strong ties of friendship, offered him a spacious room overlooking a picturesque clearing.

When the first half of the ceremonial reception was over, the piano concert began. Carmen had been preparing for it for many weeks, practicing under the watchful eye of her teacher. Doña Estefanía Belmonte y Fuentes was a famous harpsichordist. She came from Madrid and in her youth, before abandoning concerts in favor of teaching, she had even played at the royal court, where she personally met the famous singer Carl Broschi, better known as Farinelli, and the respected librettist Pietro Metastasio.

Just before the melancholic sounds of Scarlatti's *Sonata in F minor* filled the ballroom, Doña Estefanía, who arrived late for the party, took her place next to Eugenia Castro. The ladies exchanged bows and smiles, then listened to Carmen's playing as if enchanted. The teacher noticed however, that her companion's face was sad.

"What bothers you so much, dear Countess?" She asked.

"It's that Scarlatti..."

"Indeed, this sonata has a hint of melancholy to it."

"It was one of my cousin's favorite pieces..." Eugenia sighed heavily.

"You mean the late Duke de Valsombra?"

"Yes, he loved Scarlatti."

"I am so sorry," Doña Estefanía replied, squeezing her hand.

"We grew up together. Martín was a bad man, but for me he was like a brother that I never had..."

"He died a terrifying death, just like Don Giovanni, drawn into a hellish abyss..."

"What an irony of fate, this is his favorite Mozart's opera!" Eugenia said.

"Perhaps because the main character was so similar to him," Doña Estefanía suggested.

"Sometimes I think he was lured there by the spirit of one of his victims, just like The Commendatore who came to Don Giovanni's party..."

"Quite possible..."

The sonata was finished. Lord Ravendale walked over to Carmen and kissed her both hands. After the concert, the guests went to the dining room, where a dozen or so delicious dishes and outstanding wine from the best vintages, brought from the castle cellar, were waiting for them. When the guests fortified themselves with a meal, the second part of the ball began, which was enriched by the most beautiful compositions of Santiago de Murcia, Vivaldi, and other famous composers.

The ball was concluded by the famous Bach's Suite in B flat minor, which Blanca danced entirely with Lord Ravendale, and Doña Estefanía with Angelo Florentini. When the cheerful sounds of the charming *Badinerie* had died down, Carmen unexpectedly sat down at the piano again. She decided to surprise César by playing especially for him the Handel's Sarabande in D minor, a beloved piece of his late mother, which she used to played for him often.

The guests took their seats again to listen to the concert. When César heard the first two chords, he immediately understood the intention of his younger cousin. He got up and asked Blanca to dance. The bright light from the enormous chandeliers illuminated the room well enough, but Enrique also lit candles in twelve wall candlesticks, which filled the room to the brim with a warm glow.

As Carmen finished the last variation and César kissed Blanca's porcelain hand, the weather suddenly worsened. The lofty harmonies smoothly turned into the gloomy bass howl of the wind. Heavy grape vines lashed the terrace furiously, and the branches of an old oak growing just by the castle wall rattled against the windows, as if someone were knocking urgently on the window. Blanca and César exchanged glances. They both thought the same thing, but neither of them dared to put their thoughts into words.

Along with all the guests they went to the dining room, where an elegant dinner awaited them. The windstorm still tugged at the treetops and whipped the walls of Castillo de Viciosa furiously, but the guests, accustomed to the vagaries of the spring weather, paid no attention to it. Only Blanca, hearing the crackle of boughs and the sounds of shoots hitting the glass more and more insistently, instinctively looked back.

A small twig that directly touched the glass, unexpectedly changed its position under the gusts of the raging wind. When it broke away from the glass, it only touched it with its tip. At one point it made a slight vertical movement and then dropped.

"What attracted your interest so much?" César asked.

"It's nothing..." Blanca replied, turning her head.

As their silhouettes disappeared behind the door, the twig rose again, making a round line similar to the letter C. Then it rose again and fell, as it had been the first time, making the same movement twice, then half-crossed both vertical lines with one horizontal, and a moment later it drew in the similar way the subsequent letters, which formed the sentence: *ICH LIEBE DICH* [32].

32   German *I love you.*

www.ingramcontent.com/pod-product-compliance
Lightning Source LLC
Chambersburg PA
CBHW050126030726
47505CB00007B/2058